ROXY BLUE

Fiona's FURY

For my father, JDW, 'Son of Hercules'
the ultimate alpha male and hopeless romantic.

Chapter 1

Fiona

"Dripping with pleasure, relaxing into all the sensations, allowing your limbs, your nervous system, your heart to just melt into the floor and go. Let it all go...that's it. Remember to breathe. Keep breathing...good."

Does the fact that Celeste's sickly-sweet baby-doll voice makes me want to jolt my naked ass up off this paint-puddle floor, and smack her upside the head mid sentence, mean I'm an inherently bad person? And whatever in this world does 'remember to breathe' mean?

"Breathing in openness and exhaling restriction, tension, obstacles...now I want you to feel, some of you for the very first time, your true relationship to yourself as you nurture, nourish, and allow all the holding in your body to drop down through the floorboards, saturating and swirling in and around your colors...ebbing and flowing with the tides of your breath and your heartbeat. Remember to breathe... good work Fiona!" Clearly Celeste misinterpreted the sound of deep disgust that just escaped from my chest cavity.

But at least, thank goodness, it was a sign that I'm remembering to breathe. I mean, God forbid what might happen were Celeste to forget to remind us to breathe! Lord... all dozen of us dying in a miserable, sticky, rainbow-slicked heap right here in the middle of Om Wellness Sanctuary. Can you envision how that headline would read? Twelve Middle-Aged Ninnies Collectively Forget How to Breathe During Tragic Art Movement Therapy Session.

I really don't know why I let Quade talk me into this stuff. He seems to think that somehow, someday, if I have just the right moment of truth in the perfect setting, I'll come to my senses and see that we should never have divorced in the first place. And he's such a pathetically selfless sweetheart...with all that money he puts forth for my greater good. I only wish I knew how to tell him I'm a fraud and a fake.

After thirty minutes of slithering around with a room full of women of multiple ages, shapes, and sizes, I'm supposed to have mystically arrived at full body acceptance, holistic centeredness, and embodied mindfulness...all while having created my own unique 'color imprint' on the thickly paper-covered floor beneath me.

"How was it for you?" my beautiful bi-racial friend, Holly, asks exuberantly as she approaches me after the session.

"Oh I guess it was alright, if you don't mind having to fully shower and shampoo paint out of your cracks in the middle of a Wednesday evening."

"Come on Fiona...didn't you at least enjoy it a little bit?" she asks, still smiling and looking like she just had the time of her freaking life.

"Sure. It was great. It was everything I ever imagined wallowing in paint could be," I reply, attempting to sound more whimsical than negative.

"Fiona! You're the worst," she responds with a weak laugh and a tiny slap to my forearm. "Well I thought it was fab, and I expect the aftermath to move mountains of obstacles out of the way of my joyful life. So there. See you Saturday," she adds before giving me a quick hug and bouncing out the door.

I do look forward to my Saturday lunch dates with Holly. She seems to have an unending capacity for being used as my verbal dumping ground on all matters Fiona...ex-boyfriends, ex-husbands, issues at work like that new little fink I hired who thinks she can run the place. She's the best sounding-board I have, and is capable of handling the kind of brutal honesty that would get Quade's panties all in a bunch.

I drive through the Whippy Dip to grab a little soft serve, my idea of therapy, on my way back to the store.

"Hello." I answer a call from Quade, who's undoubtedly checking to see how things went at the Om.

"Hey Cookie, how did it go?"

"Okay."

"Just okay?" It instantly breaks my heart to hear him sound so disappointed.

"Pretty good actually. Really good. I feel much better now. Thanks so much for that, sweetie," I answer almost honestly as I slurp in the flavors of my butterscotch vanilla twist cone.

"Ah...well that's a relief. It wasn't cheap." Why is it that Quade, a bankruptcy lawyer and virtual bottomless pit of money, always finds it necessary to let me know how much he's spent on me?

"So...did you not really wanna spend a few bucks for me to go to a holistic art therapy mindfulness movement class? Cause you know, you didn't have to spend it, and I didn't have to go." Now he's got me bristling.

"No, Cookie, honey...listen. I want you to go. I want what's best for you and I know how much you need this."

"Well we don't have to keep—"

"No, I'm sorry I said anything. I'm so happy for you doing this." A dysfunctional silence falls between us until he changes the subject. "So how's everything going with your new flower girl?"

"Good. I think. Really good maybe."

"You sound hesitant."

"No, it's just that she's actually more qualified than what I was initially looking for."

"Really? I thought you said she was new at this."

"Well she is. That's the thing...she's like, really fast or something. She's already better than Laura and Faye put together, and you know how experienced they are."

"She sounds perfect then, right?" Quade is still on to my sense of reservation.

"Yeah. But in all honesty, she knows she's too talented to be mindlessly assembling pre-designed bouquets for the showroom, so she kind of does her own thing here and there. And I totally appreciate everything she's doing. I just feel like I need to keep an eye on her."

"Hey, honey, this is your perfect opportunity to practice what we've been talking about, right? Letting go of micromanaging everything and everyone around you."

"I know. You're right," I say with some emotional fatigue, but no resentment. He is right. For a change.

"Of course I'm right Cookie. Help yourself by letting others help you."

I'm really rolling my eyes at that one.

"I've gotta grab this call. Talk to you soon," he says before bailing off the line.

'Of course I'm right Cookie'...how dare he patronize me. I've known Quade for almost twenty years and have never once told him that I could squash him like a bug. His friendship is everything, but at the same time he's so miniscule that I feel like driving over him with a steamroller.

I yank open the door of Fiona's Flowers in full rage mode, ready to storm in, see to whatever needs to be done before close, and then get out quickly before I bite some poor, undeserving employee's head off. So much for the Om, and ice cream. All that good is out the window after five minutes on the phone with my sweet, generous, loving, make-me-wanna-puke ex-husband.

The sheer loveliness of the showroom puts my mood in check, as I enter to find Maxine's handiwork on every shelf in sight. Okay, I yield. The kid's got a real talent.

"Hey Maxine." She's in the back doing her closing cooler-work. "Got those sketches for the Hoffman wedding ready for me?"

"You bet," she answers, a little too cheerfully for my tastes. "Everything's in this envelope here," she says, pulling a file folder out from under a stack of fulfilled orders.

Maxine continues bustling around as I flip through the folder. She's learned to back off and let me look over her projects without trying to sell me on anything. As per usual, her work is excellent.

"Looks good Maxine. The sunflowers and sedum are a nice touch, very much in keeping with the barn theme. It's all gonna look fabulous once we get it put together." Maxine beams with satisfaction, but I don't need my compliments going to her head. "I'm gonna place my supply order from home tonight, so I'm outta here. See you tomorrow," I say as I slip out the back door in an already improved mood.

I pick up a roll of sushi for dinner and head straight up to my home office with it, feeling my energy steadily increase from no-longer-pissed to genuinely enthusiastic. Although I get the bulk of my supplies from the more local Florist Distributing Co, I use Big Bo's down in Florida for specialty flowers you can't find in Iowa.

By the time I was released from this afternoon's harrowing therapy session, I felt so bedraggled that I almost forgot about my looming phone date with the master of orchids. There's something about Bo's down-home personality that calms me to no end, and I can hardly contain a slight, crooked smile as I dial the all-hours order line he gave me.

"Big Bo here," he answers in his deep, husky voice.

"Fiona Turner here," I respond with a hint of tease.

"Well...hello there Fiona Turner. I was about startin to wonder when my favorite midwestern gal was gonna call me up for some orchid action this spring."

I don't realize that I'm giggling like a schoolgirl, until I happen to wheel my chair around and catch a glimpse of my grinning reflection in the ornately framed mirror hanging above my grandmother's turn-of-the-century English bureau. "I guess I just couldn't resist any longer." No sooner than the words leave my lips, I hear the thunderous rumble of Bo's bassey chuckle welling up on the other end of the line.

"Rumor has it I'm pretty hard to resist," he grinds out in his best bedroom voice, which may be the very best there is. Anywhere.

I'm a busy woman, too busy according to everyone I know, and I really have no time for this ridiculous song and dance every time I order from Bo. But then, I don't do it often...and it humors me at some primal level of simmering womanhood I haven't felt in decades. Well, barring those few weekends I spent with The Beast. But that doesn't count...in the eyes of the Lord.

"So," I clear my throat in an attempt to redirect our conversation toward productivity, "what have you got for me this time?" Did I just say something suggestive, again?

"Well now, lemme tell you all about that. I have got the biggest...most impressive...most gigantic...most unbelievable...blossom selection I've ever had to date." I'm almost doubled over in hysterics as Bo continues. "I mean I've got more different colors of everything than you can shake a stick at this year. Whatta you want darlin? Anything you want, I've got it for you. Right here right now."

I notice that I'm fixating on a vision of what Bo might look like. I truly believe I've never met any human being like him in my life, and it's impossible not to wonder.

"For now, I'll take ten flats of the purple orchids and twenty flats of the white," I reply, once I manage to reinstate minimal composure.

"Aw, this time of year...those'll sell out in no time."

"You're probably right, but if they do...I'll just have to call you up and order some more." I know I'm flirting now, against my better judgment, but I don't see any other way out of this situation. And anyway, what harm could it do with a guy I've never met and never will?

Again I can hear Bo's muffled laughter, and I feel an expanding heat when neither of us says anything for almost a minute. "Well," he starts in at last, "let's hope sales are real good for you then."

I giggle flirtatiously, in order to prevent another possible silence that feels more intimate than anything I need with a random Florida hick I order flowers from. Funny how silence has that effect. All of our flirting adds up to little, by comparison.

We get through the rest of the order and off the phone with surprisingly minimal fanfare, though that silence keeps creeping in between words. It's not an awkward silence. It's almost a too-comfortable one, as if there were now some mutual understanding between us that can never be undone. I scoff at the absurdity of it as I get off the phone. What on earth is happening that would cause my highly respectable self to even notice an aside like that? I suppose it's the natural recession of brain cells after the kind of day I've had.

Oh good...a text from Holly.

Hey Fiona, just wanted to remind you to Loosen Up and enjoy life a little. And yes, that includes activities involving nudity and paint. Can't wait to see you Saturday!

Oh please. Holly thinks she needs to remind me to enjoy life now? I do enjoy life. I love my life. I'm a beautiful, powerful, special woman, and I'm living my life to the fullest. All I want to know is, what the hell is wrong with everybody else that they think I need some kind of help?

I spin around and glance at the mirror to find an entirely different face reflected in it. The red grimace of emotional resistance. A term I learned in some other afternoon 'therapy' extravaganza. I take the recommended five deep breaths and watch the ruddiness magically drain from my cheeks. Okay, maybe some of these techniques work just a little bit. I suddenly remember that I adore Holly and can't wait to see her too. Then I hear Bo's sleazy chuckle in my head and, moment by moment, begin to feel human again.

Chapter 2

Bo

"A fine woman, Jose. I'm tellin you…she's a fine woman."

"But, how do you claim to know that only from hearing her voice?" Jose looks at me incredulously.

"I just know, okay? Big Bo knows these things…don't ever question the man, alright?"

"But man, what if she's like…gnarly or something?"

"Aw, no man. Don't even go there."

"But what…what if she looks like she fell off the ugly tree and hit every branch on the way down, man?" Now he's just plain messin with me.

"Aw no, come on man. She ain't like that…not this one."

"But you don't know that. Brother I swear, you're gonna get messed up over some old spinster, man, with weird looking teeth and everything. I swear by it, man."

"Aw hell no, Jose. First off, I ain't gettin messed up over no woman. Alright? You can get that outta your head right now. And second off...oh I don't know. I've just got a feelin about this one, alright? So just...let it go man, cause I can't explain it and it ain't worth tryin to explain to a box of rocks like you." I reach over and rustle what's left of Jose's shiny, black hair, letting him know it's all good.

"Okay, whatever you say man. Beer?" Jose shoves away our empty bottles and eyes the bartender.

"Naw that's cool. Thanks man, but I gotta get goin anyhow. I got a bunch of tender new babies at home, need checked on."

"Hey, you really do love your plants, don't you? You're a good man, you know that Bo?" Jose's eyes sparkle with a sweetness he usually tries to hide.

"I reckon so Jose. I reckon I love them plants more than anything else I have in my life." I touch the brim of my hat as I give a quick nod and turn toward the door.

I've always liked Jose. The guy's alright, but a strange calm sets in as I fire up my Chevy and head back to the farm. That last exchange is stinging me, somewhere inside. I guess I never had much of anything else in my life, after my brothers grew up enough to go their own ways. I still love em to this day, always will, but I'm not too sure I'll ever see either one of em again. Such is life in the fast lane. Ain't my thing anyway. I chose the country life and I'll stick by it to the end.

As I turn down the gravel lane, I can just make out the long strips of pink, yellow, and coral coneflowers...fading in the twilight like neon watercolors. I park next to the shed and head on back to the greenhouse to see how my orchids are doing. As I open the door, thousands of delicate babies quiver their heads at me, set in motion by the slight draft. I can feel the life in each and every precious petal, and I believe they can feel mine too. Some folks think I'm peculiar, but I talk to my plants before bed each night...even run experiments with em. The ones I talk to the nicest are the ones that grow fastest. No doubt about it.

"There's a real special lady up in Iowa who's gonna be takin care of ya'll soon. So I need you to grow up big and strong, hear me?" It tickles me to be able to tell these tiny purple orchids where they're headin off to. I can feel they're gonna have a happy life up there.

Chapter 3

Fiona

After having sprung out of bed at six thirty to do a long meditation, pick through emails over a mug of cascara tea, and soak in my clawfoot tub, I'm beginning to drift off when I receive a call from Quade.

"Hey Cookie, having lunch with Holly today?" he asks with a familiar undertone.

"Of course. What's up?"

"Well, I'll be flying in to meet a client this afternoon and thought maybe I could interest you in an early dinner? I have to be in Chicago tonight but we could take a couple hours before I go." I love my ex-husband, but it makes my skin crawl when he uses that pursuant tone of voice.

"Probably not this time, sweets. I'm meeting her in Iowa City to do some retail therapy after. She's already up there for an early appointment and I'll be hitting the road to join her in less than an hour."

"And? After that?" he says in his classic manner of perfectly calm pushiness.

"Well I don't know. I don't know how long we're gonna take. I don't know where we're gonna go, what we're gonna buy, what we're gonna do. I don't know!"

"Okay Cookie, calm...calm. Deep calming breaths."

"And second of all, how am I going to eat an early dinner after a late lunch? Huh? Riddle me that, Batman!"

"Okay, I'm gonna let you go...I'll be back in town later this week. So let's plan on a couple hours of quality time, say around Wednesday? I'll let you know when I have my schedule for sure."

"Okay fine. Sounds good. Lemme know, whatever, whenever—"

"Gotta run. Don't forget your restorative yoga class Monday. Talk to you soon." Click.

"Oh sure, I won't forget. Go ahead and schedule me however you like. My career doesn't matter at all. What was I ever thinking when I thought my time mattered?" I ask the room, well aware Quade's no longer on the line.

I step out of the tub with careless haste, splashing the tiles thoroughly with water, then successfully yank a bolt out of the decrepit towel rack sticking out of the ancient wall of my antiquated bathroom. "Shit! I don't have time for this." I dry off vigorously for ten seconds, dash the towel to the floor, and stomp toward my dresser to retrieve the hair dryer.

Having thrown on a simple pair of black capris with an oversized white button-up, untucked, I step into my thongs and I'm off. Feeling better, I smile slightly as I sit in my white Jaguar and put on a podcast. An hour of *Calmer You* ought to make the drive fly by. She's interviewing a Spiritual Life Coach in this week's episode. Oh boy.

By the time I reach our designated restaurant, One Twenty Six, I'm almost in a coma from all that excitement. As I approach the patio, I can see Holly waiting for me under a striped umbrella...her long, luxuriant corkscrew curls swaying in the breeze. She's sipping something that looks remarkably like pinot noir.

"Fiona!" She stands and hugs me with the enthusiasm she always brings to our outings. "Sit, sit. Pick out some wine." Our waitress comes by and I order the same.

"So," Holly starts in, twirling her glass and gazing at me through sparkling brown eyes, "how are things in your life this week?"

"Just the usual. A couple more seedy messages from The Beast, and a few conversations that made me wanna reach through the phone and strangle Quade is all."

"Aww, Fiona, you're so hard on him. I wish my ex was nice like that."

"I know, you're completely right. There's just a dynamic I can't put my finger on, and I feel like it's always been there. He's an excellent friend but mistake number one was marrying him in the first place."

"You really think so? If you could get all that time back, do you really think you wouldn't have spent it with him?"

"Okay...that's where it gets tricky. See, I *would* choose to spend time with Quade, just not in a romantic partnership," I say as though I've cleverly solved some confounding riddle.

"So...why is it a problem now? He's your best friend, right? Besides me of course." She sticks out her tongue for one playful moment. Holly is always like this when wine is involved. "So why are you always upset with him if you think a friendship is what it was meant to be in the first place?"

Holly's question leaves me oddly speechless. My problem is that I don't know what my problem is. "I think...I think... he just...makes me feel like screaming!" I blurt out at an inappropriately loud volume around other diners. Holly looks at me bug-eyed and I feel embarrassed. "I'm sorry...I don't know why I said that. Quade's fabulous. He's actually in town tonight but I told him I was spending the day with you here."

"Oh! You can make it back in time to see him...I don't have to take up your entire day—"

"No that's alright. I wanna be here with you today. This is gonna be so fun." Thank God, at this moment, the waitress arrives with my wine. "So, anything happening new with you?" I make an executive decision to change the subject.

"Nothing much, just finishing the same project I've been on for what...four months now?"

Holly's life is no simpler than mine, although she somehow makes it seem like it is. Also a divorcee, she works long hours as an architectural drafter before returning home to Levi, her design engineer boyfriend...whom she then gets to launder for and pick up after. I like to make fun of her for keeping a 'pet', but allegedly Levi's perfect in almost every way. To each her own.

She orders chicken linguine, but all I want is a tuna sandwich. We talk about this and that until we finish dining. And then, while peacefully awaiting the check, something possesses Holly to take a stick to the hornet's nest.

"Um, if you don't mind me asking...do you ever think about just calling The Beast back anymore?"

"What if I do mind?" I chide, sounding less annoyed than I actually am.

"Come on...you're a flesh and blood woman and he was hot. There's gotta be *something* going on in that head of yours."

I succumb, with the help of the wine, to giggling at Holly's persistence. Ulysses wasn't the worst guy, just your everyday average narcissist. Not to mention he had a lot of loose nuts and bolts rattling between his ears. He was all muscle and no charm. But that's what you get when you go to a biker bar in a neighboring town and allow yourself to make eye contact with a fit younger man. Big mistake.

"First of all," I reply, shaking my head, "I'd never go running back to him. I'd just be using him for one thing."

Holly bursts out laughing. "Do you really think he'd mind being used by you Fiona?"

"Come on...you know what I mean. It wouldn't be fair. I have no interest in him beyond his physique."

"And the problem with that is?"

"No, Holly. You're not doing this. Nuh-uh. You're not gonna talk me into giving a guy hope just so I can have a bedmate. He was interested in me Holly...you know. Like all around."

"Oh you're no fun," she says teasingly.

"Absolutely no fun at all. That's me," I concur. "And if he was a woman I wanted to use just for sex, you'd call me a misogynist."

"Touche." We finish paying the bills, toss back our last sips of wine, and begin strolling toward the shopping area.

Two pairs of shorts, four floral blouses, and six summer dresses later, we walk toward Yotopia to finish fulfilling our hearts' desires.

"I'm not trying to bug you, but you do seem kind of quiet today," Holly interjects between bites of tropical sorbet.

"Really? All that shopping and I still can't hide my deeper emotions from you?" I ask. "Some poker player I'd make."

"Come on...what is it?"

I swear Holly knows me better than I know myself. "There's nothing on my mind...really," I say before my face broadens into a smile.

"What is it? I see that smile!"

"Seriously, you think you're so on to me but it's nothing."

"What are you smiling about?"

"Just a silly, random thought. The least relevant thought ever." We're almost back to our cars and I don't want to get into this now.

"I saw that face and there's something you're not telling me," she gently continues.

"Get over here." I pull her in for a hug. "Aren't you just so happy with all our beautiful selections?"

"I am, we really scored today. Give Quade a hug for me, you rat."

As we say goodbye and open our car doors, Holly continues to look at me with skepticism. I ignore it and smile mundanely while we pull out and file down the street. I reach to put another podcast on but no longer feel the ambition. After fifteen miles of open highway, I'm unusually serene and content with the silence. My mind is clear, and it naturally settles on the foggy, faceless image of a man's mouth and the sound of his voice. And then it occurs to me...I'm smiling, again.

Chapter 4

Bo

On stormy nights like this, I love to lie in bed and listen to the sound of the rain smacking against this old shed. I could fire up the electricity and move into the big house, but what would be the point? Ain't nothin a man needs indoors besides a bed, a bath, and a cookstove. Although I could sure use a more comfortable cot. This one's gotten too old for me. Or I've gotten too old for it, not sure which.

I'm on the brink of driftin into the netherworld when a clap of thunder jars me upright, rattlin the very window panes. My thoughts come on like a water faucet...did I row-cover all the seedlings, did I tarp over the snapdragons, did I finish movin the pots and peat moss flats inside? Check... check...check. Like countin sheep, I'm half asleep again when another strike hits. This time my mind is empty, clear. I watch the shards of moonlit water slappin hard against the glass and allow the sound to hypnotize me. I see a vision, clear as a bell, of her...and a moment later I'm out for good.

Chapter 5

Fiona

After a day of phone calls and paperwork, including a video conference with the American Florist Association, I want nothing more than to slip into a deep, hot tub. But I'd be the queen bitch of the universe if I broke my dinner 'date' with Quade, so instead I'm opting for a quick shower and a fresh outfit. He picks me up at seven o'clock sharp and drives the few blocks to Shokai. We pick the quietest spot we can find, a small table tucked into a corner, and order four rolls of sushi.

"You look incredible in that dress," he mumbles between bites. He's been eyeing it ever since picking me up, with a look I could only describe as longing.

"Thanks. I bought it when I was out with Holly," I say stiffly, keeping my eyes to my plate.

"You've always been beautiful, Fiona. There's no way you could wear something like that and not look conspicuous."

I shoot him a look that says 'What does that mean?' but he holds my gaze as if to challenge me. I look away with a shrug and immerse my attention in dipping the next piece of sushi.

"So, how's everything at the store this week?" he asks to my great relief.

"Good," I answer brightly. "Maxine's really turning out to be a go-getter."

"In a good way?"

"Yes, I believe so. She's...got a lot of potential."

"Yeah, you told me you thought she should further her education."

"Ha, well...she's outdone me. She wants to go for a month at London Flower School. Can you believe that?"

"Really? Do you feel okay with losing her for that long?"

"I think so. I appreciate her spirit, you know? She'll be back. And...she'll be even better than she is now. I'm actually thinking about inviting her to AFA with me."

"You're kidding. You, not traveling alone? I can't picture it," Quade says with a smirk.

"Yeah, but you know why I want her along?" He stops eating and subtly gestures for me to continue. "I think she can win that design competition."

Quade rumples his face in mild disbelief. "Don't you think she should try something like that next year, after she's back from LFS?"

"Oh...probably. But I can always enter her again if she doesn't place."

"And I suppose you're funding all this?" he asks in a somewhat alarmed tone.

"Of course I am, sweets. She'll do great. If she even wins third we'll get to bring home a plaque," I say, as I raise one eyebrow.

"Okay Cookie," Quade says with a freshly molten expression. "Whatever you feel is best. And I do think you could use the company, quite frankly."

"Oh really?" I'm not sure why that comment takes me by surprise.

"Well of course. Seems like your work week is pretty solitary when I'm not around."

I'd hate to admit the truth in that statement, as I don't need Quade getting any ideas that I'm hankering for more time with him. I do stick to myself most weeks, but I'm just independent that way. Saturdays with Holly are plenty for me.

"That's hardly the case," I argue. "At the shop I'm surrounded by people all the time." I can hear the defensiveness welling up in my own voice.

"You know what I mean Cookie. Friendship... companionship. Ever heard of those?"

I roll my eyes and gently change the subject. I can guess where he was headed with that.

I'm feeling so happy, after we finish our meal and drive back to my place, that we didn't get into a single tiff. Until the moment when we go past the bar and I see a bike parked that unmistakably belongs to Ulysses. Like he thinks I actually hang out at my local dive bars.

"Any chance I can interest you in a foot massage?" Quade asks after walking me to my door.

He knows this is the one temptation I can never say no to, but my inner voice is screaming for me not to allow it.

"It's so kind of you to offer that, and I would love one, but I've got some business matters to go through tonight—"

"Just for half an hour Cookie. I won't keep you, I have business to take care of when I get back to the room anyway," he says with his typical calm, yet unrelenting, firmness.

I smile nervously as I open the door and usher him in. "If you insist, I won't say no to half an hour," I respond, immediately doused in an ominous sense of regret.

We settle onto a red and gold jacquard couch and he lovingly takes my feet into his lap. We've done this from time to time over the years, usually making light conversation to ward off any real possibility of pleasure. But this time feels different. Quade's eye contact and general demeanor have felt kind of sticky ever since my brief fling with Ulysses.

I remember chastising my own instinct not to tell Quade about my fling, then overruling it by reminding myself we tell each other everything. And nothing bad ever did come of it, except an ever-so-subtle tightening of his behavior around me. I guess that's natural for one of us dating for the first time, nine years after our divorce. But nothing would fulfill me more than to see Quade with a girlfriend. He's just never been very hotwired, and both of us are so focused on our businesses. It occurs to me that I can scarcely even imagine him taking an interest in a woman.

It also occurs to me that Quade's awfully quiet. Unnoticed, I side-eye the mantel clock and see it's been thirty-eight minutes. The time flew by in my whirlwind of thoughts, and we neither made conversation nor eye contact throughout.

"Okay." I awkwardly break the silence as I fold up my legs.

Quade looks dumbstruck, as though I've broken him from a trance, hands still poised in mid air. "Ah, well. It has been about thirty minutes, hasn't it."

Nodding and smiling pleasantly, I straighten my dress and rise from the couch.

"Thank you sweets. That was nice," I say as I automatically guide us toward the door.

Quade stands in front of it hesitantly, his expression pensive. "Well, I should say it was Cookie. Are you sure you don't want me to stay another fifteen or twenty? I could work some of those anxiety knots out of your shoulders."

"Oh, no. Thanks for offering though. I'm just gonna finish a couple things and turn in nice and early."

Quade gives me the disengaged hug of having given up, then quickly turns to go. I watch, through the distortion of the stained glass door, as his lights appear and disappear down the road, then lock the door, turn out the lights, and enter the kitchen to fix a cup of chamomile tea. As I sweep back into the foyer with my steaming prize, I pause at the bottom of the steps to enjoy the way the streetlights refract through the intricately etched and angled borders of the living room windows. All the wood and glass work in my home is original, restored, priceless.

As I sit at my desk, grazing through a mass of emails, I'm struck by the oddest sensation. Something about when I was downstairs...something right after Quade left. What on earth is it? It feels like when you forget what you were going to say and then remember it was totally insignificant. Except I wasn't going to say anything, unless I was planning to address it to the atmosphere. Several minutes and two emails later, when I'm still unable to shake the sensation, I decide to backtrack down to the living room.

I allow one more sip of my tea, take a deep relaxing breath, and pull on a light cardigan...feeling silly as I stop my work to walk back downstairs for no reason whatsoever. By the time I reach the bottom step, I'm becoming outraged. Why am I doing this fully pointless exercise...I wonder as I traverse the room and hover around the front door. I was actually, finally, having a perfectly pleasant evening, didn't fight with Quade, didn't lose my cool over anything, and now I'm acting stupid for no reason ...I think as I reach to open the door and step out for some fresh air.

My body becomes rigid on the spot as my hand grips the knob and it doesn't open. I locked the door. I live in Fairfield, Iowa and I locked my front door. I don't lock the door at night. The last time I locked this damn door, I was on a trip out of town for a week. This is not insignificant. What the hell is wrong with me? I decide to trust my intuition, and I back away from the door as though it were protecting me from a lion's den. Just before I turn to ascend the steps, I see headlights pulling up in front of the house...Quade's headlights.

I dash up to the top step, knowing I can't be seen in the semi-darkness. Through the glass I can make out his figure striding purposefully down my sidewalk and then reaching upward. He attempts to turn the handle...without knocking. I watch breathlessly as he raises his knuckles, then changes his mind and stalks back to the car.

Quade and I were married for four years and together for eight. There's nothing in me that could possibly fear him, yet I find myself locking the backdoor as well. Armed with a tiny flashlight, I quickly check the couch cushions and end tables for whatever he must have left. Finding nothing, I head back up and turn out my office light, huddling in front of the glowing computer screen. I have no missed calls or texts.

Two hours later, I'm still wound up from the oddity of Quade's behavior. I very much need to get some good sleep tonight, so I think I'll do some casual reading to wind down. Actually, AFA sent me the list of speakers and vendors for this year's conference. That could be sort of fun and distracting, or at the very least bore me to sleep.

I begin scrolling through the dizzying list and see several familiar names from last year. I always look forward to going and mingling with people I recognize, although I've never felt like I made close friends with any. Maxine is such a nice and charismatic young woman. She should fit right in and, perhaps, provide good company. Quade can't be wrong about everything.

Finally I'm getting sleepy, as I peruse the vendors page, a languid yawn forcing my eyes to tear up at the corners. Although I usually don't get too excited about vendors, since none of mine ever attend the conference anyway, a distinct word catches my eye as I quickly scan down the alphabetized list. It's a short, precise little word that's hard to miss on a page full of longer names. Bo. Bo Thompson. Big Bo's. Big Bo's is listed as one of the vendors attending this year's AFA Conference.

Irrationally, my heart is beating at double time. I've been getting supplies from Bo for going-on four years now, and I've never seen him at the conference before...even though he lives right there in Florida. And I never imagined I would. He really doesn't seem like the crowded-social-event type. I don't know what's possessed him to enlist, nor what's come over me that I would concern myself with it, but suddenly I'm looking forward to this conference in a way I never have before. After the evening's events, I feel a delirious combination of exhaustion and exuberance as I get into bed.

When my alarm goes off at seven, thirty minutes later than usual, I tear out of the covers and throw on my robe, ready to rush into my morning routine. I bolt down to the kitchen and begin making my cascara tea, which should theoretically give me enough energy to survive morning meditation without falling dead asleep.

As I stroll into the den, which is furnished and decorated like an English tea room, I realize with a start that I must change out of this short, satin robe before Quade drops by. He's supposed to leave for the airport at eight, so I should be hearing his knock before long. Although I don't feel any need to wear paper bags around my ex husband, my go-to house robe happens to be especially slinky...and it shows an awful lot of leg. I abandon my tea to rush upstairs and change into a lounge suit.

Back on the flowery couch in the den, I answer a few texts and emails in preparation for my workday. A smile spreads across my face when I pause to sip tea and remember what I found out last night. I glance at my phone; it's five till eight. What in the world happened to Quade? I get a text from Holly.

Good morning bright eyes! Going to yoga this afternoon?

I'm planning to, if I can make it out of my meeting on time.

You'd better! See you at four.

I'm sure I would have utterly forgotten if I hadn't received Holly's text. After a couple sun salutations on the carpet, I'm ready to begin meditation. And I'm turning my ringer off. Whatever Quade wanted will just have to wait till later.

I meditate for one hour, sleep for another, then get up and hustle to the shop...never having received any texts or calls from Quade.

* * *

I decide to show up at the Om fifteen minutes early because Holly's always early for everything. How that's possible, given her schedule, is beyond my comprehension and I rightfully despise her for it. No sooner than the entry-door bell finishes jingling, I spot her on the far side of the room, predictably warming up with deep breathing. Who warms up for deep-breath yoga with deep breathing? I don't even wish I was as perfect as Holly.

"Oh hey, Fiona!" she opens her eyes and says with total surprise, as I reach out and gently touch her arm. "You're early. What's gotten into you?" She giggles and pats the yoga mat beside her.

I sit and stare at her like an animal in headlights, trying to figure out whether to begin with the weird news or the even weirder news. "Holly," I begin in a lowered voice, "I've gotta tell you something." I break into a wide grin.

Holly gasps. "You've met someone," she says with the enthusiasm of a teenager.

"No! No. It's nothing like that. There's just something silly and irrelevant that I wanna get off my chest. That's all. But first, I need to tell you something creepy as shit and get your opinion on it. I just...I'm in a mixed space right now and I don't know what to think."

"Okay...I'm here for you," she says, reaching over to lightly rub my back.

I draw in a gulp of air and let it out in a puff. "Last night I went out to dinner with Quade, like I said I was going to. After we parted ways, I turned off the lights and went upstairs. About, I dunno, half an hour later...I went back down for something and saw him pull up in front of the house. He got out, walked up to my front door in the darkness, and attempted to turn the knob. It was locked, but what the heck Holly?"

She looks at me like she wants to care but can't imagine what the big deal is. "Okay...well he is your bosom buddy of seventeen years. I'm sure he just forgot something or wanted to tell you something, right?"

"Right, except...he never followed up. I waited all morning for him to call about whatever he left at my place, and he got on that plane and never called."

"Did you ever figure out what it might have been?"

"No." A solemn silence drifts between us while Holly composes her thoughts.

"Well...it's a little strange but I guess I don't see it as any big deal. I mean, I'd expect you to come into my house without knocking."

"This was different Holly. I don't think I'm explaining it well but it left a bad taste in my mouth."

She looks genuinely concerned now, probably more for my mental health than anything else. "Why don't you just call him tonight and ask him what he wanted?"

"Because...maybe I don't wanna know? What would he possibly have wanted that would cause him to come back to my house, clearly after I'd decided to turn in for the night, and just open my door and waltz in?" Holly looks confused by my concern. "No, you're right Holly. He wanted to talk a little longer about something and assumed I'd still be awake. And he was perfectly right...obviously I was."

We sit quietly for a moment and I almost feel satisfied with that explanation. "It's just that...then he raised his hand to knock, but didn't, and he walked back to his car." Holly recoils slightly in response. "Why would he drive all the way over to come in unannounced, but then wouldn't bother knocking to get me to answer the door? He could see my office light was on."

Holly shrugs and looks pensive, but not exactly concerned.

"Wasn't there something else you were gonna tell me?" she asks, as we begin shuffling into separate spaces at the instructor's request.

"Later," I mouth, and float into a nice, secluded corner with my mat.

After a full hour of yoga, I actually feel refreshed and relaxed for a change. I drift over to Holly to exit the studio.

"Good class?" she asks, seeing the slight smile on my face.

"Yeah," I answer. "Good class."

She follows me to the parking lot, clearly noticing my increasing smirk. "What's so funny Fiona? I thought we were all freaked out over your bestie trying to enter without knocking," she says flippantly.

I roll my eyes over her already making light of the Quade situation, but find that I can't maintain any angry thoughts. All the worry is rolling away from me like a junk-filled whirlpool on a dingy Jersey beach.

"Okay, but you're gonna think I'm weird."

"Too weird for *me*? Come on!"

"Okay...there's kind of a guy." Holly instantly begins shrieking. "I mean...there isn't a guy, there's just kind of a guy in my imagination."

She stops walking and plants herself in front of me with a goofy frown. "Fiona, what the heck is this nonsense you're speaking?"

"I have a vendor...a flower vendor...who's attending the AFA conference this year."

"Okay?" Now she's looking at me like I've lost my mind.

"A male vendor...who I'm slightly interested in meeting. That's all." Her look is slowly morphing into an unconvinced half-smile. "I know. It's perfectly idiotic. Please forget I said anything. See you Saturday." I begin booking it toward my car.

"Wait, Fiona!" Holly runs giggling ahead of me and thrusts herself between me and my Jag. "What has gotten into you all of a sudden? You're all over the place today."

"Guilty as charged. Look, it's silly. I do business with this guy on the phone about three times a year, and suddenly I've got some kind of...you know...thing for him. It's not even worth mentioning. I should never have brought it up." I would open my door and peel out, except Holly's still standing between me and it. "Now can I please get into my car and drive back to my store?" I ask, feigning irritation but still smiling.

"Not so fast missy. First of all, let me see a picture of this hot flower guy you've got a thing for."

"That's the problem Holly. I don't have any photos. I've never seen a picture of the guy. He's not even a social media friend or anything."

Holly's looking more stupified by the second. "Then how do you know you're into him?" she asks, naturally.

"I don't. I have no idea. All I said is, I have a thing, okay? A thing. I really don't have any idea what that means," I blurt out, beginning to get genuinely flustered.

"Okay...it's okay," Holly says in her most calming voice, placing her hands lovingly on my shoulders. "You don't have to know what it is or why. I'm just happy to hear there's some...thing going on in your heart again."

"I didn't say he was in my heart. For heaven's sake, let's not make a bigger thing than it probably is." I press my fingers to my eyes, feeling embarrassed for sounding so damn difficult.

"You know Fiona," Holly continues, "it's okay to let someone into your heart again. It really is. But don't go losing your head over someone you've never met...and don't even know what he looks like. Remember the way Olga got burned meeting that guy from Minneapolis?"

I nod unwillingly. "Yes, I remember all about it. Don't worry. I'm not gonna lose my head over any man, okay? I'll be fine. Just...a little excitement never hurt me and I'm looking forward to meeting him. That's all that matters. I'm sure he looks like an ogre, but he's friendly and I look forward to meeting a friendly person. You happy now?"

"Okay then, go in peace," Holly says with one of her pert little smirks, then forcefully hugs me before backing away from my car.

* * *

An entire seven days later, I still haven't heard a peep out of Quade. He's never like this. The man calls enough to make me crazy on an average week. But after the day I had at work, I'm anxious to run something by him...so I succumb to dialing.

"Cookie," he answers with a slight hesitation I rarely hear in him.

"I thought you'd fallen off the face of the planet."

"No...just had an extra busy week. What's up?"

What's up? Quade never addresses me so flippantly. "Uh...I need to talk shop. That's what's up."

"Go ahead," he responds with an insolent level of detachment.

"Uh...I will go ahead Quade. What I need to tell you is that...you know what, never mind. I don't need your opinion to run my life. Have a nice weekend," I belt out in a huff before abruptly hanging up.

Of course he calls me back within seconds. I knew he would, but that doesn't make me any less pissed.

"Cookie, I'm sorry. I'm here for you...I just...have been processing some things lately. I'm very interested in what you have to say," he ekes out in his most pathetic groveling voice.

I heave a couple audible breaths into my phone and then feel my calm begin to return. Whatever calm I even had today.

"Well Quade, she's decided to hop her ass to London for a full month to take the most extravagant floral course anyone could ever ask for, is clueless as to how she'll get that done, and expects to march back into *my* store and pick up exactly where we left off just like nothing ever happened. And that's normal, of course, because every good little employee does that, right? Everyone feels entitled to globe trot and then return back to work, whenever, so they can better themselves as a person, right? I mean...I have absolutely nothing to be the least bit concerned over."

"Whoa...slow down there Cookie. Who are we talking about here?"

"Oh you know who...Maxine. Who else? I told you she thinks she's entitled." As I feel the heat rising up my neck and face, I realize how full of unexpressed resentment I really was when Maxine gave me her news.

"Well...now...calm down and let's think about this for a minute. You tell me she's a real talent, and that you'd like to see her education furthered and even bring her to AFA to compete."

"All true," I mutter, not wanting to admit the stabilizing effect Quade's words already have over me.

"So what's the big deal? If she wants to go to the best school, and it happens to mean a month in London...the girls can handle that, right? You already said Laura was moping about her hours being cut since Maxine came along. Maybe this would help to keep *her* on board a little bit longer too. I really don't see a huge problem here."

"You're right Quade. You're so correct. See, I knew I could use your help with this one," I say with a huge sigh. "And you know what...I'm happy for Maxine. And I'm glad she wants to reach higher than the rest, I really am. She's a good kid with a bright future and I wanna edge her forward, not hold her back."

"Kid huh? I thought you said she was older than the others."

"Oh...she is. But she's not like old. She's still a kid to me." I can almost detect some wistfulness when I speak of Max this way, like her spirit is bringing something youthful back to life inside me. I really do like Maxine.

"That's my Cookie," he responds, and I immediately feel my blood begin to boil again.

I'm nobody's cookie. I'm nobody's anything, except their boss.

"Yes, well...I should let you go. I hope I didn't bother you," I stammer.

"Hey, why would you ever imagine you're bothering me?"

"Because you haven't called all week and I respect that you have your life and I have mine, and I hope I didn't catch you at a bad time. That's all."

"Not at all Cookie. Not at all. I'll call you soon, okay?"

"I don't need you to call me, okay? I'm just saying...you usually do and you haven't and I don't like to bother people. I don't *need* anyone to talk to."

"Okay, okay. How about you call me next time you want?"

"Oh God Quade, can't we just be normal?! Forget it. I'll talk to you when I talk to you. Bye. And thanks for listening. I appreciated it. Bye." I hang up feeling like the difficult bitch that I am.

I can't fathom why I'm so upset, but Quade never did address his silent treatment to my satisfaction. And I wasn't about to ask about that night last week. It still gives me the heebie jeebies...I should be *relieved* he hasn't called lately. Perching my laptop and a glass of wine on the circular, marble tubside table, I pour myself a hot bubble bath. It's time to unwind, get Quade and Maxine out of my head, and do some planning for the upcoming conference weekend.

Chapter 6

Bo

I don't often hit the bar on Wednesday nights, but I've gone and done somethin impulsive. I think I'll head out and see if I cain't find Jose tonight.

Sure enough, as I pull into the parking gravel for Cowboy Saloon, his Mustang's in its usual spot.

"Big Bo! What's up man? Get your ass in here!" Jose's never lacking in encouragement, as I enter the dim corridor of the bar.

"Hey bro, how's it goin?" I reach out and pat his back as he flags down the bartender.

"Can I get you a beer?" he asks. "Hey Kiana," he calls to the bartender without hesitation, "get this man a Lagunitas on me." He slaps my back in return and clinks his Miller Lite against my freshly opened bottle. "What brings you out on a Wednesday, man?"

I turn up my bottle and take a long pull before answering that. "Well Jose, I decided to set certain events in motion towards the possible betterment of my future."

Jose looks at me like I'm an alien. "Dude, man, you're so...nerdy for a great big fucker. You know that?" I put my head down to laugh, feelin self-conscious but humored all the same. Jose's a straight talker, and I dig that about him. "Bo, man, I wanna be happy for you, but what is it you're trying to communicate man?"

I take another good swig and half my bottle's empty. "Jose, it's about my lady Fiona."

Jose looks away with a smirk, mumbling something in Spanish.

"No come on man," I press on. "Hear me out here, okay? I'm takin steps...you should be proud of me."

"Okay. Like what kind of steps?"

"I signed up to attend a florist conference over in Ft Lauderdale that I happen to know she attends every year. That's what."

Now Jose's eyes light up. He's startin to get the picture. "So like, you're gonna meet her there and then what... you're gonna have one of those long distance relationships or something man? That ain't gonna work, you know?"

"Hey now, don't be so pessimistic. Who says it cain't work, and besides...I ain't askin you about that. I'm tellin you...I'm gonna meet this woman, I'm gonna love this woman, and I'm gonna make her mine. That's how this is gonna go down bro. And now, you can challenge me on that all you want to, but you're gonna find out soon enough." One more swig and my Lagunitas is toast.

Jose's been lookin skeptical, but now his expression breaks into the smiling laughter he's famous for. Jose's a good natured guy, among the best of men. He just doesn't ever wanna see me get hurt and I love him for that.

"Hey, Bo, I'll dance at your wedding. Okay man? I believe in you man." He eyes my empty bottle as he drains his own. "Another round?"

"Sure thing bro. This one's on me."

We sink into the next round without conversation. Jose's eyes wander between Kiana's movements and a group of dudes shootin pool. I know what he's thinkin...that I'm takin a huge risk, that I should cozy up to one of the single regulars at this bar, that I'm nuts. But I also know what I know, and I can't quite explain how I do.

When I was a boy of fourteen, one of the last things my mama ever told me was that I had the gift. She said she had it too, came from her Apalachee Indian roots. I remember the way she looked at me that day, with her dark black eyes, somberly...as though she knew somethin dreadful that she couldn't say. And the way she held onto my hug before goin out to the barn that night, and wouldn't let me follow. All she said was that Pappa needed help with the horses, and that it wasn't safe for me to go too...

I'm startled out of my reverie when Jose reaches over and pats me on the back. "You okay there buddy, you're looking really far off somewhere."

"Yeah, thanks man. I was lost in thought there for a minute."

"You thinking about her?" he asks, sounding more cooperative than before.

"Yeah. I was thinkin about...her." Jose doesn't need to know anything more than that.

The memory of Mama's long, honey-colored hair drains out of my mind and fuses into an image of what Fiona might look like. I know it's a wing and a prayer, but I keep gettin omens out on the farm. Every time I think of Fiona, somethin tells me I'm on the right track. I just can't wait to meet that woman.

"Aren't you nervous at all man? To meet someone blind like this, like a blind date?"

I take some time to think about that. "You know Jose, I oughtta be nervous. You'd be dead right about that. But for some reason, I'm just not. Maybe it's cause it's not a blind date. I mean hell, she probably hasn't got the faintest idea I'm even gonna be there."

"Wait man...you mean...you didn't tell your lady?"

"Naw bro. She's only a client anyway. What the hell would she even care?"

"Hey, that's my point in the first place man. If she's only a client, why would she want to meet you?"

"Just trust me on this one bro. I have a feelin, alright?" I fist-bump Jose and rise to excuse myself for the night.

"Hey Bo," Jose calls out as I turn to go, "not to sound weird or anything man, but you know what? You're a good looking guy Bo. I'm pretty sure any woman would be happy to meet you man. I believe in you man."

I tip my hat to Jose and saunter out to my truck.

Chapter 7

Fiona

From the almost entirely glass-paned dining room, I watch as Holly parks and strides up to the Noodle House in a short, ruffly, bright fuschia dress that is way too beautiful for our selected venue. We hug and coo over each other as we file through the line toward the lunch counter, then order our selections and find a corner table for two.

Holly gets quiet as she props her elbows on the table, rests her chin on her hands, and looks at me with the expectant eyes of a puppy. I smile to myself, knowing she's waiting to hear more about my mystery flower dealer, but I have nothing to say on the subject.

Finally conceding, I break the silence with a vaguely related topic. "Well, I got a commitment from Maxine to attend AFA with me. She's gonna compete."

"Great, I'm excited for you. Do you really think she can place in it?"

"Tell you the truth Holly, I don't see why not. She exhibits a level of creativity I've rarely seen anywhere, and you know I've been in this business for fifteen years."

"Yeah, wow...that's great you found her," Holly responds as the owner brings out our giant bowls of udon noodle soup and fried rice. "Done any more business with the flower guy lately?" she asks between blows onto a spoonful of blazing hot soup.

"Nope. Probably won't between now and the conference."

Holly looks at me with disappointment. "Couldn't you come up with some excuse? Just order an extra batch of something—"

"Why would I do that Holly? Why?"

"I don't know...to get to know him more before the conference?"

"Holly, he's just an invisible vendor I have a convoluted long distance crush on. There's nothing to know. I'll go up to his booth and introduce myself at the conference. If he looks like a warthog, I'll awkwardly flirt with him for a minute anyway because that's what we do on the phone, then walk away and go about my business."

"And...what if he doesn't look like a warthog?" she asks, giggling over my cynical nature.

"Then I'll flirt with him a whole extra minute before walking away and going about my business. Satisfied?"

"Woo! Sounds like some big exciting plans," Holly replies with friendly sarcasm.

"Yep, that's me," I say as I focus on the fine art of eating rice with chopsticks.

We fervently slurp away at our noodles and rice for some time before Holly begins her probes again. "Quade behaving himself normally by now?"

"Yes, actually. After the night I laid into him for not calling me, he's called twice and seemed normal as ever. I even thought about asking him about that one night."

"Why don't you? You keep bringing that up...just get it off your chest."

"I don't know Holly. There's something internal that prevents me from going there. There's something uncomfortable about it."

"I think you're blowing it all out of proportion and all of it would go away if you'd just bring it up to him. There's gotta be a stupidly simple explanation."

"I'm sure you're right, and I probably will at some point." I turn back to the last bites of my food, hoping she'll be satisfied with my response.

After Holly gives up on prying any juicy info out of me, she submits to chit chatting about her latest architectural assignment...which I personally find fascinating. But she always interprets it as a failure when she can't engage me deeply in gossip about my life. I keep trying to tell her that hers is more interesting, but she never buys it.

Needing to put in some Saturday work, Holly apologizes and takes off quickly after lunch. So I decide to take a stroll in the warm, sunny afternoon air, stopping by Thymely

Solutions for some gourmet chocolate. I'll need this in the bathtub later.

* * *

I arrive home tired and head upstairs for a rare nap, only to be awakened after twenty minutes by a call from Quade. "Hey Cookie, what are you doing with your Saturday afternoon?" He sounds chipper.

"I was sleeping, actually. A bowl of fried rice knocked me out I guess," I reply in a dramatically groggy voice.

Quade chuckles into the line. "Well Cookie, it's Saturday. You're entitled to spend it however you like."

"Oh, thank you Quade," I respond with barely suppressed sarcasm.

"Did I tell you I'll be in town this evening?" he asks out of nowhere.

"No," I reply, jerking myself upright and feeling suddenly alert.

"Yeah…I have a dinner meeting but I'll be free after. How about I come around eight and we'll pop some corn and watch a flick."

I answer politely against the better judgment of my arm hairs, which are standing on end. "Sure, that sounds like a good idea." I cannot explain why I'm having these palpable responses to Quade that I've never had before.

"Great. I've gotta run now but I'll see you around eight then."

"Okay good…see you then." After hanging up, an electric silence buzzes through my bedroom like a restless spirit.

Nearly thirty minutes later, I glance at the bedside clock and realize how long it's been since I moved a muscle. I feel paralyzed by lack of impetus, a phenomenon that never occurs in my life. Maybe the hot bath will help. As I slide my legs over and push off the edge of the bed, I notice I'm faint and breathing audibly. Collapsing back down, I can hear my breath escalating in speed and volume...yet I'm helpless to stop it. It dawns on me I'm having a panic attack, my first one in years, and then the thought disintegrates into a wash of blurry, dizzy hyperventilation. I writhe limply on the bed, clawing at nothing with distorted arms and useless hands, as my body curls in on itself and gives up. The roaring of the jet engine inside my head comes to a sputtering halt, and then there is only gray, blindness, and a high pitched whine in my ears. Speckled fragments of colorless fuzz reintegrate and slowly form the room around me.

I wake up at five, in a state of disbelief that I've allowed my entire afternoon to slip away. Feeling hit by a truck, I stagger up and brew some tea to keep me from sleeping through my meditation. At six thirty I'm ready to pour a bath and get psyched for Quade's visit. Shuffling a few movies around in my head, I add coconut bubble oil to the water and consciously relax my face. I should be happy, looking forward to tonight, but nothing can get my attention off of what happened earlier without any cause or explanation.

After lighting a couple beeswax candles and killing the overhead lights, I finally slip down into the soft, delicious smelling water. Within seconds I feel so much better. I reach out to my tableside tablet and put on an All Things Considered episode about baby talk, then lean back against the tub pillow and close my eyes to listen. Inane discussion about things that don't pertain to me or my life. Perfect.

Shit! A tidal wave of bubbles splashes out onto the red and white mini-tiles, as I singularly yank myself upright and slam my fists into the water. I left my fucking chocolate in the bedroom! What next? Somebody kill me now.

As I hastily attempt to snatch my towel, the crooked rack loses its last bolt and both crash to the floor in a heap. Not giving a flying flip, I storm past them and into my room...where I grab the chocolate cherries out of my purse and throw it back onto the bed, contents spilling everywhere. Stalking across the wet carpet, I begin tugging at the impossible-to-open bag of cherries. What in the hell was the manufacturer's point in creating an impossible-to-open bag? Did twenty people sit at a thirty-foot table on the seventeenth floor of a forty-eight story high rise to put their heads together and come up with *this* as a reasonable means of containing eight ounces of chocolate covered cherries?! God help us all.

I whiz around the corner of the bathroom in time for the plastic bag to pop open, depositing chocolates throughout, just as I lose my footing and stumble toward the tub...which now looks like the candy-bobbing bucket at a seriously trashy Halloween party. Seeing that there are still a few ounces left in the bag, I splash into the tub and begin unceremoniously choking them down as I feel something strange happening. Two little tears are welling up in my eyes and threatening to slide down my cheeks. I hold my mascara-coated lids open wide to avoid a smudgy disaster, but then resort to laughing so hard the same result is inevitable. Now hysterically laugh-crying while choking on a cherry, I'm convinced I've lost my mind. I haven't shed a tear in at least five years, and I can't determine whether this sudden flood is a good or bad thing.

Right after I reach over to turn off the utterly pointless podcast I've been tuning out, I hear something that alarms me out of my emotional mess. There are footsteps thudding up my stairs.

"Quade! Quade is that you?!" I yell at the top of my lungs.

"Yeah, it's me Cookie. Sorry...I tried knocking but you didn't answer," he lies as his voice gets closer and closer.

"Quade! Ever heard of calling, or sending me a damn text? I'm in the tub!"

A moment later his face is peering around the thick, dark mahogany molding of my bathroom doorway. I stare at him stupidly, rendered speechless by feelings of helplessness, when it occurs to me that my exposed C's are still perky in their childless middle age...and are floating on top of the bathwater.

"It's okay Cookie...I've seen you naked a time or two," he states calmly, in a desperate attempt to hide the fact that he's ogling me. And then the inevitable question comes. "Cookie, what in the world happened in this place?" he asks with a stricken expression. "What is going on...are you okay?"

As he gallantly tiptoes between chocolates to come to my aid, I burst out laughing like a bloody fool. I can see in the oval mirror on the opposite wall, that my face is smudged to hell. I look like a zombie that didn't even get to sleep before resurrection. At the oddest moment, as Quade stares in confusion, I replace his face with the image of Bo that appears to me whenever I hear his voice. And suddenly I'm grounded, like none of today's events ever happened.

"Quade," I begin with the steadiness of a slow train, "I'm fine. And you...are early. I do not owe you any explanation regarding why I'm bathing in a tub full of melting chocolate balls, do I?" He begins to rise and back away from the tub, looking disproportionately wounded. "It's my business what I do in my home by myself, isn't it?"

"But Cookie...what are you—"

"And right now I'm in my home by myself, aren't I? Because I don't have any company tonight until eight o'clock. Otherwise," I continue, suddenly raising my voice, "I wouldn't be sitting naked in my private bubble bath, would I Quade?" Radio silence. "Would I?"

"Okay, hold up Cookie," he says, putting his palms out in front like he's trying to whoa a horse.

"No you hold up, Quade! This is my bathroom, I'm sitting in my bathtub, and you're not invited in my house until eight o'clock. It's as simple as that!" I yell, brandishing my arms wildly and unwittingly releasing my boobs. Automatically his gaze rivets on them. "Quade!" I splash my fists into the tub, sending another slosh of frothy water and chocolate balls onto the floor.

"Okay okay, sorry. I'll just go...wait somewhere else until eight," he says as he ducks out of the bathroom looking devastated. "I'll be sitting in the dining room then," he belts out as I hear him start down the staircase.

Now too far away for me to make a reasonable protest, I sit in my tub fuming. I should never have let him have the last word. I should have requested he sit in his car, or out on the damn deck at least. Now he's down there lurking in my house, twiddling his thumbs while he waits for me to finish taking my *relaxing* bath. Again my veins are surging with the new, unfamiliar feeling I keep getting around Quade. I can no longer imagine sitting in front of a movie with him tonight. I want him out, out, out...

I close my eyes and take five deep breaths, remembering what happened to me earlier. How humiliating if that should happen now, and Quade were to come up here and have to rescue my naked body from drowning in the tub. I must hold myself together.

I hop out and grab a clean towel, shuttering over the full unacceptability of the situation and feeling powerless in a way I'm unaccustomed to. I throw on a shapeless, green lounge suit and proceed downstairs forty-five minutes early. I may as well accept my fate and enjoy the rest of the evening. Quade *is* my long-time best friend, after all. I have no idea what's got me so bitchy and paranoid lately.

"Hey," I say calmly, as I walk past Quade and grab a broom and dustpan. "Yeah..." I can see the question in his eyes. "I dropped some chocolates earlier. Little cleanup job to do up there."

"Please, allow me," he says, gently taking the cleaning articles and heading toward the stairs. "After you." He waits patiently as I lead him up the stairs, feeling like quite the ass for freaking out on him before.

As we enter my bedroom, I turn to address him about the situation but am halted by his smirky grin. "What?" I demand.

"Nothing, nothing," he replies, shaking his head but still grinning.

"Here." I snatch the broom and pan and quickly begin scooping in the balls that are still on dry areas of the floor. Then I use an old towel to mop up the chocolatey mush-water directly around the tub. The mess inside the tub can wait. I stand up and turn to find Quade leaning against the doorway with his arms crossed, still watching me with a grin. Now I'd like to slap him.

"So, what did you have in mind for a movie?" I ask instead, unable to hide my irritation.

"Oh, I haven't thought about it really. There's a family drama that looks interesting...Disobedience."

"Hmm, never heard of it." I'm aware I sound minimally cooperative, but I can't help myself.

"Well, would you like to pick?"

"No. No...Disobedience, whatever. Sounds fine."

"Are you sure?" he asks like the sweetie that he is.

"Yes, sounds good. I'll get the popper started while you find it," I respond, already feeling better about myself for making some little effort.

I reach around the kitchen for a minute, gathering salt and butter, then pour corn into the machine and turn it on to wait. Impatiently tapping my nails on the counter, I watch the corn in a daze...trying not to think about anything that might make me hostile or emotional. So, nothing. Suddenly feeling a cloud of discomfort hanging over me, I peek over my shoulder and there's Quade standing at the end of the kitchen with his arms crossed...looking smug again.

"Did you find it?" I ask to divert whatever weird energy's building up in the room.

"Yeah, uhh...do you wanna watch it in the den, or—"

"Den's fine," I cut in.

"How about the loft? Wanna watch it up there maybe?"

"The den's fine." He's giving me a disappointed look. "I just don't feel like going up and down stairs all night," I offer as a half-assed explanation.

Defeated, he takes the bowl of popcorn. We traipse down the hall behind the staircase and enter the amply comfortable den, setting the bowl in the center of the oak coffee table. Quade already has the film pulled up on the screen, and we sit down on opposite ends of the couch.

My usual position is to lean into the corner and stretch my legs across the cushions, but I hesitate tonight. I know he'll grab my feet and start massaging, and I still don't feel comfortable with Quade's new habit of barging in. I want space, and I'm willing to sacrifice his humdrum foot massage in order to get it.

As the credits begin, I can see in my peripheral vision that Quade is staring at me. Once I detect he's looking back at the screen, I shoot him a side-eye glance and notice he's actually staring at my legs now...which are extended out onto the coffee table. How silly I was to think I could look 'inconspicuous' in a pair of massively baggy shorts. Feeling self-conscious, I tuck my legs under myself and reach for the popcorn just in time for Quade to thrust his hand into mine.

"You go ahead Cookie," he says cordially, as I dip my hand into the corn with annoyance. Ten minutes into the film he's staring at me again. Definitely staring. And what the hell is this "family drama" about, really?

By the second hour of the film, I'm not sure whether Quade's watched more of the screen or me. And *every* time I reach for the popcorn his hand dives in under mine. It's too late to say anything about the film now. Having been awkward from the first minute in, this feels more like a bizarre out-of-body experience than a movie viewing. I'm so uncomfortable that I'm actually trying to will myself out of the room without moving.

"What is up with this movie Quade?" I finally blurt out when we get to the scene where the two female stars begin erotically kissing. "This is not a family drama...this is a hot lesbian fantasy!" I stare at him accusingly in the blinking light from the screen.

"I've never watched it before Cookie. How was I to know?" he asks guilelessly.

Yeah right. "Didn't you read anything about this film before selecting it?"

"Sure...a little bit. I thought you'd like it. I think it's quite good, don't you?"

"You thought I'd enjoy sitting on my couch with you and watching two chicks make out? You thought I'd enjoy that?!"

I can hear the scene getting steamier in the background of my yelling, and I'm ultra-relieved we're staring at each other with hostility rather than watching it. I wish to keep yelling at least until the scene has passed, but it sounds like it's just getting started.

In a moment of mounting anger and discomfort, I snatch up the remote and turn off the television. What's shocking about the following minute is that the dead silence between us is way worse than the sex show was. Now what??

"Would you like to try something else?" I ask, trying my darndest to sound willing and easy-going.

"That's alright. It's a little late to start something over," he replies, sounding so crushed that I almost feel bad.

We sit in terrible silence for another minute, until I nervously fish a few half-popped kernels off the bottom of the popcorn bowl and crunch into them with surprising volume.

"Cookie," Quade starts back up, his sweetness apparently restored, "how about a little foot massage before I go? I can do that, just right in here on the couch."

As opposed to?

One-hundred percent of me feels revile at the thought of Quade's touch tonight, yet how can I turn him away in such a callous manner after his attempt to make the evening nice for me? After all, he probably knew little about the film and selected it based on a long string of fantastic reviews from snooty critics. That would be just like him. Again, I've allowed myself to get the willies over nothing.

"I don't know Quade, I'm just not feeling very well. I think maybe the popcorn didn't sit well with the chocolates I had earlier." That sounds perfectly polite, not to mention realistic.

"Oh no Cookie...I was afraid of that. I could've seen that one coming," he adds with a faux-scolding wag of his finger.

"Yeah yeah," I respond faux-playfully, "I stand corrected."

Good, the mood in the room has transformed nicely. Now he can leave peacefully and we'll forget all about this off night. I grab the bowl and rise feebly, dragging my feet all the way to the kitchen to feign moderate illness. I set it into the sink, run a little water, and turn haggardly toward the staircase.

Quade closes in to hug me at the bottom of the stairs, but instead of the old pat-pat-pat he picks me up in a herculean effort to haul me up to my room.

"Put me down...Quade! Quade! No!" I quit kicking and screaming once he's halfway up the steps, not wishing to make him falter now. Quade's never been built enough to carry me up stairs before. I thought I'd noticed a recent increase in upper body size, but it's hard to tell through most of his button-ups. Nonetheless, he's panting and carrying on as if I were one big sack of potatoes.

By the time we pass through the threshold, I'm in an impotent rage...exhausted from mentally struggling against him all evening. I say nothing, but give him the death glare as he lays me across my bed with a look of pride.

"Is there anything I can get you, anything I can do for you at all?"

"No. Thank you. I just need sleep now."

"Goodnight then Cookie," he says as though he doesn't see I'm furious.

"Goodnight," I manage, softening my face enough to satisfy him so he'll leave.

I allow him to pull my blankets around me and plant a kiss on my forehead. Surely I'm a horrible person to not better appreciate a friend like Quade. I eke out a smile as he walks toward the doorway, looking lovingly over his shoulder, then turns out the light and heads down the hallway. I nervously rerun the events of the night, staring wide-eyed at the dark ceiling.

So he accidentally picked an inappropriate film for the occasion. I didn't need to make him feel like a leper over it. But then there was the gawking-at-my-legs thing. What was that?? We've been divorced for nine years and all of a sudden he's talking about my dresses and fixating on my legs. Why didn't he do that when we were married? I could have used a man with a pulse. But the notion of him having 'those' thoughts about me now is surprisingly grotesque.

I flip onto my side to get serious about sleep. Taking five deep breaths, I smile to myself in the darkness. Quade is gone, I'm in a very comfortable bed, it's been a long day... it's time to shut down the mental clutter.

At six a.m. I awaken from the kind of icky dream I have on very rare occasion. I can hear the earliest robin out on the lawn, but it doesn't save me from the muck that is my existence at this moment. I try to get back to sleep, to erase it, but I can't get the flashing, vivid images to leave my mind.

I see Quade's face of ten years ago...shiny, eager, dorky, and I recall the hypnosis I was under when I told myself that our drab, neutered connection was the stuff a proper marriage is made of. Successful, generous, and sweet to a fault...the perfect suitor. Of course my family and friends all adored him. And then I see him naked and the way he grins like a boy, like a kind, innocent boy who has no remote clue what he's doing. His penis is enormous in the dream... unrealistic and rubbery looking, though not flaccid, and he's beaming at me with pride. Then he somehow mixes it with my body as he continues grinning, looking happy and complete. I feel nothing...no pain, pleasure, or interest. Just the submissive blankness of compromise. The hollowness of detachment. I wrap my arms around him to show that I love him, but I know it's a lie. I'm empty inside. Quade is my greatest friend and he's all I know, but I'm empty. His great big, glowing member cannot fill me in the slightest.

I sit up with an aching sadness that won't leave. I'll get up and start my day, make some tea, meditate the images away. As I pour the cascara, I find it in myself to briefly smirk... Quade's penis isn't a tenth the size of that thing in my dream. At least my subconscious has a sick sense of humor.

Chapter 8

Bo

Mama would always say that when the skies are cloudy for a while, they're protecting the earth from too much harshness, too much stimulation. The rain comes to rinse away the old and cultivate new life and formation, different perspectives. If life were sunny all the time, everyone would burn out in a fire of excess energy.

I learned the hard way that rain and fire can come at the same time, cause confusion, lead to chaos, end in tragedy. But since then I've spent my life watching the cycle, the daily growth of seedlings, saplings, baby birds...forming, growing, and disappearing or slowly breaking down. Like a vase full of roses, fading from bright velvet red to rusty brown. It'll happen to every single one of us eventually. Life is about livin while you're livin, takin in everything that's around you. Feeling.

I took my mama seriously. I believe I can remember every word she ever said to me. And I aspire to act out her wisdom in all that I do, to make her proud wherever she is. I can see her in the sunset tonight, as I bring flats of lantana seedlings into the shelter of the greenhouse. In a few weeks they'll open to the sky like tall jewels, in every shade of magenta, purple, coral, yellow, orange.

As I run my fingertips over the soft, baby green leaves, I watch the sky sharpen into a blazing watercolor painting... then fade and drift slowly toward darkness. An owl hoots in the giant swamp oak around the edge of the old house. I look over at its mammoth shape in the shadows and see the last light glinting off the west facing windows. A spark burns within me to fix up the house, get the water and electric on and move into it for the first time in thirty years. It's not a desire I felt in the past, but every time I see a sunset I can hear Mama telling me it's okay. It's okay to go back in and live with the luxuries I've denied myself. And I know she's right, but I won't – I can't – go it alone.

Chapter 9

Fiona

Tuesday morning I receive a text that Quade will be in town for the night, and I do something I've never, ever done before. I ignore it. Maybe he'll think my phone service glitched, or that I read it at a busy moment and it slipped through the cracks. All I know is that I stood in the back of Fiona's Flowers for what must have been a solid ten minutes, fingers poised over my phone, unable to manifest any possible response I'd be happy to send.

I don't want to visit with him tonight. I don't want to tell him that. I don't want to make up an excuse. I don't want to pleasantly submit and go along with whatever he has in mind. I don't want to hurt his feelings. I don't want him to be in town. I don't want to deal with responding in any way. So...I didn't.

The potential flaw with this plan was that Quade would continue texting throughout the entire day, annoying the heck out of me and eventually becoming worried. The reality? He didn't.

It's seven o'clock; for the past three hours I've been helping Maxine prep for an upcoming graduation party, and I dread going home. I've even stayed to help clean up. By now Maxine must be wondering what I'm angling for, but the fact is that Quade will knock on my door at some point...and I'd love to not be home when he does. Unless I'm lucky and his evening's full of meetings or paperwork. Maybe that's why he didn't try harder to reach me.

"Okay, everything looks good," I reluctantly say to Maxine once there's nothing more I can conjure up to do.

"Thanks for staying and helping with all this," she responds graciously.

She'd kept assuring me everything was under control, but I'd insisted on staying.

"Are you excited about our big weekend coming up?" I ask as I finally gather my things to leave.

"Yes! I am so excited."

"Me too kiddo. The conference is always fun, but I have the feeling this one will be extra special." I'll leave it at that.

I stop to order a couple fish tacos for dinner, then meander through the south end of town for a while...cruising by a couple houses Holly's having work done on. I eventually sit in a park with my windows down and force myself to eat the tacos at a leisurely pace. Then, after a twenty minute walk under the old oaks and walnuts, I submit to going home. It's after eight and I simply have to get to my office and get some things done. Surely Quade would have texted by now if he was coming over.

As I enter the dark, quiet house and head toward the kitchen for tea, I feel myself truly relax for the first time all day. I briefly consider calling Quade to let him know I'm alright and was too swamped to respond earlier. That would reduce my guilty concern that he's feeling ignored. But he's obviously piled up with work or he would have tried reaching me again anyway...bless the guy. I guess I'll just leave it. Quade's a big boy and he'll be fine.

After setting my tea on a bedside table coaster, I fetch my laptop from the office and carry it into bed to resume with work. I guess it feels less like I'm still working if I prop myself against pillows to do it.

At half past ten, I catch myself dozing off in the middle of an email and decide to call it quits. I carry my teacup downstairs and lock the doors, a surprising habit I've developed since that first night I did it. I still don't feel any real need to; I guess it's just an OCD thing now. A shortened condensed version of my bedtime routine relaxes me further, but I lie awake for a few minutes feeling guilty about how relieved I was not to hear from Quade. All because I thought I detected him looking at my legs a few nights ago. Surely he could sense my discomfort and he's either trying to give me space, or just avoid the trajectory of my latest surge of irrational moods.

Oh well, tomorrow I'll apologize for missing his text, and next time he comes we'll have our usual nice hour or two together. The last thing in my awareness is the lovely pitter patter of fat raindrops hitting the windows on either side of my bed, as I drift off to sleep.

The next thing in my awareness is the patent creak of my bedroom door opening. My eyes pop open and my body goes frozen. Do I have a ghost? Stuck facing away from the door, I squint through the blackness at the glow of my alarm clock...which reads eleven twenty-two. Paralyzed with fear, I remind myself that I've been in this house for nine years without witnessing anything mysterious, and I don't believe in malignant spirits anyway. After taking five deep breaths and hearing nothing further, I'm tempted to reach over and turn on a lamp to demystify the atmosphere. It must have been a draft or, God forbid, a large mouse that bumped the door open. I only had it pulled to, after all. But some primal terror has fixed my body into a wooden plank and won't allow it to move.

Feeling like a silly child, I commit to taking another round of five breaths before I'll reach over to the lamp. I imagine Celeste's simpering voice 'reminding' me to breathe during therapy, and it brings a relaxed smile to my face. By the time I get to breath number three, I feel released from my foolishness and begin to extend my arm. At that moment, I detect the slightest sinking at the foot of my bed...a vibration as though something had hopped up onto it. My arm ceases its motion, still under the blanket, and my heartbeat becomes deafeningly loud. The worst scenes from the few horror films I've ever watched flood my mind with images. I squeeze my eyes shut in the darkness and tell myself I imagined it.

When the foot of the bed sinks again, I enter into a wild panic like never before. Within a fraction of a second, I bunch my legs up into my chest and reach for the lamp...a foreign guttural sound bellowing out of my chest. I click the lamp on and snatch it off the table in one fluid movement, wielding it over my head like an ax. In the flashing moment of light before I yanked the lamp too far for its cord, I was able to make out the figure leaning on the foot of my bed.

"Quade!" I scream out like a savage. "Quade you fucker!"

As my body goes limp and I curl into a ball of hysterical crying, he says nothing. Is Quade now staring at me through the darkness? Sobbing, I blindly hurtle the small lamp toward the foot of my bed and hear it crash onto the floor. A moment later I feel Quade's hands grappling for me, quietly, finding my wrists and wrapping around them.

"Quade! Quade! What are you doing?!" I scream in a panic, flailing until he tightens his grip and holds my arms still.

"Why did you lock the doors Fiona?" he asks with all the calmness of a psychopath. "Why didn't you answer my text Fiona? You knew I was in town...why didn't you answer me?"

"I'm sorry," I plead. "You're hurting my wrists. Quade... Quade...please let go of my wrists. I promise I'll talk to you, just please let go," I say in the most neutral voice I can muster.

"Can I trust you?" he asks with sickening condescension. "I can't have you throwing things at me. You could have hurt me. I bought you that lamp, you know. I don't appreciate you throwing our things."

"I'm sorry…I'm sorry. You scared me, that's all. I didn't know who you were Quade! Why would you surprise me like that?!" As I begin to raise my voice again, I feel his hands automatically tighten. My fingers are shriveled into claws, with no blood or feeling left in them. "Quade, please." I sweeten my voice back to a gentle beg. "I can't feel my hands Quade, please…that's too tight. I can't feel my hands anymore."

"When did you start locking up at night Fiona?" he asks as he loosens his grip enough for me to wiggle my fingers again.

"I don't know. I just did it one night without thinking and then it became a habit. It doesn't mean anything. It's just a habit now. Quade…I wasn't trying to lock *you* out. I thought you were busy. You haven't texted since this morning and I just had a busy day and forgot about it…I'm sorry," I say in a strategically agreeable tone.

I'm shaking like a leaf and have never felt so physically helpless in my life. Quade wouldn't have even been strong enough to grab me and hold me like this before…who has my ex husband become?

Finally he releases my hands completely and I fall forward onto my two numb, useless stumps, tears streaming from my eyes. I try not to sniffle, not to let Quade hear that I'm crying, that I'm weak. I lie motionless, waiting for him to say or do something, anything, but he holds still in the darkness. He does not turn on any lights, but I can make out his hovering silhouette in the shadows my eyes have adjusted to.

Oddly, I have no instinct to kick and scream or call the police. I mentally rehearse it; I could bolt away from him in the darkness and lock myself into the bathroom with my phone. But my intuition tells me not to do this, that he wouldn't run out to his car and flee, that he would break down my old bathroom door if he had to. I don't know this powerful new Quade and I'm terrified out of my mind.

It seems like an eternity as he watches over me, lying still on my bed, trying not to make a single move that might incite a response from him. My fear only escalates throughout this expanse of unknown. What is he doing? What is he thinking? Should I try to say something? I get the sinking feeling I should not.

Finally...something happens...but it's almost a worst case scenario. I feel the side of my bed sink down again, as Quade lowers himself and reclines. I'm curled on my side in such a way that I can see him behind me, propped on his elbow to peer over at my face. I keep my eyes squinted, pretending they're closed, until he reclines fully and places his hands on my naked shoulders. In an instant I roll off the other side of the bed and stand with my arms across my chest.

"Well I can feel my hands again...that kinda freaked me out Quade," I say, sounding like I don't want to make a big deal out of it. "Lemme just throw a robe on and we can talk, okay?"

Without taking my eyes off the dark blob on my bed, I slip an arm into the closet and grab my thick, long, full-coverage winter robe. But before I can get it on, Quade's standing inches in front of me.

"That's not necessary," he says, grabbing the edge of the robe so I can't finish wrapping it.

"Oh come on sweets, I'm cold." Now resorting to tender placation, I fear what he might do if I get hostile.

"As I said, that's not necessary. I'm here to keep you warm."

My instinct is to freeze up like a statue and shut him out, but I'm afraid I must yield something lest he become aggressive again and take even more. My body's been next to his thousands of times; this shouldn't be scary...but it is. I'm grossed out to an almost inexplicable degree. I stop struggling against him with the robe and allow him to move forward, farther into my personal space. He's fully clothed but I can feel his body heat searing with mine, not a sensation I'm used to. He was always on the chilly side before. Again, I don't recognize this new alien Quade.

He leans in and breathes onto my neck, placing his open lips against it. To bolt out of the room, I would have to move around both Quade and my bed. I would not be able to detour to the bedside table and grab my phone. As Quade tests the waters further, now opening my robe to place both hands on my hips, I feel that slim window of opportunity shrinking to something even more minute.

I make an executive decision to do the only thing I see possible, to play it cool. I slowly raise my hands to my shoulders and drop the heavy robe to the floor.

"How did you get in here anyway?" I ask with a phony giggle, as he continues kissing my neck and tightens his grip on my hips.

"With my key, Cookie. You know I've always kept keys to my own house."

Of course. In nine years it's never come up, but he never turned over his copies of the keys. Sensing my sudden lack of resistance, Quade moves toward my lips and I put a manicured fingertip against his with a smile.

"Not so fast," I say seductively, and he actually allows me to move around him...bending onto the bed and crawling across it on all fours.

Mouth gaping, he is fully transfixed. I roll over and lie back, stretching the length of my body across the top blanket, presenting. As Quade rips his shirt over his head, I can make out his rows of muscles even in the shadows. His arms, chest, and abs make him look like a different person, impressive yet simultaneously chilling. What would possess him to suddenly take to hard workouts in his middle age?

He reaches to unbutton his khakis and peels them down with his underpants. As they roll to his lower thighs, I seize that exact moment to exit.

"Hang on...I'll get my vibrator," I quip as I roll off the edge of the bed nearest the door, leaving him on the other side.

I try to look unhurried as I disappear around the doorway, then grab a towel from a bathroom down the hall and quietly sprint down the stairs and out the front door. The moon is full and the yard is bright. With two acres of property, there's a lot of room between me and my neighbors and I can now hear Quade yelling in the house. I'm naked; surely he thinks I'm sane enough to hide somewhere inside. But if he gets near a window, he'll easily see me streaking across the yard in this moonlight. And my pale pink towel will give me away if I hide under the bushes.

I stop breathing when I hear the front door slam. He's out here with me. I run around to the back of the house and then panic, having no idea which side he'll pop out on. My heartbeat is in my ears as I take off at full speed, straight across the backyard and toward the road...desperately clutching my tightly wadded towel. I slide down the steep bank that separates the yard from the road, my feet scraping noisily across mud and leaves, and wrap the towel around myself at last.

As I glide down the road toward the other houses, I can see everyone's lights are off. I have nothing but this towel and no phone. I'll walk the few blocks to Holly's townhouse and yell at the door if I have to. Frantically looking behind me every few seconds, I race over asphalt and gravel... unconcerned with the battering my feet are taking.

Once I get within two blocks of Holly's, a car rolls up beside me and slows to my pace. Just a madwoman on the loose wearing a towel, I keep my gaze straight ahead...and then I hear the sound of an electric window sliding down.

"Where you going Cookie? Are you running away from home?"

I keep walking, refusing to respond or look in his direction.

"You know, your home is my home Cookie. I was only paying a visit to my own house...as I'm entitled to do."

Finally I break, but continue walking and facing forward. "I'll call the police and get a restraining order on you Quade! You can't barge into my residence, my bedroom, my bed...in the middle of the night! You have no right!"

"Oh! Cookie...I wouldn't recommend you do that. You know, I ran into Frank tonight at dinner, and he invited me to join him...since you were missing in action. I really like my friend Frank and wouldn't wanna cause him any grief in his little town. I really don't think he'd appreciate my crazy ex wife trying to make life difficult for me. What do you think?"

Frank Vernon is the local Chief of Police, and has been buddies with Quade since high school. He's got me over a barrel.

"Hey, Cookie, get in the car and let me take you back home. I promise I'll leave you be and you can get back to sleep." I continue walking as though he said nothing. "Cookie, come on, let me take you home. You look ridiculous out here."

"I don't care what I look like!"

"You know Cookie, it's not gonna do you any good to tattle to Holly about this." We're now half a block away from her front door. "Leaving the house in my name is your problem Cookie. You could have taken me for all I was worth, but you were always so cooperative...so forgiving... so patronizing. Did you think I wasn't a very smart man, Cookie? Did you think I was just going to share my home with you forever, without asking anything in return? Did you think I was going to fund your business from the ground up, and then let you walk all over me? Walk away from me? Ignore my texts?"

I'm now standing at the edge of Holly's yard, breathing so hard I can barely keep the robe around my ribs. If I go to her front door, Quade can easily park and remove me before she can get downstairs. I could just stand here and have a screaming fit, even though he'll tell Vernon I'm nuts. Quade was an upstanding community member for decades before moving, and he pulls a lot of weight in this town.

"If you come with me now, quietly, I'll drive you back home and we can forget this ever happened." I continue to stand, breathing, psyching myself to not have a panic attack. If I hyperventilate here and now, he'll drag my limp body into his car and do God knows what with it.

"Cookie...I'll strike a deal with you. How about...you get into my warm car, I'll drive you home and you can go upstairs and get into your nice comfortable bed, you'll be quiet about this incident...and I'll let you keep your home *and* your business. Doesn't that sound like a nice idea Cookie? Huh?"

I have to think fast...think fast. Quade could take away everything that means anything to me. But I cannot get into his vehicle. He's insane. What if he tries something horrible? What if he takes me to the woods and leaves me in a ditch somewhere? What if he's psychotic? He *is* psychotic! My sweet, placid ex husband has gone completely off his rocker and he's a psychopath. The full reality of the situation sets in, as I stand in the night air...shivering in deafening silence.

"How about...how about I walk home next to your car. You can see me home and I'll walk next to the car, okay?" I manage, finally making eye contact. Quade's eyes are blazing with a look I've never seen before.

"Okay. Let's go for a walk then."

As I turn and head back into the shadows toward my neighborhood, I'm torn apart by the sensation of leaving Holly's yard. The security of knowing she loves me and would take me in, and hold me while I break down and have a desperately needed cry...all of it dissipates as I walk the other way. As we traverse the long blocks, I begin to feel the bruising in my feet. I consciously soften my face to create the illusion of trust, or even slight friendliness. Anything to keep Quade from becoming riled and possessive again.

Once we reach the beginning of my driveway, I turn to him with a falsely grateful smile.

"Okay, I think I'm okay now. Sorry if I overreacted. I think I'll be okay from here."

In essence, I'm begging him to stay in his car and let me enter the house by myself. But he continues to follow, slowly, down the long, gravel lane. Seeing in my periphery that he's watching me intently, I maintain my phony look of pleasantness.

"Thanks for seeing me home. I think I can sleep now," I turn to him and say, as we reach the front of the yard.

"Oh Cookie...promise me you'll get to sleep," he says sweetly, his tired eyes reflecting an entirely new demeanor.

"I will...you too," I say with a smile, as I turn and head down the walkway.

In a calm and collected manner I open the front door, then raise a hand over my shoulder to wave him off. To my relief, he puts his car in reverse and backs down the driveway. I watch rigidly until his lights disappear and then the panic comes. I exhale a deafening scream as I limply collapse into a ball on the foyer floor, and then I hear myself screaming and screaming, eyes dry and open, until it feels like all the contents of my insides have been expelled into the room. I snap to my feet in a frenzy, on my last shred of adrenaline, and scan out the windows for his vehicle. He could turn his headlights off and creep back up my driveway, but I have a deep feeling he's done for the night. He looked so different at the moment he left, like he, too, was going to have to reckon with the aftermath of the damage he'd done.

Entering my bedroom to retrieve my phone, I feel a wave of weakness and nausea as I look around and see the glimmer of the broken lamp base on the carpet. How will I ever sleep cozily in this room again? I cross the hall and enter my office, which faces the front of the house. I leave the lights off, so I'll have high visibility out the windows if Quade returns. I sit at my desk and futilely dial Holly, who turns her phone off at night.

"Fiona?" she answers to my surprise.

"Holly!" I can't get another word out before my voice breaks into sobs.

"Oh my God, Fiona...what's going on?" Through all our years of friendship, I don't believe Holly has ever heard or seen me cry. I'm just not the crying type, especially in front of others.

I'm about to say 'Quade' when I realize he could have snuck into my house through the back, and could be lurking somewhere...watching my every move. I know I'm probably alone, but I also don't know what he'll do if he's monitoring me and I slip up. "It's just...I can't sleep with this moon and...I'm just feeling emotional. I just needed to hear your voice and cry I guess."

"Oh Fiona...honey, I'm so glad you called...gosh, I can't believe I had my phone on. I couldn't sleep either. The moon is huge and I've been lying in bed for hours."

It kills me to know she was awake while I was standing in her yard in a towel. If only she'd been looking out a window, or sitting on her porch.

"Holly, what's your schedule like this week? I could really use a girl date before my trip."

"Of course! I'll make time for you. How about lunch Thursday?"

"Okay."

"Yeah...I woke up at around midnight and then couldn't go back to sleep, happened to turn on my phone when I went to the bathroom...and then you called. It was perfect timing."

"Oh." I nervously laugh, glad just to be on the phone with the voice of love and reason. "So, what are you so restless about?" I ask. I may as well sit and listen to Holly talk about anything that keeps me from telling what happened.

"Oh God Fiona, it's so stupid. Seriously...Levi's not here tonight and I'm just skittish for some reason. It sounds dumb but I just woke up scared. I went through my condo and turned on about twenty lights."

Uncontrollable tears are quietly rolling down my cheeks again. "So that's why your lights were on," I mumble, almost choking on the words.

"What?"

"I was out taking a walk...and I noticed your lights were on."

"Fiona you sound terrible, and that's a pretty hardy walk for this hour. What is going on?"

I let out a heavy sigh, verging on telling her, then remind myself Quade could literally be hiding within feet of me.

"I've just had an emotional day. Any chance you can do lunch tomorrow?"

"Oh dear...I would love that but I have a call that's going to cut my lunch down to about twenty minutes, at my desk. Maybe I can put it off—"

"No...no, Thursday's fine. Don't do anything drastic. Well, I'm excited about the AFA weekend." I don't quite know how to fill the space without telling my story, but I know we both want to linger on the phone after our respective fright nights, so I may as well lighten the atmosphere if I can't discuss anything relevant.

"Yeah! Maybe it will be a little bonding experience for you and your star employee," Holly says, already sounding brighter.

"Should be something like that." We're silent for a moment, neither of us wanting to mention the Bo factor.

"You know what," she abruptly starts back in, "there's no way I'm going to sleep right now. Even with all the lights on. Any chance you'd wanna come back over? We could have a slumber party...or I can come over to your place? I know it's absurd but I don't feel like being alone tonight."

I'm dying by inches as the words come out of her mouth. Holly's company is *exactly* what I need right now, and I'm determined to stay on the phone forever if I can't have it. But the possibility of Quade listening or watching has got me in a paralysis. If I try to leave, he could be out there...obsessively stalking, waiting to pull up alongside me and follow. And having Holly over is simply out of the question. I wouldn't be able to talk about anything real. Not to mention, what if my ex husband's so psychotic that he attempts to take on two women? I know that's not going to happen, but I can't be responsible for putting Holly in a possible situation. This is all so new to me, and I have no idea what I could actually be dealing with.

"I know...it was a silly idea. We should probably both just try to sleep," she says after being met by the silence of my indecisiveness.

"No...actually it's a great idea. But, can we stay on the phone while you come over?"

"Of course. Please, yes, let's stay on the phone. Okay...so I'm coming over there?"

"Yeah. Is that okay?"

"Sure. My empty condo's giving me the creeps and I wanna get out of here anyway. I'm already walking down to my car."

"Perfect." I'm sure she'll be safe in her car, and if Quade's spying on me he'll flee before she arrives. It's not like we're dealing with an ax murderer...

"Okay, ignition on and garage door opening. I feel better already. This will be so fun!" Holly says. I force out a giggle in response.

We make chit chat until she pulls up in front of my house, at which point I finally brave moving around and turning on some lights. I figure if Quade's in the vicinity, I'll act like I don't suspect it. I manage to walk down the hall and stairs to meet Holly without any hiccups, which increases my sensation that Quade's done here for the night.

I watch her safely leave her car and walk to the front door, then throw it open to greet her. We hug each other too hard for a couple of friends who saw each other three days ago, then enter boisterously and begin bustling around the kitchen, heating up tea water and digging out snacks. As we sit down to celery sticks and Cesar dressing, clutching our hot mugs of tea, I'm almost convinced that I feel happy and normal. But, after a few minutes of conversation, the guilt seeps in when Holly asks me about Bo and I'm resistant to answering it. How could I compromise another woman by luring her into my unsafe home?

After I shrug off the Bo question, Holly cheerily changes the subject to the huge, pink hot tub in my attic. "I have the best idea," she says. "Let's go up to the attic and get nice and sleepy in a big hot tub full of bubbles."

Again, I'm stricken with guilt at the image of the two of us, giggling in the hot-tub with Quade peeking out from a closet. My one comfort is, if he drove away from my house, parked on the next street, hoofed it back over here, and stealthily entered without making a sound, then he's not going to be able to follow us up to the attic without being detected. Oh...until we turn the jets on and begin shouting over the top of them. Or worse yet, he comes out of hiding and corners us in the tub, naked and vulnerable, because he no longer cares about consequences. Plus the law is on his side. We're not getting in that hot-tub.

"Ooh yeah...that does sound nice," I start in by means of explanation, "but the attic's kind of a mess right now. I need to clean the tub out actually."

"Aww, that's okay. I'll help you clean it real quick. I'm sure it looks as great as the rest of your house anyway." Both of us glance around as Holly says that.

She's right. I'm a neatness freak and the place is always spick and span.

"No really, I haven't used it in a while and I've got some stuff stored up there right now. I feel exhausted just thinking about tackling it," I lie.

Holly makes a pouty face but concedes to hanging out in my office, which also has a bed in it. I welcome her to stretch out on it while I sit at the desk.

"So...how are the vibes in my house tonight? Better than back at your place?" I ask, since Holly apparently is pretty tuned in to me.

"Actually...I don't know. I feel like we need to meditate. I'm sure there's something going on with me and the moon tonight. I don't feel really comfortable anywhere."

Her intuitive admonition gives me a bad chill. "It's not just you," I mumble.

Holly gives me an intense look and slight nod, like she knows there's something 'off' about me.

"So what's your story? Insomnia too?" she asks.

"Yeah...I get this way during the full moon sometimes."

She looks at me with apprehension. Apparently she ain't buying what I'm selling. "Okay, I would assume you're just excited about next weekend except you don't look excited. You look like a frazzled alleycat. Are you nervous about meeting that guy?"

Bo is the absolute last thing I want to talk about right now. "Oh...no," I say, casually swatting my hand to blow off the thought. "No, you were right. I was being silly over nothing at all. I have zero interest in meeting any man these days, much less some limp wristed flower vendor." I nod a few times to drive my point home. I'm done with the flower guy.

"Oh hon, when are you gonna get out there and find someone to date again?"

"Hey, you were the one who knocked me for my enthusiasm over meeting flower vendors. And I'm only interested in expanding my friends within the industry anyway."

"That's not what it sounded like when you told me about that guy," she says with a smile.

"I'm sorry Holly, you misread me is all."

Holly frowns slightly and shrugs.

"Are you getting sleepy yet?" I ask right after Holly's first yawn.

"Yeah…I think I might be. Any chance you'd be comforted by sharing a bed tonight?"

"Yes!" I blurt out with more enthusiasm than she was probably expecting.

"Okay," Holly replies, laughing at me. "Shall we go to your room?"

"No!…sorry. I accidentally broke something in there earlier and there's glass shards in the carpet."

"Oh, please, let me help you clean it up Fiona. I'm sure it would take five minutes and then we'll only be more ready for sleep."

There's nothing in me that wants to re-enter my bedroom tonight. "Let's not…seriously, we might have to dig shards out or something. Honestly, I haven't even looked at the wreckage."

And with that, Holly rises from the bed and marches straight out of the office, down the hall, and into my bedroom as though in a trance. Arriving just before me, she flicks on the light and her jaw drops.

"Oh my goodness," she says, covering her mouth with her hands. "How did you...drop your lamp?" As she turns around, I can see her confusion.

"I kind of...had a nightmare." The words come out in the faintest whisper.

"Fifi...why didn't you tell me?"

"I didn't want to freak you out more. And I lied about the attic earlier. The place is neat as a pin. I just didn't wanna go up there."

"Understood," she says, nodding grimly. "But...how can this be?"

"It's simple. I woke up from a bad dream and threw my lamp before I could come to full consciousness."

Without another word, we exit the room and head back down the hall...leaving the light on behind us. At least I feel satisfied that if Quade is in our presence, he knows I'm not ratting him out.

With an arm around Holly's shoulders, I guide her back to the office bed and we crawl in, fully clothed, and lie down with every lamp in the room still on. We face each other and lie still for a while, staring like two scared rabbits in a headlight.

"You actually threw the lamp," she finally says, shaking like a child.

"Maybe we shouldn't talk about it."

"We have to. This is too crazy...there's no way I'm going to sleep now. Did you really throw an object in your sleep?"

"Yes. I woke up in time to feel myself picking up the lamp and hurling it."

Holly's eyes show a faint glimmer of tears. I want to cry with her, but I'm hard. And angry. Extremely angry that I no longer have the freedom to tell the truth to my best friend in my own house. I watched Quade drive away long ago. It's very late and he has a flight tomorrow. There's no way he's obsessively hiding around the corner right now, without making one single sound, and every ounce of my reasoning knows that. Yet the stakes are so high if I'm mistaken, I cannot take any chances.

"What do you think it means that we're both freaked out under a full moon?" Holly asks, unwittingly pushing me into territory I don't want to go in.

"Absolutely nothing, sweetness. Nothing at all. Just a couple planets out of alignment tonight."

Chapter 10

Bo

It may be only a two hour drive, but headin to this conference feels like the biggest thing I will have done in a long time. Not only because of the extra work involved, but because I don't normally socialize in groups and it takes a lot to get me to go to somethin like this. After spending the past couple days gettin my orchid crates organized, I've still got birds of paradise and numerous miniature sunflowers to sort and stack before I can begin to think about loading. But I have an unusual motivation for this trip; call it a hunch that it's the right time in life for me to get out and meet people. I try not to read anything more into it, but I shouldn't have to. Makin a new friend or two will be good enough for me.

As I peel off my gloves and head back to the shed for lunch, I decide to take a detour around the old house for a minute. The siding has held up extremely well, but I need to put up a steel roof before it starts springing leaks. I walk all the way around, peering in through the dusty windows. There's almost nothing left inside the place, most of it having been gotten rid of long ago.

I'd kept a bed and a couch to move into my shed, added a small bathroom with shower, built a partition to divide the place into two little rooms, and put my kitchen facilities in the main room along with a washer and dryer. I redid all the interior walls, floors, and ceilings with beautiful, knotty pinewood, pale and reflective to maximize the windows I installed throughout. All in all, the shed turned out to be my perfect tiny house.

Even so, I sometimes long for a larger kitchen to prepare my homegrown meals in. I continue my trek around the house, stomping down the long overgrown weeds to get a closer view. I cain't remember the last time I looked inside some of these windows, maybe never. Peeking into the den gives me a bad funny feelin in the pit of my stomach. Regardless of it being too empty to resemble its former self, the mood of family evenings in front of the TV is still in there. I can hear the conversations and laughter now, echoing through my memory like ghosts. One small table stands at the back of the room where we used to play cards and board games. Oh to go back in time.

Snapping back to my senses, I pull away from the windows and trek back to the shed...wanderin first around the long abandoned swimmin pool. I never do this engaging-in-old-memories nonsense. Hurtin over the past never did no good for nobody. I've got a bright life right here in the present, surrounded by all the lovelies. I pass my hands over the soft, rubbery petals of a pale purple rose bush as I brush past, realigning myself with the present. It's a good life out here, and I have every moment of the day to remind me of that.

Removing my boots at the door, I enter my little kitchen and grab the chicken salad out of the fridge. I spread it across soft whole grain bread and layer it up with garden grown cucumbers and thick slabs of avocado. With no room in here for a table, I simply crash down on the couch with my sandwiches and wolf them down while I soak up the air conditioning. I've put in a righteous amount of prep work already today, and it's turnin out to be a hot one.

After a long afternoon in and out of fields and greenhouses, I get the firepit goin and grill up some shrimp with corn and potatoes...New Orleans style. I usually find it hard to sleep under a full moon, but not tonight. Tuckin into my bed, I'm sufficiently exhausted and snug as a bug as I doze off.

At half past midnight, I spring up in bed as a bolt of lightning and thunder hit the farm like a sledgehammer. It was a clear, starry night when I turned in; this one must have moved in fast. The first thing I did after inheriting the farm thirty-three years ago, was to put lightning rods on each building...so I don't have a lot to worry about. But there's a strange feelin in the air, and I don't like it.

Not to mention, I was havin a restless dream. Downright disturbing actually. Images of the same woman I always dream about, except she was in distress with a shadowy man hoverin over her. The man restrained her, and her long hair shook wildly as she screamed and tried to escape. I seemed to be empathically inside her body, and was helplessly tryin to free myself from his grip when that thunder hit. It was a damned unpleasant way to wake up but I'm glad for it, all in all.

I need to get back to sleep, but my mind is now stuck in a quandary over what it's like to be a woman, or a smaller man for that matter. I've never in my life had the experience of somebody grabbin me and tryin anything. It was a terrible feelin, not one I'd wanna repeat, and it gives me a compassionate rage for all the women out there facing domestic abuse.

The memory of Fiona's phone voice flashes through my mind, as if tryin to soothe me from my angst. But now it's mixed with the screams in my dream and the vague image of shiny hair swishin in the darkness. I don't like that one bit. I have a good feelin about that lovely woman, and I don't like it marred by this sinister fusion of dream and reality.

Now of course, I know Jose's right about the lady...she could be ugly as sin and not even nice for all I know. But this won't be the first time I followed my nose and it led me to do somethin I otherwise wouldn't. And I always find that things work out best if I abandon myself to my inner callings.

An hour later the storm's died down, but I still can't sleep. I get up and open the windows all around my bed, ushering in that beautiful post-storm air. There's a sense of deep dread hovering in my room, invisible but dense as an object. I haven't felt nothin like it in the longest time. Disturbed, I turn on the bedside lamp and grab a book off the built-in shelving. I'll distract myself the best I can until

I get sleepy. I've got much work to do tomorrow. Ahhh...a little Isaac Asimov outta do it. I've always been a fan and I haven't read this one in years.

Five pages in, the remnants of screams have cleared my head and I'm becoming sleepily enraptured by a magnificent, alien world. But just as I feel my first yawn comin on, the stillness of the night is pierced by an actual scream...loud and right outside my window. Big Bo ain't scared of nothin, but I drop my book and scramble to my feet as another hair-raising screech cuts through the other side of the room. My sense of panic melts as I gain clarity on the fact that the shed's surrounded by barn owls. And once more...they scream in unison, lighting up my bedroom with the bone tingling stereo of raspy discontent.

I pull the windows shut and try to laugh at myself as I get back into bed, but there's no question that somethin just ain't right with me. Stereo barn owls is a bad omen if I've ever heard one. For the rest of the mornin, I get scarcely two hours of sleep, tossin and turnin under the weight of an indiscernible moroseness.

Chapter 11

Fiona

I survive Wednesday, again sleeping with a lamp on. In fact I didn't sleep in any bed, but crashed on a living room couch instead. I figured if Quade decided to enter, I'd hear him coming through the front door and wake up sooner. It would be less shocking than letting him surprise me in a bedroom again; not to mention I wouldn't be cornered. Theoretically I could hear him in time to sneak off the couch and head for the back door. I slept in pajamas.

As previously agreed, I meet Holly at a Mexican place for lunch, and we rush toward each other upon sight...as though we've recently survived a shipwreck together.

"Holly, we have so much to talk about," I say, clutching her arms too tightly before she can sit down.

Her eyes grow big with worry. Undoubtedly she'd thought the other night's spooky shenanigans were a thing of the fading past.

"Okay. Shall we sit and order first?" she asks with a smile, apparently hoping some normalcy will lighten my mood.

"Yes, of course." I try my best to concentrate on the menu for a minute, but all I see is an incomprehensible jumble of letters before me. My brain is scrambled.

When a young lad comes by to take our orders, Holly requests chicken fajitas. "I'll have the same," I say, casting my useless menu aside.

Sensing my tension, Holly smiles and waits for me to begin.

"Okay, listen up girlfriend," I say with my voice lowered. "Quade still has keys to my house, from the old days. He helped himself in Tuesday night and appeared in my bedroom at eleven thirty p.m., in the darkness. I threw my lamp at him because I didn't know who the hell was in my room." Holly sharply inhales, slapping her hands over her mouth. "Yeah, creepy right? Well it gets worse. He grabbed my wrists in the dark, never turned a light on, and restrained me till I begged him to let me go...claiming it was self defense. I was stark naked, so I reached into my closet to pull on a robe and he stopped me and held the robe open. I pretended I wanted to get sexy on my bed and he fell for it and started pulling his pants down, which gave me enough time to bolt off the other side of the bed and run out of the house." With her hands still over her mouth, Holly takes in huge, panicky gulps of air as her eyes begin to tear up. "In the end,

I grabbed a towel and walked all the way to your house with it wrapped around me."

"Oh my God Fiona!" Holly blurts out as the tears begin to fall.

"Please, please." I begin looking around the restaurant frantically. "He has eyes and ears everywhere, important friends. He said some things...I can't even describe how serious he was about this but something inside him has snapped. I don't know this man at all. He's physically bigger and stronger, and mentally...not like anything I ever imagined my husband would be in a thousand years."

"Okay...okay." Holly dries her eyes and drops her hands, sitting up straighter and trying to look normal. "So you couldn't tell me anything the other night..." She's putting two and two together now. "Oh my God, what if he'd come back while I was there?" She looks petrified, and maybe a little angry.

I glance at her self-consciously. "Well, I watched him drive home but...yeah. That's why I protested the hot tub. I was so afraid that if I went to your place he'd track me down and stop me. I figured if he was hiding in my house, our conversations would only serve as proof I wasn't gonna rat him out."

"Oh my God...okay." Holly shakes her head and stares at the table, assimilating what actually happened that night.

The waiter sets our steaming plates down and we both stare at them in a stupor, having no comprehension of how to eat at the moment. I abruptly pick up my fork, determined to have as normal a lunch as possible, and poor sweet Holly begins to break down again. "I...I just...I can't...," she says with a cracking voice.

"Me either," I say with a heavy sigh, tossing my fork back down.

"What are you going to do?"

"Well, since Quade's in bed with our local Police Chief, there isn't much of anything I *can* do. He already threatened that if I report him he'll tell Vernon I'm crazy." Holly raises her hands to her mouth again. "Quade owns my house, owns my business, and has me fully by the balls. So I'm now living every moment of every night in fear that he'll waltz in my front door and attack me. Maybe force me. Frankly that seemed to be the direction he was heading in the other night."

"Oh God Fiona...you have to do something. You can't live like that."

"You're right, I can't. But if I pack my bags and move into your condo, Quade will know I told you everything."

"Do it...who cares? As long as you don't report anything, don't try to make legal trouble...don't you think he'll leave you alone?"

I think about this hard for a couple minutes, even taking a bite of my food. "Well, now that you mention it, I don't suppose he could freak out over what you know as long as I keep the law out of it. But Levi would have to swear on his life not to spread this anywhere. They have mutual friends you know. If this got out to anyone, I don't know what Quade would do. Aside from pulling my home and business out from underneath me, I don't trust him on any level. Holly, I can't exaggerate how deranged he acted the other night. He was totally unrecognizable."

Holly puts her hands over her face, and I carefully pull them away. "Remember, nothing happened," I remind her.

We quietly pick at our plates for several minutes, then resign our meals to boxes before both of us have to go back to work.

"How about you spend tonight at my place, and then tomorrow you'll be off to Florida and won't have to think about things till next week," Holly says, as we make our way to the parking lot. "Just assume that when you get back, you'll be staying at the condo with me. Next time Quade comes around, it will send him a strong message that you're not making yourself available to his abuse."

"Holly." I can't think of what else to say as I crash into her welcoming arms. "Thank you for saving me."

"Are you kidding?" she asks, holding me out where she can look me in the eye. "I cannot believe you've been sleeping in that house of horrors for the past three nights alone. In light of everything you just told me, I truly don't know how you haven't gone out of your mind."

"I about have," I admit, tears welling up again. "I've been sleeping in the living room so I could bolt out the back if he suddenly came in. I don't think I've fallen into a deep sleep once. I've been napping through lunches out of desperation."

"Fiona," she says, clutching my shoulders, "never again. Don't you ever go without telling me something like this again. You should have been with me all week."

"I was afraid to tell you over the phone. It dawned on me that it could be tapped." Holly looks stricken by my revelation. "I'm serious. I know that sounds paranoid, but after Tuesday night's performance, I don't think he would stop at anything. I know how obsessive he gets over projects and clients. He's always been that way...it was just never projected onto me before."

"God...I'm late," Holly says, glancing at her phone. "I'm so sorry—"

"No, don't be. I have to get to the store anyway. Your timing's perfect," I assure her as I reach for my car door.

"Okay. You'll come to my place as soon as you get done today?"

"Unfortunately, I've still got all the weekend's packing to do." Her expression falls. "But I'll hurry and try to get over there before dark. Don't you worry...I bought a bottle of mace."

"Oh good!" Holly says, slapping her hand over her heart. We hug once more and then drive away.

* * *

At four thirty I leave the store, also dismissing Maxine so she can do her own weekend preparations. We've got a couple of big days ahead of us, and I must find some way to get my mind out of my own personal dread and start looking forward to it again.

As I pick an assortment of nice dresses out of the walk-in closet, I begin to feel more like my old self again. Being in my bedroom isn't so bad; my body's aching from all my tossing and turning on the couch. I'm almost tempted to just sleep in here tonight. Quade never flies out twice in the same week, and I'm sure he flew home on Wednesday. So I'm probably being silly to pack it out of here now. It's a surprisingly hefty inconvenience to move my things over to Holly's and then have to get on a plane tomorrow. I'd love to have a long bath and one night of good sleep before all this, in my own bed.

Three hours later, I'm almost finished packing and never even stopped to eat. Still a little way from twilight, I dig some leftover curry out of the fridge and sit at my desk with it, plugging away at a few last-minute details. As darkness approaches a certain melancholy seeps in, reminding me that I want to enjoy my own home before the weekend away... and also that it will be a hotbed of fear the moment the sun goes down. I shoot Holly a text and she quickly responds, encouraging me to get out and come over as soon as possible. Taking one last sad glance around my house, I gather up my luggage and leave.

Holly's response to my arrival, squealing and rushing into my arms, is all I need to get over my away-from-home blues.

"Levi's on his way out," she says with an excited glint in her eye, apparently loving the idea of a girls' night.

"Hey Fiona, how are you?" Levi asks in a tone of mild concern, grabbing my bags with one arm and wrapping the other around me.

"I'm alright," I reply, wondering what he knows.

"Good, good. So you're about to have a big weekend in paradise, huh?"

"Well...if that's what you call Florida this time of year. I plan to either be in a building or a pool the entire time."

"That would work for me!" He seems chipper enough as he gives Holly a smooch and scoots out the door.

But as soon as he's gone, Holly turns to me with eyes of knowing...sadness and shock still in their corners. She motions for me to follow her up the steps and toward her bedroom. "Guess what I have," she says with a clever look.

"What?" I ask, my mood beginning to elevate.

"I have a hot tub...we can actually use!"

I clap my hands together in glee, as she swings the master bath door open and begins pouring the tub.

"Oh Holly, you're such a mind reader."

She throws me a quick smirk, then rushes out of the room and returns a minute later with a bottle of champagne and two glasses.

"Voila!" she says, presenting one of them to me.

"Oh gosh," I gently protest, throwing up my hands. "I really shouldn't get into anything before the conference. They keep you plied with free booze at this thing." Holly makes puppy-dog eyes and I surrender, taking the glass and stipulating that I'll have only one.

We settle into the huge, granite-encased tub and fire up the jets...sighing as we lay our heads back and sip.

"So, you completely lost your enthusiasm for that one guy huh?" Holly asks after several minutes of grateful silence.

"What guy? The flower guy?" I'm both surprised and relieved she's back in the mood for idle girltalk.

"Yeah."

"No!" I accidentally shout with a laugh. "Not really, I just couldn't talk about anything with my Quade paranoia going on, remember?"

"What...you think he'd be upset that you were meeting someone?" She looks incredulous.

"Honey, I have no idea what would upset Quade at this point. But, yeah, I'd suspect he could potentially harbor jealousy or spitefulness over something like that. I mean...his behavior rather pointed to possessiveness in the extreme."

Holly grimaces and shudders her shoulders up around her face. "I guess you're right. I still can't believe what happened..."

"Me either. At all. And I haven't heard a word from him since. It's almost as if neither of us wants to believe it ever happened."

"If only. I'm sorry though...I shouldn't have brought that back up," Holly says, already pouring herself a second glass and offering to top mine off.

"That's okay. It did in fact happen and there's no use denying it," I return, brushing off her refill attempt.

"So...then you are still crushing on flower guy?"

"Bo's the name, and I never said I was crushing. As a matter of fact, I haven't even been on the phone with him in months now and the entire notion seems like a silly, distant fantasy. I guess I'm finally getting lonely in life. Perfect time for my ex husband to start ruling over me with an iron fist." Holly has slapped a hand over her mouth to contain her apparent mirth.

"What?" I ask.

"His name is Bo?"

"I know! He sounds like the classic central-Florida hick farmer, does he not?" I can't help but laugh with her. "See what I'm getting at...it's not worth calling a crush, or even an interest. He's simply the first theoretically heterosexual male I will have ever met at this thing and...well I guess I'm easy to please these days."

Holly is fully guffawing now, so I will myself to drop my bashfulness and join her.

An hour later we're out of the tub and winding down, Holly fishing through films to watch despite my protests. My flight isn't that early, but I'm still wiped out from everything about my entire week that could cause someone to feel like a zombie. I figure I'll humor her until I start dozing off on the couch, then happily transfer myself to the guest bed.

But instead, Holly puts on the chick flick, I gently recline down one length of her luxurious wraparound couch, and I awaken seven hours later in a puddle of drool. So much for a night in a real bed...Holly's living room couch is apparently more comfortable than anything I've ever slept on.

* * *

At eleven thirty I'm boarding a plane next to my sweet little protege, Maxine. This kid is the stuff every employer's dreams are made of. In addition to being an ace floral designer, she's conversational, full of smiles, and has an adorable...albeit cheap...fashion sense. I only hope she won't expect me to be great company on our flights, after the sleep deficit I've recently accrued.

I am, however, willing to chat her up during the initial half-hour flight to Chicago. It goes by in a flash and we're dumped into the O'hare for a ninety minute layover. After hitting the bathroom and securing lunch, we sit at our terminal...Maxine's face buried in a book and mine in my phone, which has exploded with texts and messages from Quade. After our days of silence, my hands are shaking as I read them.

Hey Cookie! How was your week? I know you're on your way to FL but please check in with me when you get there.

Hey Cookie, you at the O'hare yet? Maybe give me a call. If you can. Please.

Hey honey, sorry if I was overly aggressive the other night. Lately I feel like you're drifting away and it scares me a little bit. You can't blame a guy for caring too much.

I officially want to hurl my phone against a wall and break it after reading that last one. Can't blame a guy! What a zinger! I excuse myself and begin rapidly pacing down the aisle as I pull up the voice messages. The actual sound of him takes my repulsion to a whole new level. I feel my breathing escalate as my shakes become almost too violent to hold the phone. I want to vomit.

Hey Cookie...are you almost there yet? ....Okay...... well...give me a call. I hope you're out there having fun. Just not too much fun without me...heh heh...just kidding. Love ya bunches, talk to you soon. Bye.

Aaand...he's back to the same old sickly sweet doormouse of a man he ever was. All breathy into his phone and calm as a hindu cow. Next message, while I still have the nerve to even listen to this shit.

Hey there...gotta land sometime. If you didn't have time at O'hare...just......call me as soon as you get into Fort Lauderdale, okay? There are some things we need to discuss before you're gone for the entire weekend, okay? I'll be waiting for your call. Have a nice flight.

Some things we need to discuss before I'm gone for an entire weekend? An entire weekend? What is that even supposed to mean? As if I owe him some sort of check-in before I'm allowed to go on a field trip. My mind is spinning with the sheer number of trips I've taken over the past nine years, never having gone through any sort of exit requirement by Quade before. The guy has gone bananas, and I've a mind not to call him at all. I continue storming indignantly in the opposite direction of our gate, not wanting Maxine to see me with my blood boiling this early in the weekend.

On the other hand, I do have a good half hour before boarding...and I know what happened last time I ignored him. Maybe if I get this over with now, I won't have to think about Quade after I'm in Florida...which would be quite the perk. After making a quick pillow and bottled water purchase, I stroll into an empty gate and sit down to dial him, fingers wobbling with nervous rage.

"Cookie! I thought I'd never hear your voice again!"

And the truth comes out. After his outrageous stunt the other night, Quade clearly thought he'd lost me. Suddenly he doesn't seem so powerful and scary after all.

"Well ta-daa! Here I am. Just trying to do diligence to a bajillion messages before boarding my second flight. As requested."

My response is met with a surprising interval of silence. "There's no need to get sarcastic with me," he says at last, that eerie, calm control having returned to his voice.

My memory flashes to the creep driving beside me at five miles an hour, the threats about my business and the home I live in. I remember with clarity that this is not a guy I want to piss off.

"Quade," I start back in with a laugh, "I'm just playing around. What did you wanna discuss? Just a heads-up, I have about ten minutes before I need to hightail it back to my gate."

"Ah, well." He clears his throat nervously. "I don't really think that's adequate time for the topic I have in mind Fiona. Maybe...why don't you just give me a call from your nice quiet room after you get there. After Maxine's gone to the meet-and-greet."

My heart sinks through the floor. I love the damn meet-and-greet. It's the best part before the weekend gets bogged down in tedious, note-taking lectures. The thought of spending it in a hotel room, crouched over my cell phone with Quade in my ear, is destroying my soul by inches.

"You wouldn't wanna make me wait, would you? Curiosity might kill me on the next plane," I sweetly implore, prodding him to launch into whatever it is.

"No Cookie, I wouldn't want to do that," he responds like a man under a spell. He lets out one long, loud exhale and begins. "It's just that...I want to talk about...us." I meet him with silence. What is this 'us' he speaks of? "You know... where our relationship is going. Sometimes I think you're pulling away from me Cookie, and I don't like it. I don't like it at all."

I'm now sitting in the middle of an empty row of seats in an empty gate, looking like a dufus with one hand on my cheek and my jaw fully dropped. I cannot believe what I am hearing. My ex husband wants to know where our relationship is going?? I must have died a few days ago and gone to hell.

"Quade," I start in with another softening chuckle, "I just don't know what you mean. We've been close friends ever since our divorce...I don't know what you think has changed."

"Please...please don't use the d-word. It was hardly a divorce...more like...a minor adjustment from our original agreement."

My jaw drops a little farther, which I wouldn't have thought possible. I had never, in my wildest dreams, imagined our lack of legal finality would come back to haunt me this way.

"Well it does sound like something we should talk about when I'm home Monday," I stammer out, realizing my time is draining. And if I let him call me later we could easily kill an hour or two, opening a can of worms like this. "Not that there's anything to discuss," I reassure him. "But if you feel things are changing, we can certainly talk it over." I'm using the most benign tone in my inventory of voices, and he still isn't responding. This is not good. "Quade, whatever you have to say, I'm listening," I say encouragingly, feigning calmness as I breathlessly hustle back toward our crowded gate.

"Fiona...are you seeing someone?" Two ladies trip over my carry-on as Quade's question stops me in my tracks.

Who in the hell does he think he is to press me about something that's none of his business? I quell my rage as I remember he's merely the madman pulling the puppet strings of my entire life.

"No Quade! No! I don't know why that would be relevant to you, but I've told you before that I'm not. Now what is this about? God knows you didn't seem to care when I was dating that stupid biker."

"Exactly. Because the guy was an idiot. He could never fulfill any of the purposes that I do in your life. What I want to make clear to you Cookie, is that you're not going to be able to replace me, ever, with anyone who's capable or willing to do half the things that I do for you. Do you realize that? Do you realize that your world turns because I say it does, and that I have the power to stop it just like that?"

Somehow, out of the distortion of Quade's icy voice, combined with the muck of airport chaos, I manage to distinguish the boarding call for my flight. "Now boarding all remaining rows," the attendant says.

I look around and see Maxine, standing at the edge of the masses and looking distraught. Finally we make eye contact and I know I have to bail off the phone. I do not want her worrying about me and my personal business.

"Quade, listen...I would never try to replace you in my life or imagine that I could. My plane's all boarded so I have to go…I'll be the last one on. Let me call you Monday when I'm home and we can talk longer, okay?"

"Okay Cookie. Okay…I would like that very much. You go do your thing, make lots of good connections, have a nice time with Maxine. And good luck to her…tell her to break a leg."

"Okay, talk to you in three days. I've gotta board now. Bye bye."

I hang up feeling the sweet relief that Quade likely will leave me alone until Monday. I'm going to have a fun time in Florida, and I'm not going to have one single thought about my disgusting ex husband or my teetering life.

Last in line, I dart down the ramp behind Maxine. "Hey, are you okay?" she asks.

"Yes, fine sweetie. I had to take a last minute call from Quade and I thought he was never gonna let me go," I respond, smiling like it was the greatest thing ever.

"Whoo…you scared me for a minute there."

Once we settle into our seatbelts, I'm happy to see Maxine's headphones come out right away. I'd love to engage in as little conversation as possible, since I can't think of anything that wouldn't be a whole lot of negative complaining about my life. And I definitely don't need to be sharing those types of personal problems with an employee. But oh, what I wouldn't give to be sitting next to Holly right now. I can't tell whether I want to scream or cry, and the confusing combination is pushing me toward another panic attack that I really cannot have on an airplane full of strangers.

I close my eyes and do my best to get comfortable against my new rock-hard airplane pillow, which doesn't resemble anything a human being would ever be able to sleep or relax against. But I just paid thirty-five bucks for this bitch and I'm going to use it. I'll pretend I'm asleep until Maxine's deep into her headphones and the most extreme danger of eye contact has passed.

To my surprise, I'm overcome by a feeling of serenity after a couple minutes with eyes closed. I feel distant, separated from the bustle around me, and a comfortable sense of presence overtakes my previous turmoil. I decide to run with the feeling and begin clearing my mind for meditation. The din of the crowd grows silent as we begin our ascent, my thoughts of Quade and my freshly ruined home slipping further and further away. I imagine that I'm leaving them behind with the Earth, and begin to drop into the transcendent. Something awaits me there that's subtler than thought, more like a sensation of peace...which then morphs into a vision. I see a pair of eyes, large and brown, darkly lashed but not feminine. I feel rested in the line of their gaze, as though they're seeing through all the foibles of my life without judgment. My emotions are held still by them, contained, pacified at last.

The next thing I know, a flight attendant is handing Maxine a fizzing cup of something on ice and a packet of peanuts. As I crack my eyes open, the attendant asks if I'd like anything. I decline and have a couple pulls on my water bottle before checking the time. We're about ninety minutes from touchdown and Maxine looks happy enough to be left alone, apparently immersed in some dreamy headphone world, so I close my eyes and gratefully resume my state of inwardness.

I do not become sleepy this time but remain in a state of relaxed alertness, my mind successfully running a series of pleasant, motivating thoughts in place of the ones I've been having lately. Somehow flying toward Florida is creating the illusion that I'm leaving my life behind, entering an alternate reality with no worries. I've felt so backed into a corner for the past week that total escapism is my only chance for enjoying the weekend. I must wipe all future concerns from my mind; after all, Monday is just around the corner.

I attempt to settle into the space I was in earlier, with that mysterious pair of eyes softly penetrating my soul. But they don't return to me, and I slip back into the blackness of desperately needed sleep. Eventually awakening to the harsh clang of a stewardess gabbing through the intercom, I look over and smile at Maxine...who seems pleasant and happy as usual. It's time to prepare for landing, to return our seats to the upright position and tuck away our belongings, and I'm feeling surprisingly refreshed and renewed...maybe even a little excited again.

"Feeling pumped about tomorrow?" I ask brightly. I may as well begin the pleasantries now since I'll have an entire weekend of this.

"Yes! I definitely am, but I also don't wanna think about it too much beforehand. I figure I'll make the most of tonight and just try to have a relaxed attitude, since I have no idea what kind of flowers we'll be working with."

"Have you put some thought into what direction you're going to go in with your design?" It actually feels unbelievably good to be talking and thinking about something outside of myself.

"I hope this doesn't alarm you at all but...no, I haven't. I mean I've tried to think of something, looked online at winning entries from the past, picked a few styles that appeal to me, but I just have the feeling I'm gonna do something totally unique and I have to wait for the moment to see what it'll be."

And yes, I am slightly alarmed...but no, not terribly. I trust Maxine's ability, and I like her Zen attitude about in-the-moment design. Granted, I'd be more thrilled if she had something planned out that she could share with me and get my professional opinion on. But she probably wants the money as badly as I want the plaque, so I expect that when the time comes...she'll give it her all.

"Well...you've done your research and that's about all you can do. I think you're wise to allow some room for spontaneity," I tell her warmly, trusting she'll do her best and do it well.

* * *

By five we've checked into our suite, and I'm perfectly pleased with it. It offers me a completely private bedroom, apart from the living room pull-out Maxine will be on. She's already rushed off to the newcomer's meet-and-greet in a sparkly, pink dress that I think is a tad overdone for the occasion. I zip open my garment bag and carefully hang up the dresses I brought, mulling over which one to wear to tonight's party. I'm not in a frivolous mood and I need to get into it, but I think I'll settle for a long, comfortable, cotton wraparound. Aiming to be fashionably late, I spend a good while touching up my makeup. Then, buckling on a pair of low platforms, I'm ready to go.

For the first time, I feel some nervousness setting in as I stand before the full-length bathroom mirror. Adding a couple inches, I'm about five foot ten in these sandals. It's been days since I actually indulged in looking forward to this weekend, much less thought about the prospect of meeting Bo. And with Quade's complete personality shift, the last thing I should even consider is looking for a man. In fact, I feel cold feet at the mere thought of it. How foolish of me to flirt on the phone like that. Of course, at the time I had no idea he'd be attending the conference this year. I'd have never engaged in such behavior, had I known.

Oh well, at least I'm dressed more modestly than someone whose name I won't mention. I'm just going to suck up and walk in there, mix into the crowd and relax for once. And tomorrow I'll search out Big Bo's booth and introduce myself with politeness and professionalism. He'll find out what I'm made of...not some silly hussie flowergirl you can toy with over the phone. Enough with that already.

Grateful to all that is sacred for no more messages from Quade, I meander toward the convention center and find it too brightly lit and already roaring with conversation. Strangely trembling, I make a beeline for the refreshment table and practically stumble into Maxine along the way.

"Yay...glad you're here!" she says in a tone that's too cheery for me just yet.

"Yep...made it. Have you made any new friends yet?" I ask, hoping she'll take the hint not to hang around me all weekend.

"Oh, you know...everyone's super nice but I haven't exchanged contact info or anything."

"Well you look gorgeous. You just work the room a little and they'll be following you around like puppies," I tell her in all honesty. Yes, the sparkly dress is a little Britney Spears for my taste, but she wears it like a charm.

I pretend not to hear Maxine's reply, and hustle off toward the drinks. She'll find her feet eventually. I'm not here to babysit. I dip into a large, crystal bowl full of champagne punch, and ladle myself a full glass. The longest week of my life ends right here, right now, with the comfort of this perfect deliciousness.

"Fiona!" I turn around to see Zoey Norton, a sweet fellow florist who comes most years. "How are you? You look beautiful!" she says, giving me a half hug while balancing her punch.

"I'm great Zoey, how are you?" I lie.

"Oh you know...living the good life! Have you met Cora Lee?" She introduces me to another friendly yet equally vapid looking gal, and we gently take hands as we visibly size each other up.

One hour and two drinks later, I am maximally taxed on meaningless conversation. Again I'm longing for Holly, for someone I can really talk to. I want to stand in the middle of this room and scream for help over the top of everyone else's rambling. Maxine seems particularly intelligent, like someone I could confide in and take advice from. But there's no way it would be appropriate to involve her in anything going on with me. I'm resigned to playing the socialite game for the rest of the weekend, then going back home to discuss my relationship with a lunatic. So I may as well make the very most of the next two days.

On my way back to the punch bowl, I scan the room for pink sparkles and spot Maxine way off in a corner... surrounded by about five chattering women. She's in good hands; I can relax. As I turn back around to continue on my champagne punch quest, I collide with another familiar face.

"Fiona Turner...so good to see you! How are you?"

"I'm good Lenore. Business has been booming this year. How are you?"

"All good here. I've had a good quarter especially... business is blooming!"

As Lenore bursts out laughing at her staggeringly humorous pun, I notice a very tall man gazing at me from a neighboring group of people. I can't tell whether he's engaged with the group or just standing alone at their perimeter, but it appears he can't take his eyes off me.

"Are you attending the digital marketing series tomorrow?" Lenore asks as I toss the man a half-smile before returning my attention to her.

"Yes, probably. It's so critical in today's business climate."

"Oh I know, but it gives me a headache. Anyway...I'll be there too. See you tomorrow then." We give each other the pat-hug, and I'm back to my pursuit of cocktail.

I dole out another coy smile for Mr. Tall, Dark, and Handsome as I brush close by on my way, then turn to peek over my shoulder while I pour my glass. Okay, he's definitely not engaging with any group, and in fact looks a little out of sorts. I don't want to say awkward, but. I don't blame him one bit. Not everyone's cut out for all this tomfoolery. My only question is, what is *he* doing *here*? Surely he's not a florist. Or a marketing coach. Or a board member. He stands out like a lion in a cat shelter.

I quickly look away as he turns his head and catches me staring. Oh well, two can play. After a minute of sipping and scanning the crowd for friends, I subtly glimpse in his direction to find him gone. Feeling some combination of relief and vague disappointment, I file back through the throngs in the direction of Zoey until a veritable brick wall steps into my path.

"Fiona?" he asks in a husky voice that matches his face. "Fiona Turner?" My world turns upside down, again, as it dawns on me where I've heard that voice.

"Big Bo?" My mouth opens wide as I stare at him like a crazed woman. I cannot believe what I am seeing.

"Bo's my name," he says with a big smile. "Great to finally meet ya." He clinks his glass delicately against mine as I continue to stare, mesmerized.

"Ah...uh...how...how did you know it was me?" I finally manage, clamping my mouth shut before the drool can come out.

"I heard those ladies over yonder call out to ya. Plus, I just took one look at you and knew." He chuckles smugly, seeming to enjoy my state of confusion.

All at once my face lights up in the type of grin I haven't experienced all week, and we stand silently gazing at each other amidst this room full of noise.

"Well Bo, I...I...I'm so pleased to meet you too," I say after a lengthy pause.

I never stammer. I took courses in public speaking and was tops in my class. I've given florist symposiums in front of hundreds of people. I take another swig of my punch. Nothing could have possibly prepared me for this.

"Would you like to step out and get some fresh air?" he asks.

"Yes! I can't hear myself think in here," I reply, and we begin pushing our way toward the doors. "Oh, do you think we can escape with our drinks?" I ask, not yet ready to sober up this evening.

"I'm pretty sure nobody's payin any attention around here. Plus, invisibility's one of my super powers," he says as we cruise straight through the double doors, without turning so much as one head.

I can't help but laugh at the concept of this huge man becoming invisible, as we excitedly wind our way down the carpeted hall and out into the humid night air of the well landscaped yard. We take a moment to catch our breath from laughter, like two high schoolers who have snuck out of a pep rally.

"Wow, I didn't think you'd even be at the party tonight," I say to break the ice again.

"Oh yeah? Why's that?"

"Mm...I don't know. You seem like the elusive type." I hope he doesn't feel offended that I wouldn't have guessed this was his crowd.

"Dern right I am. Slippery as an eel," he responds, sending me into yet another fit of laughter.

I don't know who I am right now, this happy, smiling woman. I've been huddled inside my home and inside myself all week, in a state of panic over my horrible new life. Yet tonight I feel light as a feather, like I could accidentally float away if Bo weren't here to catch me. Either this is one hell of a strong punch, or I'm in exceptionally good company. It must be the combination.

"Allow me," Bo says, as he gently locks my arm in his and begins walking us through the garden.

Chapter 12

Bo

I guess I've been a pretty nice guy most of my life. I went through a few rough teenage years after my parents died, but got myself straightened out on time to grow into a gentleman the best I could. I never dated much, never felt like I met the right one and didn't wanna go around takin love and breakin hearts.

But nothin could have ever made me believe a woman as beautiful as Fiona would walk into my life. After all the dreams and premonitions, I should have been better prepared. But I still wasn't. I knew the moment she stepped through those doors who she was. When she made her way to a nearby woman that called out her name, I felt the rush of affirmation hit my heart like a golden ray of sunshine.

Tall and bronzed, with a streaming torrent of honey hair, she walks with me now...arm in arm through the humid coastal air. As if underwater, time stands still and I watch her laugh in slow motion, the sound of her voice husky and worldly, experienced and tired, musical and feminine. She's everything.

We stop at a bench among a grouping of luscious ostrich ferns, and I offer for her to sit. She accepts, keeping her elbow locked in mine, and gazes at me through the dim light.

"Who are you?" she asks with a brilliant smile.

"I'm just a lonely country boy who loves to grow stuff and pretty much keep to myself," I tell her.

Her smile fades and she gives me a penetrative look, as if trying to see all the way through me. Her light brown eyes are challenging and intense, sad and drained at the corners. I love her complexity.

"I'm sorry," she says with a giggle, as she releases her arm from mine. "I didn't mean to hold you hostage." She suddenly appears shyer than before, yet does not break our eye contact.

"Not at all ma'am. You're welcome to hold me as long as you please." Her eyes melt at my interpretation of her words.

We sit quietly for a spell, not needin the interference of conversation. Once she begins to nervously cross and uncross her long, tan legs, I take the cue.

"What do you think of all of them stars up there?" I ask, turnin my gaze toward the cloudless, black sky.

"They're breathtaking."

"Ain't it funny how we've both been sleepin under the same stars and planets ever since the day we were born?

I think that's really somethin." She turns her eyes back to mine and gives me that stunned look again, then nods very slightly. "Would you like me to sneak in and fetch you another drink?"

"No," she answers resolutely. "I can't imagine there's a single thing I need that isn't on this bench right now."

In a moment of bravery, I reach up to touch her cheek with the back of my hand...and she closes her eyes to savor it. She looks like a miracle as her lashes fold down to curtain her face. I run my thumb along the extraordinary curve of her dark eyebrow, and she slowly opens her eyes and levels all the way into me.

"Did you imagine it would be like this?" she asks under her breath.

"I knew that it would," I tell her in honesty. Her perfect lips part ever so slightly, and she releases a long sigh.

An unknown passage of time escapes us as we hold each other's gaze in perfect silence and calm. At long last my heart feels like it's really alive, and I thank the heavens in every moment that Fiona seems to feel it too.

"Oh," she unexpectedly starts in, "I've abandoned Maxine in there...my employee I brought with me. She'll do fine on her own, but I should probably check on her before she leaves for our room."

Sensing Fiona's slight onslaught of nerves, I rise with her and take her arm in mine again. We stroll slowly back into the building as though we hadn't any care in the world. Standing at the edge of the now thinning crowd, she spots her friend and gently breaks our hold.

"Please excuse me just for a minute."

As I watch Fiona stride away, I notice her perfect posture and proud bearing. Her simple, golden-brown dress matches her skin and cinches her delicate waist with a sash. Her absolute elegance takes my breath away. She has a brief exchange with a young lady in a pink dress and then heads back my way.

"She's good. I didn't think she'd have a hard time socializing and she's going to bed soon anyway. So I'm off the hook."

I look past Fiona to find the lady in pink checking me out. I nod to her and usher Fiona back out of the crowd.

"On second thought, how about that refill?" Fiona asks, as she grabs my hand and pulls me to the punch table.

"As long as you keep holdin my hand."

"Deal," she says with a smile, ladling up a new drink for each of us.

She then hands me my glass, grabs hers up, and clasps her free hand in mine, pulling me playfully through the crowd. She seems to be tryin to rush me back out of here, and I'm more than fine with that.

"Fiona!" another gal calls out, waving us over. Fiona looks back at me with an eye roll, then reluctantly pulls me toward the woman. "Hey, how's everything with you?" the lady asks.

"Couldn't be better," Fiona replies in a tone that strikes me as phony. "The store is booming, I've got a fantastic new designer, and my ex husband is stalking me while I sleep. How are you?"

I almost laugh at Fiona's audacity, as the woman struggles to answer, but suddenly I'm hot under the collar at the mention of an ex-husband who oversteps his boundaries. That ain't the sorta thing that goes over too well with me.

"Uh…great, great," the lady answers. "Yeah, everything's going good with business this year." An awkward silence ensues as Fiona stands with her phony grin plastered on, waitin to be released. "Well it was nice to see you Fiona, enjoy your weekend."

"You too Eva," Fiona throws over her shoulder as she speeds away with my hand.

I can't even hide what her prickly personality does to me. Something tells me I'm in for a wild ride, and every inch of me is up for it. We're almost to the doors when we pass by Fiona's pink employee; they exchange a polite wave and we're out of there, dashing back down the carpeted hall.

"Oops!" my lady exclaims as a quarter of her champagne sloshes over the edge.

"Someone's in an awful big hurry to get me out of here." That comment earns me a sharp look, followed by girlish laughter, as Fiona flings open the door to the gardens and drags me along. And never was there a more willing captive.

"So, what made you decide to come to the conference this year?"

She's goin straight for the kill now. Will it be overbearing if I answer honestly? I'm bettin Fiona can handle about anything.

"Are we playin truth or dare?" I tease.

"We're not playing at all," she answers in a way that floors me. "I want the truth and nothing but."

She's stopped along the path and angled herself in front of me, still holding my hand. Being in the line of her direct gaze is so stunning, I almost can't catch my breath enough to answer.

"I came because I wanted to meet you," I answer without flinching.

She gives me the coyest look, then drops my hand and turns to head down the path in front of me...laughing. "You have no idea what you're getting yourself into, Bo. I am not an easy woman, and my life is not flowery."

When she turns to face me and continues walkin, backward, I see her glass is already empty again. Apparently noticing at the same time, she quickly grabs mine and takes a rather unladylike swig.

"Careful there princess," I try to warn her.

"Princess? What do I look like to you, some kind of a nice gal? You think I'm a sweet old-fashioned mannerly lady you can pick up with all your...charm and...good looks?" she asks, sweepin her eyes up and down me like a predator.

"I think you're a damn wild woman," I answer, catchin her waist with both my hands as she almost stumbles backward into a crepe myrtle bush, "and I hope to pick you up with everything I've got."

Now holdin both our glasses, she takes another gulp of mine before lookin down at my big old hands engulfing her middle. Hating to have to release my grip, I gently take the glasses and set them under the bushes. As soon as I stand back up, Fiona takes both my hands and places them back onto her waist. As someone exits the hotel bar, a slow, jazzy tune drifts momentarily out the open door and we begin to sway. She places her arms over my forearms and moves with me, almost imperceptibly, while I revel in the feelin of that long, lean body captured by my very own hands.

"How did you know? When did you know?" she asks with refreshing directness.

"I think I've always known. The first time I ever heard your voice, it hit me that you were her, the one I'd seen in dreams and visions. After hearin from you a few more times, I knew it could only be a matter of waitin."

"Tell me about these dreams and visions," she says, takin my hand once more and pullin it toward the nearest bench.

"Well, alright then." I let out a heavy breath before beginning. She's askin me to walk her into some pretty mystical territory already. "It really started when I was a youngster. You see, my mother died when I was fourteen and I believe she sent me a vision. She wanted what was best for me and used to send me all sorts of images and messages. Like she was guidin me from the beyond." Fiona keeps her eyes scored on mine, riveted. "My first vision was a woman. I was so young, but I still could feel who the woman was. I wasn't really thinkin about women yet, but this woman was so beautiful...and strong, so strong, I knew beyond doubt that she was my destiny."

"That's incredible."

"Oh it goes beyond that...I've seen her countless times throughout my life, maybe once every two or three months. Always the same face, same eyes, same hair. One time I tried to reach out to her, but she disappeared before me...as if to say 'not yet'. Then about, oh...five, six years ago, I started havin a different sorta dream about her. These dreams have been restless, disturbed even. Like she comes to me on nights when she's in distress."

"And you believe this woman is— "

"Beyond doubt. Beyond doubt I do. Now you can make of that what you will, but now that I've seen you in the flesh...I have no question yours is the face I've always seen. Always."

She looks at me with an expression I can't quite read, but I know she's unafraid. I know this woman, somehow, and she has a strong tenacity for life.

"Well I think you're the most interesting man I've ever met." Fiona may be emboldened by a few drinks, but I can read her sincerity. This one's as real as the day is long.

"Why thank you," I respond with a smile, as we both lean back into the bench...loosening our grip to a hand hold.

"So your mother passed away when you were fourteen... were you raised by your father then?"

"No ma'am. Both my parents died together in the same night." Fiona gasps and I give her a moment to process it. "Lightning ignited the horse barn aflame while they were in it," I tell her solemnly.

Those events occurred too long ago for me to feel any more pain, but I know it must be a shock to new ears. She squeezes my hands tighter and her lips impart a faint smile. She sees that it's all okay with me now; she gets me.

"Did you go into foster care then?" she asks gently.

"No...I have one sibling who was eighteen at the time. My big brother, Mack. Being raised on a farm gives you a lot of life skills you wouldn't otherwise have. Plus, we had crops and we knew how to keep em goin. Mack never had any real interest in all that, but he delayed college to stick around and help me. He knew I'd sooner die myself than leave the farm and live with some strangers in the city, and he saw to it that would never happen."

"Are the two of you still close?"

"Oh not really. Our lives went separate ways...you know, different interests and all. He co-owns a small chain of bars out in California these days. But I love him and I'm most grateful for everything he did for me."

"That's beautiful. So...one day you decided to turn the place into a wholesale flower farm?" Fiona asks with a look of fascination.

"Yes ma'am. It happened just about like that. My parents had owned the house and property outright, so my expenses were low. I shut off the electric and water in the farmhouse, which happens to be way too many rooms for one man, and fixed up an old toolshed. Put new wood paneling in it and moved in a kitchenette, made the place quite nice. Then I set to work cleanin up the property, got rid of old junked vehicles and whatnot, expanded the garden till I was growin a hundred percent of my own produce. Nowadays I get my meat from local farmers, but I kept my own cattle and hogs till I was about thirty-five. Around then I began focusing on flowers and business picked up fast. Almost too much for me to handle at first. I've got a couple guys now who put in part-time help and the place runs like a top."

"No kidding...that's quite a story. So did you get to finish high school and all?"

"No ma'am, I didn't. But you know what, I never really missed it. My uncles taught me everything I needed to know about home construction and electric work, and me and Mack about worked ourselves to the bone the first few years. Eventually we refined our systems, updated equipment, got to where we could take care of the farm and still find a minute to fish or sit out on the porch, catch a movie here and there."

Fiona stares into my eyes with a look I can only describe as awe. "So, did you ever marry?"

"Can't say that I did, no. I meet women here and there through my work or at the local bars."

"No takers, huh?" she asks with that gorgeous, flirtatious smile.

"Oh there are plenty of takers, none that have really interested me though."

She gives me a sober look, like she's tryin to see all the way through me again, and it feels good to be taken seriously by a woman as real as Fiona. We sit in silence for a good while, soaking each other up through our eyes. I consider grabbin this opportunity to ask about that no-good ex, but she starts back in before I can.

"So...have you lived on the original property all your life? Is that where the flower farm is?"

"Yes it is, and yes I have." We mutually drop our gaze and fidget with our fingers together.

"I'm sure you have great friends and workers, but it sounds a little lonely," Fiona says quietly, lookin back up at me.

"Well, I reckon it is in a certain way. But I've got them thousands of plant babies to look after, and owls and songbirds all around the place. It don't seem too lonely to me...but I am always aware of what's missin. Make no mistake." She looks at me now with hunger in her eyes, and it feels like we're devouring each other without makin a single move. "What about you? Born and raised up in Iowa?"

"No," she answers with a laugh, "not a chance. I grew up in Oakland, with all the privileges of the only child to a clinical psychologist and a chiropractor." Fiona drops her eyes again, lookin slightly embarrassed by this revelation.

"Well there ain't nothin wrong with that now is there? Both your parents still around?"

"No actually, they were older when they had me. My mother passed away at age seventy-five but my father's surviving. He lives in a care facility in Fairfield where I can keep an eye on him, but dementia's made my visits pretty obsolete in recent years," she says matter-of-factly.

"Well, you can only do what you can do for him." Fiona nods her agreement. "Have you lived in Iowa long?" I ask.

"Almost twenty years now. I moved there for the meditation movement in Fairfield, which seemed like a nice place for my parents, and then I met my husband...now my ex, and ended up opening my store there. The community's been really good to me but I get stir crazy a lot. And the winters drive me nuts. I used to winter back in California before I opened the store, but that's not so easy with a business to run."

"I can only imagine what winter must be like up there. So do you do meditation then?"

"I do, twice a day, and I love it. It's my lifeline. I'm sure I would have pulled my hair out long ago without it," Fiona says with a laugh, but I can see the lines of stress on her face.

"Well we wouldn't want that happenin to that beautiful hair of yours." She smiles and pretends to be bashful. "But seriously, I think meditation's a great concept. I can't say I've ever learned any official instructions how to do it, but I sorta do my own meditations all the time. Like when I'm waterin or plantin a long row and I get into a rhythm with it, I'll focus in on the sounds of the grasshoppers, cicadas, breeze blowin, that sorta thing, and my thoughts go quiet and it's like I'm in an amphitheater of realness where there's no interference, ya know? Like everything I'm doin is ultra-lucid when there's nothin in my mind stoppin me from being right there in it."

"I know exactly what you mean," she says with the biggest smile. "That's amazing how you've stumbled upon it without being taught any technique." She's lookin at me like I'm a god.

"It's the drone of all them cicadas taught me how to do it," I tell her with a wink. A musical giggle spills out of her like a mountain stream, cool and crystal clear.

Fiona's forgotten the punch I stashed under the shrubs; her unyielding attention tells me she's not wanting for anything more than what she has right here. A group of boisterous people passes by, breakin our focus briefly before she turns back to me.

"So, you said the dreams about…someone who looks like me…have become restless in recent years," Fiona mentions with some concern.

"That's correct," I affirm with a nod, not feelin quite ready to broach the subject.

"Like what kind of dreams...how are they disturbing now?" She's brave enough to ask and has every right to know.

"Well, it's usually more of a stressful feelin than anything specific. She seems a little frantic, dissatisfied." Fiona isn't quite ready to refer to my dream woman as herself, so I'll tread lightly. "Like when your life's fittin together tight like a puzzle...and everything's doin okay, except there's this one piece that ain't cut right. And you keep tryin to cram it in there a million different ways but it won't go. And that one doggone piece keeps everything else from workin together properly." She's starin at me wide-eyed and noddin her head constantly. "Now I did have a truly strange dream just a few days back, but until then they were pretty vague."

"My God Bo, that's the description of my life. And the craziest part is, I don't really know what that odd piece is. It's like something gnawing away at me day in and day out, yet I can't put my finger on it. Then again lately...some things have come to pass that are definitely specific." I wanna ask Fiona what she means by that, but she jumps in first. "So what was the strange dream you just had, if you don't mind my asking?"

I watch as her body language becomes giddy. She shivers a little, even though it's still hot out, and I detect a faint shaking in her voice.

I have to take a big breath for this one. "Now Fiona, these are just dreams, okay? And I have been known to take my visions and dreams very seriously a time or two, but the psyche can kick up all kinds of dumb stuff that don't mean nothin." She's lookin more alarmed by the moment; I'd better spit this out. "Well it was too dark to determine the face, but judgin by the hair it was the same image I always dream about. And she was bein restrained by...some man in the darkness." Fiona claps her hands over her mouth and begins to tear up. "Fiona...darlin."

I lean forward and take her into my arms, finally holdin her heart against mine the way I have wanted to for so long. Her trembling intensifies, and she leans into me and allows it to come in dramatic bursts.

"Did you hear what I said to that lady in there about my ex husband stalking me?" she asks against my shoulder.

"I sure did, and I've been wantin to ask."

"Well, let's just say he's got the upper hand."

I take her by the shoulders and hold her at arm's length where I can look into her teary eyes. "Fiona, you tell me about this man. What's he tryin to do to you?"

"Nothing...I just...it's a long story."

"Well...I've got all weekend." Now that my blood's rushing to my head and all my veins are standing up, she sees I can go from Zen to t-rex real fast.

"When we divorced nine years ago, Quade moved back to California and left me the house...but it's still in his name."

"So he's threatenin to pull the rug?"

"Something like that."

"No!" I growl with disgust. "What would make him wanna do such a thing after so many years?"

"To tell you the truth, I really don't know. He seems to be sensing an increased loss of control over me? I don't know how or why, but he's been saying things lately...to indicate he thinks I'm slipping away from him. Quade and I remained best friends over the past decade, and I've never seen him like this before."

"Slippin away?" I have to cut in. "What right does your ex-husband have to exert any control over you whatsoever?"

"Well, he doesn't. Apparently he's been living under the delusion that we're still essentially married. I guess maintaining such a close friendship has been a huge mistake. There's no way I could have predicted it would come to this."

"Come to what exactly, if you don't mind my askin?" I'm askin regardless of whether she minds, but I figure she'll only give me more information if I'm diplomatic about it.

"Well, I don't know exactly. That's the thing. Several nights ago he threatened to take everything away from me. And he freaked me out a little bit."

"What did he do to you Fiona? You can tell me anything," I try to implore calmly, though she can probably sense I'm about to run to Iowa to sucker punch this guy.

"He just...I think he might be spying on me. Maybe has my phone or my house tapped somehow. It's just paranoia I'm sure, but I moved into my other friend's condo right before leaving for Florida. Holly's offered to put me up until I feel confident about living at home again."

"My God woman...you can't even sleep in your own home because of this guy? That ain't cool."

Fiona looks away, like she doesn't wanna deal with my directness. I think I read a little embarrassment, but there's definitely somethin she's not disclosing to me. I can see it in her flighty eyes.

"Do you really mean to tell me that your own ex-husband, and pretend friend, would tap your phone or your house?"

"Oh...I'm sure not. I'm known for my hysterics. It's just a thought I had that's been freaking me out and I need to stop considering it."

"Well I don't know darlin. I put a lot of stock in intuition, especially a woman's intuition." I also can't imagine that a ten-year-old ex would tap her phone, but I don't wanna see her shut herself down if she's onto somethin real... especially considering the potential severity of the situation. "Quade. I don't like it. He has the name of a wounded ego," I practically bark.

"That's him exactly," Fiona affirms, shaking her head in dismay. "He's a weak, little man who never made a good husband for me. But he used to be kind. I've consulted him over business details every step of the way and he's been indispensable. He's a big pushover who's never gotten his hands dirty in his life. I found him insufferably insecure as my husband."

Now I can see how her expression contorts into the stress lines on her forehead. I know exactly where they came from.

"It was all wrong from the start but my family adored him and I thought they'd disown me if I turned him down. He's such a weasel...he actually got on his knees and proposed at a family event. I said yes but wanted to privately redact it later, but then he was sharing his wedding and honeymoon ideas with me a mile a minute. He was excited like a schoolgirl."

"You were manipulated." I've said my piece, and I know I need to back off. There's a time and a place to deal with somethin like this, and now ain't it.

"Oh I definitely was. But I still could have bailed out and wasn't brave enough to do it." She looks down quietly, and I have a sense that there's a lot more to say. This woman isn't easily manipulated. "My parents let me know, in no uncertain terms, that my inheritance would go elsewhere if I 'made any mistakes' with Quade. He was like the son they'd always wanted and never had. My mother had two miscarriages trying for another child before doctors discovered she had endometriosis and recommended her hysterectomy. They were torn up over never being able to bear a son." Fiona holds her head high as she tells me this, always maintaining her dignified stance.

She needs comforting right now, but I'm anxious to get back to the details of her dangerous, current situation. "They were fools to imagine they could ever need more than you," I tell her, as I pull her close again.

Fiona feels like a doll in my arms, so precious and vulnerable. How life can try to beat down such a perfect creature is hard for me to fathom.

Slowly she lifts her head, eyes glazed with tears, and leans her face toward mine. I sit like a statue, waitin stoically for the kiss I've been dreamin of, but she stops just short and gazes at me...breathin with me nose to nose. Her breath becomes heavier as the tension mounts into almost a desperation.

"Bo, am I moving too fast?" she asks breathlessly.

"Well you've only been hauntin my dreams for thirty some odd years. You tell me." And with that, she gives me the kiss of life.

Chapter 13

Fiona

There are no words to describe this man, or what he makes me feel, or why. All night I've been on my guard for hasty and reckless behavior. Did I drink too much? Am I rebounding from Quade-induced PTSD? Yes, and yes. But...what I'm feeling is real, and my current mental and emotional state has nothing to do with it. Some part of me fell in love the first time I ever heard Bo's voice. The falsehood has been my relentlessly attempting to squelch and deny what I was feeling all along.

Now that I am here, face to face with this god of a man, I have no choice but to surrender. Aware it can't possibly go anywhere, I may as well enjoy it for all of two days. There's not a flesh and blood woman on Earth who would walk away from this, regardless of the futility.

The heat from Bo's hands on my shoulders is spreading through my body like a wildfire. I wish we were in his room...it's a good thing we're not. I can see the hunger in his eyes and I don't know how long I can resist the urge to kiss him. I was in high school the last time I experienced a welling of desire so swift and intense. I hold my face up to his, breathing in his breath.

I hope it doesn't seem inappropriate for me to open myself at this moment. After listening to the marital sob story a total of one other person has ever heard, Bo's trying to be stoic for me...responsive but strong. I know he wants to kiss me, but he's too good a man to do such a thing at a time when I might be vulnerable. I'm pretty sure the ball's in my court...and I'm rolling it.

As I close the distance between our lips, his meet mine in a succulent embrace. Unmoving, we inhale each other with eyes closed tightly for what has to be a minute. And then we lose control. As our mouths engulf each other, he places a hand at the small of my back and pulls me into him. My legs swing onto the bench to wrap around his waist, and suddenly I'm in his lap. His enormous hands are everywhere, up and down my head and back, gripping me like baseball mitts. My moans get louder and hungrier as I run my fingers along the dense back muscles his button-up is unable to hide.

Suddenly becoming cognizant of the scene we could create out here, with my dress rumpled up to my waist like a teenager, I attempt to break away...but Bo hungers forward, pulling me back to his lips with a firm hand on the nape of my neck. After one last kiss he draws back and looks into my eyes, both of us panting for breath. He rests his forehead against mine and gazes at me from inches away, stroking my hair with those hands, sending dazzling sensations through my spine.

"Fiona, I could never think a thought that trivializes you, and I know I would have felt the same about you no matter what, but you are the most beautiful woman I have ever seen in the flesh."

"Oh...Bo...I've never felt so attracted to a man in my entire life. Not only are you a massive hunk, you have the perfect face. You're exactly who I dreamed up in all my girlhood fantasies about the man I'd meet one day...that were then beaten down by reality."

"Well reality's a changin, woman," Bo says, retightening my body against his lap with a firm pull of his arms.

This sends me into a fit of dizziness, panting to the point of becoming light-headed. I don't want to ever move from this bench...unless it's to march directly to Bo's bed. But that hardly seems like the appropriate or becoming choice for a woman he's never met before. Then again...he *has* known me all his life. I inexplicably believe every word out of the man's mouth.

The greater emphasis should go to the fact that I've never seen him before, but I couldn't possibly care less. Every fiber of me wants to make love to Bo. Who am I trying to kid? Still, it feels a little aggressive for me to say it, yet I know he'll be a gentleman till the end. It's just...only three nights! The thought of it is killing me already.

"Fiona—"

"Bo—," we start in, reading each other's minds.

"Fiona, it's after midnight by now and I'm sure you're tired after your flight—"

"No! Actually...I slept through the whole thing."

He chuckles at me in his sexy way, a low rumble originating deep within his barrel chest. "Well then sweetheart, we can sit here on this hard bench all night long if you want to. I can go a couple months with no sleep as long as you're sittin on my lap. But I should at least take you somewhere more comfortable, if you'd allow me to."

"Bo," I respond before breaking into a giggle, "I'm afraid I can't be held accountable for anything I might say or do tonight. The alcohol's long gone...it's just...you."

Bo pulls me back into a long, hard kiss, and my body goes limp. Clutching me against him, he stands and then picks up my legs with one arm...laying me back against the other.

"Bo! What are you doing?" I cry out in a weak protest, laughing.

"I'm gonna carry you across the threshold," he says, striding toward the hotel while I giggle and kick my feet.

Cleverly avoiding the curious eyes of other people, he forgoes the elevator and carries me up the back stairway... to his fifth floor room. I'm astounded by his total lack of huffing and puffing when he at last enters and lays me on the bed, gently, as though I were one of his flowers. He then proceeds to stroke my hair, my arms, my hands, until my eyes close and I go into a deep state of relaxation. To heck with all those bizarre yoga-therapy sessions. This is the real deal.

Feeling his breath against me, I crack open my eyes to see Bo peering lovingly down. A smile comes to my lips and I close my eyes again, not wishing to rush or change anything about this beautiful moment. I know I'm completely safe and, although I would jump his bones in a heartbeat, I also know he's doling out his affection at his own perfect pace. I must surrender to the temporary nature of our situation and allow it to unfold as it will. My mind quietens and my eyelids grow heavy.

I awaken from a fuzzy love-haze sleep, in a puddle of heat radiating from the body I fell asleep next to. The clock reads four a.m., and I turn over to lie face to face with a peacefully sleeping Bo. I set an alarm on my phone and remain, eyes open, watching his chest rise and fall...until my sleep deficit overcomes me once more.

When my alarm goes off at seven, Bo reaches out and pulls my back flush against him. I can feel his turgidity as he growls and kisses the back of my neck, causing me to push even farther into his embrace. He finds my lips as I twist around to see him, and strokes a hand cautiously down my chest...sending a shivering sensation through my breastbone without even touching my breasts. His fingers are electric... nothing like I could have guessed about such an impressive pair of worker's hands.

His kisses are smooth and caressing, drinking me in like nectar. Bo makes me feel not only recognized, but worshiped. I long to return the favor in a thousand ways. How can there be only one weekend of this, when a lifetime couldn't be enough?

He kisses me till he can't resist turning me around, then pulls me into a tight embrace and kisses me more as he runs his fingers through my hair. Still in our clothes, I can feel his full readiness through his jeans. I know how difficult it must be for a man like Bo to resist me, yet he refuses to act in haste. He's wonderful, perfect even, but part of me wishes he was a tad less noble.

The hour disappears in a brilliant tangle of tasting, caressing, and breathing until I simply have to leave. Maxine's undoubtedly already at breakfast, wondering what in the world became of her boss.

"Bo," I whisper between kisses, "it's almost eight. I have to run. Maxine's entering the design competition in one hour and she must be beside herself with nerves."

"Okay sweetheart. I'll meet you for a quick breakfast?" he asks, clasping my fingers in his.

"Yes." And I kiss him once more. "I can hardly wait to see you at breakfast," I reply, reeling from the difficulty of leaving his side for half an hour.

Bo tears himself away, rises from the bed, and picks me up out of it, setting me on my feet with one last luscious kiss before releasing me. I stagger toward the door and look over my shoulder as I open it. His manhood is outrageously visible through jeans, and my mind somersaults into a quandary over his size. I've never had, or even encountered, a man of such dimensions. Trying not to stare, I offer a finger wave and I'm out the door.

I practically sprint across the tunnel that connects Bo's building to ours, then get to my room and unlock it to find Maxine already gone...as expected. Surely she'll be disappointed if we don't get a little time together before she competes. I pull off my overused dress and slip into a crinkled silk duo in moss green...a button up blouse with soft, flowy shorts that are cut high enough to show plenty of thigh. I'm dying to call Holly but what would I say over my potentially-tapped phone? Strapping my go-to wrap sandals around my calves, I'm out the door in a hurry. My mind is being pulled in so many directions, I feel like a crazy person... but I'm happy. Invincibly happy. In fact I'm so enthused about life, I have to keep myself in check so I don't power-walk myself sweaty again.

No sooner than I enter the lobby, my eyes settle on the most distracting man in the room. I want to rush up and jump into his arms, but I force myself to behave, instead tilting upward for a kiss on the cheek while our fingers discreetly interlock. A moment later, I'm pulling him through the throngs of people toward a frantically waving Maxine, detouring only to snatch some mimosas off the beverage table. Morning drinking is a thing I rarely do, but this may be the first and last weekend I'll ever enjoy this much. I've thrown caution to the wind.

Looking greatly relieved, Maxine leads us to her table where I introduce her to Bo. I have such a strong feeling about her success in this contest that it makes me proud to have her with me. To be realistic, she is a novice and probably won't win any higher than third place...but that would be huge for my store and her career. And the important thing is that she had the moxy to come all the way here and do this today.

When Maxine asks, I offer a quick explanation that Bo is one of my suppliers, but I can tell she's waiting to hear more. After all, she did see me with him late last night...and then I was altogether missing in action this morning. She must think I'm a loose cannon after all.

I only wish I could introduce Bo as my boyfriend, but I can't do that to either of us when our time together must be so brief. I cannot even imagine how we'll recover from any of this, so I refuse to think about it for now. I just want to lose myself in this mimosa and soak up the big man next to me.

"Do you enjoy growing?" Maxine asks Bo once we're settled in.

"Oh you bet yer britches I do. To start a livin plant from seed, hold that tiny little delicate thing in the palm of my hand and then plant it in earth, watch it grow up and unfold, day by day, hour by hour, into somethin as amazing as a flower...that right there's about the most beautiful thing I ever saw in my whole darn life." He throws me a devilish smile. "Just about."

I can see that Maxine's as enthralled by his response as I am. Every word out of Bo's mouth takes my breath away.

"You sure are eloquent for a farm boy," I tease.

"Well you see, my mother majored in English and was well versed in all the great literature. I grew up readin everything from Fitzgerald to Bradbury to Rumi. I could never get enough...I think expression is the true spice of life."

I'm so floored by Bo's brilliance, I can't even respond. I must look pretty goofy sitting here with my mouth open, but he continues to surprise me by the moment.

I'm rescued from my dumbfoundedness when a woman pipes loudly through a microphone. "Lily Cup Design Competition entrants, please head to the long tables at the west side of the convention center. Lily Cup entrants...please head to the long tables now, thank you."

"Ready for a little excitement?" I turn to Bo and ask.

"I'm ready for plenty," he responds with raised brows. My head spins from that comment as I watch Maxine rise from the table.

We wish her luck and, as soon as she rushes away, Bo covers my hand in his. He must have a sense that I wish to remain discreet about things. I want to leap across the table, to make the room full of people vanish so we can finish everything we resisted last night. But I instead settle on gazing into his smiling eyes for another minute before we get up and head toward the gathering crowd of viewers. I'd like us to be right in front of Maxine's exhibit if possible.

Arriving at the perfect spot, we stand in the crowd with our hands clasped tightly together. A minute later the countdown begins and the contestants tear into their boxes.

"Fiona darlin, I've got to get over to the Supplier Expo and get set up in a little while here. I won't get to see all of this but I'll stay as long as I can."

I can't get over the sound of Bo saying my name. 'Fiona' coming out of his husky chest sends a delightful sensation through me.

"That's okay Bo, two hours is a long time to stand here anyway. You just take off whenever you need and I'll catch up to you afterward." I wonder if he feels the same thing when I say his name.

When we finally focus our attention on Maxine, she's looking a little disconcerted. Poor girl...I should have guessed the box contents would be tropical flowers. She has zero experience with those, but I'm sure she'll be fine. The crowd has hushed to almost silence, and I grip Bo's hand tighter as we watch Maxine look around nervously. That is not what she needs to be doing. She needs to be focusing, and instead she's all bug-eyed like Alice in Wonderland.

Oh give me a break...she just glanced straight at me, and now she's fidgeting around like a putz up there. Well I guess that's something, at least. I almost wish Bo would leave now because I'm going to be embarrassed if Maxine freaks out on us here, and she looks like she's about to freak out. I steal a glance up at Bo and somehow he looks totally unruffled. My gaze lingers on him as I take in everything. Regardless of Maxine, or the competition, or the AFA Convention, or Fiona's Flowers, or my loss of privacy and sanity, or Quade...I'm standing next to a man who I would put more trust in than anyone I've ever known. Everything about this weekend will be perfect because nothing matters except being here beside him. I can feel his very energy healing me. I'll go back into my life a stronger woman because I met him, and that's above and beyond anything I could have asked for.

By the time I refocus on Maxine, she's moving with stealth. I've never seen her use those hands so efficiently and so...beautifully. She's sculpting up there with confidence now. It must be the way Bo's been projecting his unwavering attention on her from the start. The guy's got some magic that defies explanation.

Maxine's creating a ring of flowers that I'm guessing will be a headdress, and it's going to look stunning with the yellow and white dress she's wearing. The yellow pistils of those white calla lilies and red anthurium are an exact color match, as though she'd planned this. Bo finally looks down at me as I slowly shake my head from side to side, almost unable to believe how gorgeous her piece is turning out.

He places his hand on the small of my back and leans down to my ear. "I've gotta get goin, but I see she's off to one heck of a good start. That gal of yours is gonna nail this competition."

"You think she will?" I ask, fascinated by his level of confidence.

"Yes I sure do." He steals a kiss at the very edge of my mouth that leaves me starving for more, and then I watch the crowd part to let the big man through.

During the second hour, Maxine continues to feverishly fill out the ring with every imaginable type of lush greenery. It looks magnificent, and I'm overjoyed when she finally places it upon her lovely curls during the countdown. Incredible! I can't keep from jumping up and down with excitement. She looks right at me, beaming, and I tell her a clear and definite yes. She's got this.

The judges' walkthrough is excruciatingly long, but the women in my vicinity are onto the fact that I'm here for Maxine. They make the time fly by closing in on me with compliments. All of them are betting on Maxine to win this.

I'm just a little pissed that the judges took more time with the first thirty or so contestants, and then started picking up their pace. Nonetheless, I believe they saw exactly what they needed to. Poor Maxine is being mobbed on her way toward me. I hop and wave to get her over here but she's waylaid by the praise of several excited viewers, as well as other contestants. The surrounding crowd explodes with compliments when she at last reaches me, and I don't know how I could be more proud.

On the way back to our room, Maxine quizzes me about Bo. I play it cool but she's onto us. Oh well, it's not exactly as if I'm embarrassed to be seen with him. I just don't want her to think I'm mindlessly hooking up with a guy I'll never get with again, but at this point I couldn't really care. I want to spend every possible minute of the weekend with Bo, and I'm sure that's plain for her to see.

Closing myself into my room of the suite, I fish around for a dress to change into but decide to skip it. I'll save the big guns for later. Right now I just want to call Holly, and Maxine looks wiped out so this is the perfect chance. Sure enough, when I walk back through her room she's all but passed out. I wave and head out the door with my phone, feeling illogically empowered by my confessions to Bo last night.

Stepping into the pool and garden area, I find a grassy knoll where I can get some privacy. After taking a few minutes to formulate what I would feel safe saying on the phone, I dial Holly up.

She answers on the first ring. "Fiona...it's so good to hear from you. How's it going down there?"

"Hi Holly, good. How are you?" I feel like a total phony already.

"Holding down the fort. So...did you meet any interesting vendors yet this year?"

"Yes actually. You know that Fort Myers vendor I use? Well she is the greatest lady."

"Oh really?"

"Yes, delightful. She's super solid...an incredibly strong and interesting person. Not to mention, she's a total knockout."

"Oh wow! Well I hope you'll remain good friends."

"Yeah well, you know how bad I am at long distance friendships, but it's been great to meet such a nice person I'm doing business with."

"Hmm...well maybe you two will keep up with each other."

"Sure...yeah. Christmas cards and all that." I giggle awkwardly, just wanting to change the subject now. "Oh, and guess what?"

"What?"

"Maxine was brilliant in our contest!"

"Oh, that's such good news! Do you think she might place?" Holly asks heartily, embracing the new topic.

"I do. I genuinely do, and I don't even think I'm being biased. She actually sculpted a headdress up there and put it on with her dress and...I'll text you a bunch of pics here in a sec. You'll see...I think she was far and away the standout, but there were some others that were also amazing. We'll be on pins and needles until they announce winners tomorrow night."

"Yay Fifi...I'm so glad you have a lot of great things going on this weekend. What you need is a vacation, so just allow yourself to soak up all the good stuff you can while you're there."

"You are so right. Thank you for reminding me."

"Of course," she responds, and then sits in cautious silence...having almost said too much.

"Well...Quade called a couple times on my trip down Friday."

"Oh yeah? What's he up to?" she asks with feigned enthusiasm.

"Oh, he just wanted me to chat with him that night but I didn't want Maxine to have to navigate the meet-and-greet all alone." I laugh phonily. "So we decided to talk Monday instead."

"Oh, that's good."

"Yeah...he wants to talk about us a little. Says he feels like I'm slipping away," I say in a sing-song voice. "Quade's so silly sometimes. I don't know what's gotten into him lately."

"That does sound silly Fiona. Why would he imagine you're distancing from him?"

"Seriously, I have no idea. Maybe he's just jealous of you Holly," I say as though she's the only other person in my world.

"Well...I could understand that I guess," she responds with a giggle.

I check the time and it's almost lunch here. If Quade's been listening, my mission is accomplished. We get off the line and I hightail it to the dining hall, eager to sit next to Bo again.

Chapter 14

Bo

Waitin in a noisy public dining room for the most beautiful woman I've ever seen is no exercise in calm. I'm not a high-strung fella, but I've never felt anything quite like this. Some question how a red-blooded man can simply lie next to a woman like Fiona, but my answer is simple. If you know how to truly love then there is no absolute need for anything more. The emotion of connection is soul food, in and of itself. And the desires of my body are secondary to the nourishment of a heart bond like that.

With that thought, a blaze of light drifts through the entrance and across the room. She's all legs, long and bronzed, as she strides toward me with purpose.

"Good afternoon Big Bo. Long time no see," Fiona says with a laugh as I stand to embrace her.

Now that she's in my arms again, I don't know if I can let go of her. We pull back just enough for eye contact, and I can hardly stand not to kiss her. The way she smiles at me... her entire face simmering with need, her eyes blazin through me like bullets. I wanna make the room disappear.

"Shall we fix ourselves some plates?" I force myself to ask, out of politeness.

"Okay, sure. That's probably a good idea if I want to survive the afternoon," she replies without movin an inch.

I pull Fiona's waist tighter against me before releasing her, and feel her breath against my face as she sighs. This woman will be the end of me if I can't figure out some way to cope. I already wanna tell her she's comin home to live with me. It's all I can do not to toss her into my truck and hit the road.

Once reseated, I tear into my potatoes au gratin while Fiona picks self-consciously at her coconut shrimp and glazed carrots. I can see she's got those first-date nerves; she's quiet and bashful about eatin in front of me. It's damn cute, but I've gotta fuel up good for the day. I demolish my plate and go back for a couple more trout filets.

"So, what are you signed up for this afternoon?" I ask her once my mouth isn't stuffed.

"Just checking out the Supply Expo until three, then the retailer workshops go on till almost dinner. I'll try not to fall asleep."

"Someone keep you up last night?"

"Tried to," she answers, giggling.

"I'll walk on over to the Expo with you then, if you're ready to go," I tell her as we rise and make our way to the doors. She smiles, nods, and links her lovely arm in mine without a word. I love it when I can render a woman speechless.

* * *

No sooner than we arrived at my booth, Fiona was waived off by other admirers. Clearly she's got a solid base of friends and contacts from her years attending the conference. And I've had a steady stream of retailers checkin out my orchids and brochures all afternoon, but I steal a glance around the room every chance I can get...doin my best to keep an eye on Fiona's whereabouts.

Finally I spy her makin her way in my direction. I busy my hands in order to look like I wasn't keepin dibs on her, and she's standin in front of the booth in less than a minute. I've a mind to reach over and pick her up, set her down back here beside me. Just as fate would have it, three women approach with an exhaustive list of questions. Fiona steps back to wait patiently, but I hate for her to feel like second fiddle. After ten long minutes, she approaches again.

"I could have answered ninety percent of those questions," she says coyly. "I guess I have a pretty good handle on your business."

"Is that so?" I ask. "Well why don't you just come on back here and help Big Bo run this booth." She laughs like she appreciates the gesture. "I'm perfectly serious. That is... unless you're gettin antsy on me already."

"Oh no," Fiona answers with haste. "I think I've seen most of what I need to see in the room."

"Well come on back then if you like. You can help me fend off all these intruders."

She laughs again and takes my extended hand, as I guide her around behind the booth. Suddenly standing within a foot of so much woman, I wonder how I thought I was gonna pull this off. Fiona prances nervously for a while, fingering orchids and studying flyers, lookin as spunky and streamlined as a Tennessee Walkin Horse. I lean against the countertop and watch until she finally settles down and looks up at me. One hot moment later, she's thrown her arms around my neck and we're duckin behind the tallest edge of the booth for a kiss. After glancin around quickly and determining nobody's headed our way, we give ourselves over to another kiss...this one deep and still, mostly breath and little movement. Fiona pulls away as I stroke down the lengths of her gorgeous, silky mane. She looks around again but the masses are dyin down. People must be filing away to various other activities; our corner of the room is pretty quiet.

Just as she begins to pull me back to her, I notice Maxine entering through the far doors. I have the feelin Fiona wouldn't wanna be seen in any compromising position. I don't understand why she's such a private woman, but I'm pretty sure she is.

"Look who's comin this way," I announce calmly, givin her plenty of time to back out of my arms. She does and then stands next to me, smiling unnaturally as Maxine gradually approaches. It takes her about five minutes to work her way over to us and we get mobbed by a couple small groups in the meantime. But it's worth it to see the sneaky looks Fiona gives me between customers...grabbin my hands under the booth and wigglin over to me, then darting away like a skittish goldfish.

Finally Maxine walks up and I have to laugh. "Hello you two lovebirds," she says with no qualms.

Noticing Fiona's agitation, I jump to the rescue. "Well hello Maxine. I heard you were the star of the show this morning."

"Ha...I hope so. We'll see!"

"Fiona and I were just back here lookin over my new inventory lists, and choosin some new beauties for you to work with this winter." I can't explain what's come over me, but I have a wild impulse to make some demonstration of my feelins. "And we're havin a dern good time doin it, too," I say, as I wrap my arm around Fiona's waist and pull her in faster than she can react.

Quickly I notice her concern disappearing. Yep, I had the feelin that was all she needed.

"Well, I won't distract you two from your important business back there," Maxine says with a witty smile.

"Okay hun, see you at the party tonight?" Fiona pipes in, lookin so much more relaxed than before.

"Yes, see you around six. I'm gonna head to the pool until then. Have fun!" And Maxine's off, leavin us to our shenanigans once more.

I turn to Fiona and retighten my hold, tipping her back just a tad. Those brown eyes look so right staring up at me. Our area's almost empty now and she doesn't resist when I kiss her again. When I feel her growin limp in my arms, givin me her full weight, I wanna tell her I'm keepin her forever, but I reckon she don't know that yet. Anyway, I have the feelin she won't fight it when the time comes.

"Fiona, sweetheart, I want you to understand that I have the best possible intentions for you. I don't intend to take advantage or have some kind of a fling." Her eyes go wide with a mixture of curiosity and vague alarm. I have no idea why she wouldn't wanna hear those words, but I can detect that somethin's up.

"That's okay Bo. I won't blame you for taking advantage," she says with one eyebrow raised flirtatiously.

"Now Fiona, why would I wanna do a thing like that to a woman like you? You ain't the kinda gal Big Bo can take to bed and then walk away from. You understand that, don't you?" She smiles and distracts me with a kiss, negating my question.

She's killin me right now. It's all I can do to resist abandoning the booth and rushing us back to my room. But no way did I come here to play games with this woman. Now that I've discovered what she's like in person, there's no turnin back for me. I can only pray she feels the same way, and if not...I need to hear the truth.

Fiona rises up to kiss me again, and I pull away just an inch. "You know I'm being straight with you now, don't you? I recognize a quality woman when I meet one, and I've always wanted to meet you. I believe in serendipity and that there's a grand reason for all this."

"Bo," she finally responds with difficulty, "I do have to fly home to my store and my life tomorrow. I'd love to imagine I could stay here with you forever, but you know I can't."

"Would you love to imagine that?"

"Of course," Fiona laughs, "but I have to be realistic."

"Well sweetheart, we'll work somethin out...okay? We'll just figure somethin out, you and me." She smiles, but I can see the doubt in her eyes.

We continue our song and dance for the next hour, stealin as many kisses as we can and gazin at each other in between. Eventually Fiona has to excuse herself to her next activity, just as I become swamped by another group of ladies with questions, and it kills me that I can't hold her just one more time before she's outta my sight.

Chapter 15

Fiona

As I book it from one end of the building to the other, I fiddle with my phone...hot in my hand. What a lot of nonsense, this idea that I'm tapped. As the events of last week fade into a new improved reality, all this paranoia seems ludicrous. But then I remember what Quade actually did and said that night, and it serves as a reminder of just how insane he is and how far he'll go. I simply cannot take any chances until I at least have someone examine my phone.

That's what I'll do. There must be plenty of people out there who specialize in this kind of thing. I'm sure someone can accurately determine whether I'm holding a tapped phone. The thought of having no more personal conversations with Bo is absurd. I'd feel terrible if he had to sit around wondering what he did wrong, when he's done everything so right. What a great guy.

Yet, our behavior the last time I ordered from Bo is the only thing I can think of that could have led Quade to begin questioning my personal life. It curdles my blood to imagine how long he's potentially had access to my calls. Or perhaps he'd just let himself in and was hiding somewhere in my house when I made that call to Bo. I physically shudder under the weight of that thought, as I enter the conference room and find a seat in the back.

* * *

After attempting to quiet my thoughts down throughout two hours of lecture, I'm raring to get to tonight's dinner party. I stop by the room to throw on a cute mini wrap dress and head straight out. Bo will want to eat me alive in this, and I'm not above torturing him.

As I enter the glamorous banquet hall, Bo swoops over to take me by the elbow and the sight of him makes me go breathless. Dressed in a dapper button-up and dark pants, with a slick looking pair of cowboy boots, he's country-boy-hot in a way I never knew I was into. I'm not exactly the country-boy type, but Bo seems to be the exception to every rule I have.

After a few minutes of introductions among the group we're sharing our table with, Maxine makes her appearance. Speeches begin soon enough and it's all I can do to behave myself. The passing out of wines and cocktails helps, but it seems that we're doomed to sit quietly listening to floral industry drivel for the rest of eternity.

Our dinner arrives in the nick of time to prevent me from sliding under the table. Having eaten a light lunch, I'm unable to hold my drinks as well as usual, plus I'm experiencing the giddy loss of appetite that I remember getting around high school crushes. I'll take it as a good sign that this is not something I ever experienced over Quade.

I proceed to eat every last bite of my linguine marsala, in spite of myself. They never skimp on serving quality food at this conference, and everything on my plate is heavenly. Afterward the room divides into various groups doing all sorts of cutesy games and recreational activities. Not exactly my thing, but I guess I'll play along. I don't need Bo to witness what a maddeningly uncooperative dame I actually am.

I head with Maxine to the cocktail bar, where we grab Irish coffees, and I decide to commit to my good mood. I only have to survive all this social idiocy long enough to politely exit, with Bo by my side. He approaches us smiling, beer in hand, and stands there a little awkwardly. I'm positive he wants to grab me, but isn't sure how I'd respond in the middle of a crowd.

"Well guys, I think I'm gonna go join the flower trivia table. Find out how much I really know," Maxine says finally.

She's so polite. I know she's trying to allow me my space with Bo.

"Ooh, that sounds like fun," I lie. "We might join you after we look around the options a little while," I respond with a reassuring smile.

Maxine stands before us grinning stupidly for a few seconds, almost as if she wants to hug me, then subtly nods and disappears into the crowd. That was weird. Bo takes my arm in his and walks me to the perimeter of the room, where we pass the next half hour strolling around and watching different group activities. He asks if I want to join in a couple of times, but I can't get a clear read on whether he's serious. I guess I'm stereotyping, but it's difficult for me to imagine this tatted, muscle-bound hunk participating merrily in some chintzy group activity with a bunch of hoity toity strangers.

Eventually Bo tries to pull me into a group that's doing some sort of goofy challenges, which makes me giggle, but I really do not want to do this. "What's the matter?" he asks. "I just wanna see em spin you blind-folded like that lady up there," he says, referring to a woman standing on a small platform. After they release her, she crawls around on all fours feeling her way through a pile of plastic flowers until she finds the one that's supposed to be a chrysanthemum.

"Um...why the heck did they get her dizzy first?" I have to ask.

"Now that I couldn't tell ya. Entertainment purposes? A little added disorientation?"

"She's already digging through a pile of fake flowers blind-folded!"

"True. But you know...a little extra drama never hurt... made her wobble around more on all fours. Sure you don't wanna be next?" he asks, shooting his eyebrows up in a suggestive way.

I laugh and elbow him gently in his cavernous ribcage, then boldly interlace my fingers in his and pull him toward the next group. But almost immediately I'm balking again.

They're doing a timed trivia game where you have to come up with the name of an incredibly obscure flower within ten seconds. Personally, I think faster than most under fire. But not tonight. Between the cocktails and the man in the boots, I'm distracted beyond all mental function.

Nonetheless, Bo looks fascinated by the game and stalls to watch for a while.

"Would you like to join us? We're about to begin a new round," a woman calls out with a smile and a beckoning hand.

I begin shaking my head, just as Bo responds. "Sure thing, ma'am," he says. "I think we're up for a little challenge tonight, aren't we?" he asks, looking at my apprehensive face.

I smile and nod along, pretending to be a sport. But after she ushers us over and slaps a tacky-ass nametag directly onto my dress, I politely bow out.

"I'll be your cheerleader," I assure Bo when he shoots me a disappointed look.

"Suit yourself sweetheart," he says. "I'm gonna ace this game for ya."

I grin at him, feeling foolish, wondering why my stomach flutters when he calls me sweetheart. I've never been one to respond to traditional pet names, but words have a different sound and meaning when they're rumbling out of Bo's mouth.

The woman begins holding up illustration cards, first for the guy competing against Bo and then for him. The other guy struggles through the first three, one right after the other, failing to name them in the allotted time frame, while Bo gets everything right...card after card after card. I've never heard of most of these flowers in my life. Apparently Bo is a genius. He must have a photographic memory. How and why anyone would know these freakish flowers is beyond me. Once he gets to The Rothschild Slipper Orchid, I'm so proud that I'm almost teary eyed...yet I feel quite a bit dumber than before. After completing a round of five, they put him up against another contestant...and he proceeds to crucify her as well. Eventually he grows weary of toying with these poor sods, grabs my hand, and retreats back into the crowd. I must look like a bimbo as I stagger away with him in a state of slack-jawed wonder, but then I'm pretty certain everyone else at that table reacted the same way.

The party's beginning to wind down; the room thinned out a lot while we were immersed. I scan for Maxine until I spot her in the middle of a group of ladies. She appears to be the center of attention...perhaps they're fans of her now famous headdress. Satisfied that she's well taken care of, I turn to Bo with a hungry look, wishing he'd drag me away right about now.

Reading my mind, he says the magic words. "What do you say we get on out of here and make ourselves comfortable?" Newly elated, I smile and nod with the enthusiasm of your average everyday hussie.

I don't exactly want Bo to read me as easy, since I'm not, but I've also never before experienced the desire to sleep with someone I just met. I'm inexcusably eager to get alone with a man I can't even have a relationship with.

"Wanna tell Maxine we're takin off?" he politely asks.

"Nah, she'll figure it out. Look at her...she's having a great time," I reply, glancing in her direction and finding her well engaged. "Let's go," I request with an energetic smile.

Bo interlocks his tremendous fingers in mine, and escorts me out of all the frantic noise and movement. It feels wonderful to be rushing down the halls again, swinging our arms and laughing together. Every moment with Bo makes me feel like I'm about to board a roller coaster...nervously excited, giddy and giggly, thrilled to be terrified.

As soon as the heavy door of his room slams shut behind us, he looks at me like a bull at a rodeo...his body radiating nuclear heat, his nostrils slightly flared. Bo's level of total focus wipes the smile off my face and causes me to go weak in the knees. He quickly whips off his button-up to reveal the white muscle shirt underneath. Momentarily he fists his hands, causing the bolderous muscles of his arms to tighten and flex. His chest looks like it's about to rip out that undershirt.

During what has to be a solid minute, Bo inches closer and closer while I inch away...until the backs of my thighs finally hit the mattress. In another second he closes our distance and scoops me into his arms, literally sweeping me off my feet, then gently lays me across his bed like Sleeping Beauty. I find myself flailing in a way that's alien to me. Hyperventilating from the exertion of my breaths, my arms and legs are writhing with no direction, my mid-body scooting and wiggling downward to scrunch up my dress. I desire Bo with a dysfunctional urgency that defies all common sense.

I watch the way his suit pants stretch and crease over the contours of his leg muscles, as he straddles me and hovers. Staring downward with fire in his eyes, growling just a little...like a lion over its kill. I reach up and run my fingers along the shapes of a gorgeously ornate tattoo sleeve that extends down one arm. It's floral but decisively manly on Bo, an intricate garden of multiple types of blooms in black ink.

Bo then peels off his tank and tosses it, revealing the full view of his long, toned torso I didn't get to see during last night's encounter. My hands trace from his biceps to his moderately-haired chest, then follow the trail down to his hard packed abs. I shiver as I take him in with my eyes, astonished by the way my luck has turned. Once more, I find myself gulping for air as I notice the size of him, pushing against his slacks with barely containable force. I want to keep going with my hands, to get a feel of his incredible fixture, but I resist...waiting in suspense to see what he'll initiate next.

Chapter 16

Bo

Of all the things I've ever accomplished, the decades of physical labor and hard work I put into making the farm somethin my parents would've been proud of, I've never felt more powerful than I do right now...as I hover over this magnificent woman, Fiona Turner, writhing beneath me in a helpless state of desire. Her face is my inspiration, her eyes my motivation, her body my muse.

As badly as I want to ravage Fiona, all I can do is look at her, mesmerized, and fight off the temptation. I can sense she's an eager woman; she would not resist if I were to take her. But her mental tightness has her locked into a world where we can't be together, due to the simple impracticality of it. Of course I know that's nonsense and two adults can do anything they darn well please, but this conference has hardly been the time or place to work on convincing Fiona of that. And she may not fear the repercussions of a one-night-stand, but I do. There's already no turnin back for me. I will find a way to get her to see. I'm just not too sure that a full-blown seduction is the right way to secure her sense of attachment. She may act like a wild woman, but everyone with a heart has vulnerability. It's a delicate situation. I force myself to bail off of her and regain some bearings.

Fiona's already managed to wiggle her dress skirt up to her hips, leavin her exquisitely shaped legs stretched to the end of the bed. She watches in a state of mild dismay as I walk around to her beautiful, perfectly formed feet and take them into my hands. I could see her disappointment when I got up, but now she's meltin like butter as I stroke deep into her insteps with my thumbs. Her left leg bears a gold chain that glistens brightly against the skin of her delicate ankle. She closes her eyes and purrs as I take each foot and press it to my lips, kissin my way across her toes and licking her arches. Her increasing gasps and moans make it damn near impossible to resist her, but I'll stretch this night out as long as I possibly can.

Her dress has worked itself all the way up to the apex of her legs, and I can see the tiniest peak of her panties...a translucent, netlike fabric that slightly reveals the dark tuft of curls beneath it. I'd like to imagine Fiona was anticipatin me when she packed these things, and I have a hunch she was. The skin of her Barbie Doll legs is soft and smooth, supple and ageless beneath my hands, as I stroke up and down the length of her calves and work my way to her thighs.

She looks at me through half closed eyes, her mouth open, her arms splayed out. When I get to Fiona's hips, I turn her onto one side so my big mitts can access her beautiful derriere. Feelin her muscles melt against the warmth of my fingers, I stroke her languidly through the soft fabric of her dress. My heart pounds as I gaze down at her. She's all I've ever wanted...what more could a man need? Yet I have a powerful intuition that she's not fully receptive, not ready to give herself to me. And what's an old boy like me to expect anyway? I've been seeing her in visions my whole life, but she's only just met *me*. I can tell she's smitten, but perhaps not enough for me to lay everything I feel and want out on the table in one weekend. I'm gonna have to be more strategic than that. She may seem like no delicate flower, but all women truly are...deep down underneath.

Carefully watchin every response, every nuance of her face, I untie her waist sash and begin to slip the dress upward. She eagerly raises her arms to facilitate me, and I toss it unceremoniously onto the nearby chair...a lovely puddle of white and yellow daisies on a bright blue background. The full site of her body in nothin but underthings, raises my temperature another twenty degrees. Fiona's wearing a strapless corset-style bra that matches the see-through panties, and she's givin me a look that says I was intended to see her like this.

Overcome, I plant my face on her lean torso and smooch it as she wraps her legs around my neck. The slight perfume of Fiona's bodily scent, combined with her glorious sounds, throttle me into an unstoppable sense of mission. Now arching and bucking into me, she's essentially beggin me to get her naked. Still hovering over her in nothin but my pants, I delicately unclasp her bra to reveal the perfect chest of every man's dreams...well, every man in his right mind. Two firm mounds of pure gold with bronze centers, none too slight but not bulky...they're the boobs Goldilocks would've picked.

Fiona moans and grinds against me as I gape, fixedly, at her unbearable beauty. She's shootin me the look of desperation when I slowly envelope her breasts with my hand, one at a time, delicately cupping the entire mound and stroking softly from the outside to the center. Having not kissed in hours, she lunges at me with her mouth when I get mine close to her chest. But I pull just out of reach and settle my lips on a breast instead, which elicits just the response I was hoping for. Takin my time, I work each one in equilibrium until I can feel an abundance of moisture exuding through the mesh of Fiona's panties.

Before scootin lower, I raise up to make eye contact and can see that Fiona's on fire. We both wanna kiss so badly, it only makes me wanna torture us longer. I kiss a trail from her breastbone to her belly button, and then peel her sweet panties down inch by inch as she twists beneath me. I slide off the foot of the bed and pull them down her legs and off the ends of her pointed feet. As I lunge forward to resume my position, she plants one of those gorgeous feet right over my mouth and I kiss the bottom of it for several minutes before movin on to the next one.

Finally I replace Fiona's limp leg and crawl back toward her mid-body. She looks down and reaches as though she wants to remove my pants, but I stop midway for an essential detour. To have this woman in such a way is almost too great an honor for me to bear. My life feels like it's been one long rehearsal for this moment. For the next hour, my mouth dances across the waters of her ocean...inciting ripple after ripple, then wave after wave, until a tsunami washes over me of such proportions that I learn somethin about a woman's capacity I'd never known before.

Chapter 17

Fiona

I cannot believe what is happening here tonight. For me... for my mind, body and soul, for my quality of life going forward, for my entire experience of being. During the meager moments I allowed myself to anticipate this trip, I hadn't imagined I'd experience both the worst and best days of my life within the same week. Bo is everything a woman could dream of having in a man. In fact I've been constantly 'pinching' myself, checking in with reality to make sure he isn't a fabrication born out of the trauma I experienced last week.

And here I am, lying panting beneath his ultra-masculine frame, an eager and willing slave to whatever he decides to do next. Although the past hour has left me with few precious remnants of my mind, and even less energy to move a single muscle, I still find myself hungering for the penetration Bo hasn't yet graced me with.

Holding a view of him through the dazzling distortion of my damp lashes, it hits me that Bo never did remove his pants. I still haven't seen the full enormity of his flesh, nor the exact sculpting of his lower body. The longing that suddenly fills me is almost unjustified in light of what he's already given, yet it's imperative that I have him completely. I don't know how my body will take him, but apparently it possesses a determination of its own.

After somewhat regaining my bearings from Bo's magnificent pleasure-overload, I reach down to caress him... but he pulls slightly away. He holds my gaze, surely seeing the eagerness and longing in my eyes, but something in his tells me he has reservations. I feel my face flush when I glance momentarily at his pants and notice a sizable wet spot. There's no question he's ready to go, and I wonder what's holding him back.

I want to ask but our togetherness has been so perfect, I wouldn't want him to think I'm complaining or feeling lack. And, as much as I'm used to controlling, it's a surprising comfort to leave all decision making up to someone as powerful as Bo. I trust him. Maybe he's being wise. Would any greater intimacy be too much for either of us to handle under the circumstances?

As I begin to get lost in rumination, Bo breaks the silence with a question I'm inadequately prepared to answer. "What is it you want most out of life, Fiona? I wanna hear about everything that makes you tick," he says, still stretching his pants to the brink of their structural integrity.

His sudden change of strategy catches me off-guard, makes me laugh. "Uh, well...right now I wanna find out what else you can do to me," I answer in all honesty, swiping one knee across his conspicuous bulge.

He gives me that deep chuckle and buries his face in my neck, sending me into another layer of unravelment. "I like a woman who can't be satisfied," he groans into my hair. "I could play with you all night."

"Yes, you can," I encourage him, plunging my fingers into his short, thick, brown hair.

"Fiona," he says with a serious look, "will you call me when you get home tomorrow night?"

"Sure," I reply, slightly astonished that his request could be so simple.

"And will you call me Monday night after work?"

"Okay." Now I'm starting to wonder where he's going with this.

"And will you call me Tuesday," he asks before planting a kiss on my forehead. "And Wednesday." He kisses me tantalizingly close to my mouth. "And Thursday," he says, nuzzling behind my ear and putting one there.

I begin to giggle. This is getting out of hand, but not turning me off in the slightest. "Now Bo, why would you want me to torture you like that?" I have to ask.

"Torture? Havin you in my life on the regular ain't any kinda torture."

Bo's accent drives me wild. In a moment of sobriety, I cup his face in my hands and raise up to kiss him full on the mouth...for the first time tonight. In an instant this accelerates us into a kissing and panting frenzy, as we attempt to grind and push our way through the cloth barrier between us. Again I reach down, and this time I get a handful of rock hardness before Bo escapes me. He lets out the kind of groan that makes me wet all over again, before disengaging and rolling beside me on the bed.

"Woman, you'll be the end of me," he mutters, our heads turned to face each other.

"You'll be the end of me," I retort.

"Good, cause I plan to finish you off."

"Oh yeah? Then what will you do with me?"

"Well, that's up to you ma'am. Let's just say I'll go as far as you'll let me."

This comment jars me a little, as I'm no longer certain we're talking about the same thing.

"Let you...?"

"Let me take you into my life, Fiona." Bo props himself onto an elbow, which raises him approximately to the height of me sitting.

"But Bo," I say, reaching out to stroke his chest, "we live so far away. How could we be anything besides an unhealthy long-distance obsession?"

"Well sweetheart, we can't." I know he's right, but my heart feels like it's crushing from the sound of those horrible words. "Not unless we have vision...intention...ideals," he says with a look that's relaxed, yet pierces through me like a blade.

My mouth opens but nothing comes out. I'm continually astonished by the brilliance, heart, and absolute honesty I see in Bo. I've never before questioned whether I was good enough for someone, but I find myself blinded by Bo's light. Am I strong enough, do I have what it takes to deserve such a man? It's clear that his resistance is every bit as difficult, his disappointment just as poignant as mine...but I know he won't buckle. I'm going to have to take a step toward him, but I don't want to tell him any greater details of my situation. If for no other reason, I suspect he's the type of guy to take the law into his own hands and hustle up there to kick Quade's butt. Not that I'd mind, except...well there is that whole issue of me losing my personal empire.

"Bo, listen...people think I'm a strong, independent woman with the world as my oyster, but I'm telling you it's so different from that. And the less you find out about me, the better for both of us." He looks at me with a mixture of skepticism and hurt. "Can't we make the most of our time together and then go back to our lives? I just don't wanna waste our time discussing me and my problems," I say, reaching out to stroke his chest again...hoping I can divert him back to the physical. But his relentless stare won't let me off the hook. He regards me stoically, as if my response isn't going to cut it. "Okay," I say, taking one of his hands, "I have a situation with someone who co-owns my business." Bo's eyes go wide. And no wonder; he probably thinks I'm alluding to a relationship with someone else. "A jealousy situation," I attempt to clarify, realizing that didn't help at all. "I have a situation with a jealous owner who could pull the rug on me if I piss him off. He could...potentially force me to close doors."

"And what exactly is it that would qualify as pissin him off?" Bo asks with narrowed eyes.

"Well, for instance…if I were to suddenly carry on a romantic relationship, without discretion."

"So, you're in a situation where you're tryin to run a shop with someone who won't allow you to have another man?" he asks, sounding like he's barely repressing anger. "I take it you opened your store with Quade?"

Suddenly I feel affronted by Bo's tone. "It's my personal business who I opened it with," I say quietly, trying not to be too offensive.

"Yes it is, and I can't make you wanna share it. But I can draw a line at what I will or won't do with someone who isn't ready to be open with me."

Immediately Bo's words hurt. An instant later, they incite my fury. "Just what exactly is it you think I'm trying to get you to do?" I ask with foolish indignance, knowing good and well my desires are transparent.

I stealthily roll off the bed and snatch up my dress, jerking it over my head without bothering to fetch my undergarments, and I'm out the door before Bo can hardly respond.

"Fiona, sweetheart," he calls down the hall, lunging after me with monstrous steps.

As there's no way I can outrun him, I turn around to stand my ground. "I'm sorry Bo, I just need to think right now. By myself," I say as he gently clutches me by the forearms.

"Darlin, why don't you come on back inside and we'll talk this out. No pressure. You don't have to tell me nothin…I'm just wantin to get to know you before one of us gets hurt. That's all."

The sound of Bo's voice, combined with the exact phrasing of his words, would melt any woman. But I don't want to buckle. I don't want to be seen as weak, but my eyes have already glazed over.

"Oh Bo," I sigh, pressing my face to his bare chest so he won't see the tears. "I'll tell you the details some day, but I don't have it in me now," I promise, wondering why as the words come out. Like Bo's going to hang on by a thread until one day Quade settles down and I decide my phone isn't tapped.

Bo's a stud and after this performance I'll lose him in a flash. He thinks I'm the literal woman of his dreams, but he'll go home starkly disappointed and move on. By all means he should. These visions stab me as they form. I can't stand the thought of not having Bo, of him wrapping his great big arms around some hot Florida girl. He believes I'm meant to be his...how can I argue? But I'd be manipulative to keep him hanging on to the impossible.

Bo picks me up gently and carries me back into his room, then sets me on the bed and kneels before me...wiping away the rogue tears I couldn't contain.

"Darlin, you're a woman of passion, and I know there's a lot in you that you need to tell me. And I trust you'll soon want to. But for now, let's just relax and enjoy this vacation. I never meant to get you all riled," he says, stroking his fingers through my hair.

His words make me smile, more at myself than anything. I feel embarrassed about the scene I made. I finally raise my eyes to meet Bo's, then lean forward and melt into his kiss.

Chapter 18

Bo

Tenderness shoots through my fingertips like a soft electricity, as I kiss and caress the love of my life. Wild wisps of her hair tear away from the herd and lash down her face, threatening interference until I corral them back again. I love her angry, sad...every way. Fiona doesn't need to hide nothin from me. She'll learn to trust in time, but for now I'll have to leave it.

It's already late and Fiona needs sleep too, but she kisses like fire. If there's one thing I know, it's never to turn down a woman in heat if you love her. I'll have to let Fiona call the shots...she'll never forgive me if I don't.

Sure enough, Fiona grabs my hands and pulls me toward her, then sits on the edge of the bed as I stand before her... my throbbing body inches away from her panting lips. She leans forward and kisses me through my pants, the heat of her mouth permeating everything as she rubs with her hands...findin my zipper and releasing it. I revel in the sound of her gasp when she sees me for the first time and wraps her hand around my girth. Partially closing my eyes and allowing her to take control, I peek down at the incredible sight of her perfect mouth around me. She moans and purrs, the vibrations enhancing her talents.

Almost unable to bear any more, I pull away and step out of my pants. Fiona lies back and pulls her dress over her head. The sight of her is overwhelming. She giggles with excitement as I growl and crawl over her, pausing a while just to tease. When she grabs and kisses me at the same time, I release a long, low murmur of satisfaction. Fiona then wraps her powerful legs around my waist and pulls me down, kissing me madly as I enter her. Her sigh of satisfaction is the most beautiful sound I've ever heard, as I work her slowly, thoroughly.

Fiona squeezes me with her thighs, whimpers into my ears, runs her long nails gently down my back. She's so much more than a man could ask for...better, greater, more beautiful. Rapidly escalating to the edge of her tension and then remaining there, she sustains as I slow the pace to contain us both. Eventually I go all together still and we lie face to face, breathing, for what feels like an eternity in paradise, until all it takes is one slight movement to send us over the edge.

I collapse beside her and take her into my arms. She rolls over and presses her backside against me, snugly filling all the gaps between us. I pull her close and hold her as our breathing slows together. Prying open one eye to glance at the clock, I see we've been in bed for over an hour. It's past midnight, so I lie still to allow her to slumber peacefully, knowin I probably won't sleep a wink. And I don't want to. I wouldn't wanna miss a single moment of Fiona in my arms tonight.

"Bo," she says just when I think she's fallen asleep, "I hope you know I've never had anything like that."

I don't quite know how to respond. Here words satisfy me to my core. "Darlin, that goes for both of us. I thought you were already sound asleep," I say, tickled to find she's still restless.

"No...just basking in the afterglow." Fiona twists her head around to flash me that sublime smile. "And you know what else?"

"What my sweet lady?"

"I've never...um...you know. I've never...done that to a guy before," she replies, makin a slight gesture with her hand in front of her mouth.

"No kiddin? I don't mean this to sound crude, but you're a serious talent." She giggles and reaches back to slap my arm. "I mean it," I tell her. "And you might be interested to hear that I've never done that to a woman either."

"What?" Abruptly she pulls away and looks at me. " Are you telling me the truth Bo?" I nod fervently, and she bursts into her bawdy laughter. "Well...I've never really received that before, but from what I've heard...most men don't possess your level of talent either." She looks at me incredulously for a minute. "How can that be true Bo? A man like you? Surely you've had dozens of women...at least."

"No ma'am. Now see, that's where you're wrong. Big Bo don't go for a lot of women. I've only had a couple through the years, and I knew pretty quick it wasn't gonna go anywhere."

"Why Bo? Why would a man like you be all alone in life?"

"I guess you could say I'm too selective?"

With that, Fiona reclines again, facing me, wrapping her arms around me...piercing me with her eyes as we breathe into each other. "I am so honored to be the one," she says with abundant feeling.

"As am I, my lady. As am I."

"You're such a mystery," she murmurs to me between kisses.

"I'm not the only one. I wouldn't have taken you for Little Miss Innocent."

"Well you see," she says, proppin herself on an elbow, "after being in my dead-end relationship for nine years, then getting wrapped up in the business, I just haven't been on the market for a long time."

"What about your wild and crazy youth?"

"Oh that...well, my parents were a little upper-crust and kept me under lock and key. I only had one boyfriend before my husband...in college. I gave him my virginity, regretfully. He was sort of a dud. Then there was a younger guy I met a couple years ago...a biker. I fell for his type. He turned out to be an actual narcissist though, so I cut him off after a few dates."

"Aw, terrible. Terrible! A narcissist is not what a lady needs. So what about that husband of yours? Ya'll seriously never did any 'favors' for each other?"

"Oh goodness no! God...no...gross!"

"Gross? You were grossed out by your own husband?"

She hangs her head like the very subject is a source of shame. "Believe me, if you met Quade you'd understand. He's...well, let's just say he's the polar opposite of you."

"Oh yeah? How so?" I fully believe her, yet I wanna hear her spell it out.

"Well Bo, Quade is a bit of a prude. Honestly...for years I feared he was gay. We consummated our marriage and that was about it. We focused on kick-starting our two businesses and abandoned the bedroom, slept in separate rooms and everything."

"No...a woman like you? All pent up with a guy like that? Why would you do that for so many years darlin?" I can't adequately express my shock.

"Because I wanted my parents' approval more than anything, and he was the first thing in my life that ever made me feel like I was really getting it."

"Oh Fiona...that ain't right. That just...that ain't right sweetheart. Nobody deserves to go through all that, least of all you."

"I told you my life's complicated."

"Well that's where I come in. I'll be your knight in shinin armor. All you have to do is let me."

She puts her head on my chest and studies me. I can see she's takin in my words, but the sadness is still in her eyes. Like she's had too many hard times to believe things could change now. I need to convince her, and it kills me that tonight is all I have to finish my pitch. I already know I'm gonna have to head up to Iowa and crash-land on her doorstep to let her know I'm for real. I just need to figure out how to do that without causing any more complications in her life.

Finally her eyes close and I watch her fall asleep, listen to her breathin change, as she lies tucked up under my arm... her sweet, lovely head restin on my shoulder. One more day of this. I've got one more day of Fiona.

Chapter 19

Fiona

I awaken with a lustful moan, only able to comprehend the man I'm lying next to. Seconds later, I look at the clock and panic. It's seven thirty and the early programs are already beginning. Oh well...none of it is all that important in light of what happened to me last night.

When I lean over and attempt to plant a gentle kiss on Bo's lips without waking him, he springs to life and grabs my shoulders...sending me into a laughing frenzy.

"You scared me!" I slap his chest playfully and try to force myself away, but it's to no avail.

"Just where do you think you're goin?" he asks, pulling me in for his juicy kiss.

"I'm going to breakfast, and meetings, and lectures, and programs, and...to find Maxine."

"Well you're no fun at all, are you?" he jokes.

"Just because I'm a responsible adult doesn't mean I'm no fun," I say, running my hands down his torso.

As soon as Bo loses his guard, I roll away and bounce off the bed. He bolts after me and throws me over his shoulder. Laughing like I haven't in too many years to remember, I kick my feet and pound on his back until he releases me.

"Alright woman. See you at breakfast?"

"Yes," I reply, and we kiss once more before I gather up my clothing.

I scroll through messages of all sorts as I book it toward my room. Maybe Maxine's sleeping in and I can sneak in without her knowing I was gone. I slip my key into the door and open it slowly and quietly...to find Maxine standing ready to go.

"Good morning!" she calls out like this is a perfectly normal situation.

I look straight ahead and keep moving till I've slammed my bedroom door behind me. I'm sorry that I cannot deal with her energy level right now. I have no earthly idea how I'm going to sit through a morning of lectures with Bo on the brain. Tomorrow I have to deal with Quade again, and I just cannot be a friend to everybody all the time all at once. I don't even have time for a shower.

Quickly, I throw on a cute leopard-print outfit and a little makeup, then dash out with Maxine trailing behind me. Immediately my phone lights up with a text from Bo.

These will be in good hands til they're back in your beautiful ears.

It includes a photo of the dangly pearl earrings I forgot on his nightstand. I text him back as Maxine and I step into the elevator.

good hands indeed...

I'm smiling to myself as we saunter into the dining hall. Bo and I quickly locate each other and begin closing the distance between us. When we meet next to a half empty table, he hands me the earrings and bends to kiss me...but I turn just in time for it to land on my cheek. I don't think I could give him a friendly-family-sitcom kiss right now, and I'm not ready to make out in front of everyone, so I have to exert a little distance. But the look in his eyes is telling. We get through breakfast with good humor before going separate ways, each of us needing to attend different meetings.

"How about the rooftop bistro for lunch today? My treat," Bo asks both of us as we're about to part.

"That sounds wonderful," I tell him, Maxine nodding her head graciously.

After a two-hour Advanced Bouquet Design class, I fish through the crowd during the networking break. This is certainly the largest turnout I've ever seen at the conference; I hardly recognize a soul here. I can't help that I keep scanning the room for Bo, even though I doubt he'll come to this and we'd be wasting each other's time anyway. Eventually everyone disperses to their next classes, and I head off to a Flower Trends Forecast session to see what the upcoming year will demand of our inventory.

Arriving a few minutes early, I sit in the middle of the fourth row so I'll be front-and-center enough to help me focus. But all I can really see or hear is a running image of Bo...and the things we did last night.

As I settle in and set down my purse, I see Maxine filing into the second row. Isn't she the go-getter. I didn't know she was planning to sit through this one, but I'm relieved she is. Design trending is a highly important topic that I'm afraid I don't have the brain-space for today.

An hour later, I rise to catch Maxine as she files out behind the rest of the attendees. "Hey Max. Excited for tonight?" I ask as we shuffle away and head toward the bistro.

"Yes! I'm trying not to set myself up for disappointment, but I feel pretty confident about at least placing. Basically, my intuition is allowing me to feel excited...so there must be good reason for that."

"I'm behind you all the way, kiddo." I tell her with a pat on the back. I think she has a fine intuition.

We make our way to the roof to discover a spectacular bistro. Bo's already saved us a lounge area next to the tall glass panes that separate us from the abyss. Looking down, we have a view of the pool with all of its palm trees and loveliness. He kisses me on the cheek again as we gather into our upholstered chairs.

"Bo, thank you for taking us out. This place is even nicer than I'd imagined," I say with a fawning tone. Everything about Big Bo just melts me to my core.

"The pleasure is all mine," he assures me with a breathtaking smile.

Maxine thanks Bo and then disappears into the menu, not noticing when I slip off my shoe and run my foot up Bo's big, hard calf. I've got one more day to enjoy driving this man up the wall, and I'm going to do it. Heaven knows what will even become of me after today.

We order nigiri and Japanese dumplings and enjoy trading bites all around. Although I'm too excited to have much appetite, the food here is truly excellent. Our ninety minute lunch break soars by in a flourish of light conversation and laughter, Bo teasing both of us in his charming way. When he heads off to the restroom, I have to ask Maxine for notes on our last meeting and I can tell she's picked up on why I'm so distracted. I guess there are more embarrassing things in life, but I do appreciate how Bo moderately flirts with both of us to create a neutral atmosphere when Maxine's around. Not to mention, it's probably good for her. I'm always mystified that she seems forever single.

"I have solid plans to play some hooky this afternoon and spend more time at the pool. Any chance you'd be able to join me?" Maxine asks.

I inwardly wish she'd be studiously attending classes all afternoon because I already was planning to lure Bo to the pool. But Maxine's such a sweetie, and nobody likes to hang out all alone.

"You bet," I tell her. "I'm going to a couple more lectures on how to address my staff with mindfulness and calm, and how to refuel burned out employees when the going gets rough." I wink at Maxine, knowing she's witnessed me at my worst. "Then I'll be along...sometime mid-afternoon?"

"Sounds great!" she sings out, as we walk in opposite directions.

When I turn back to Bo, he has a subtly apprehensive expression. He can't possibly think he's not invited.

"You're coming too, right?" I ask, to get this squared away from the get-go.

"Sure thing darlin. I've only got one priority today," he assures me with a crooked smile.

Needing to rush off to class, I move toward Bo for a kiss and he takes me warmly into his arms and peers down at me with love in his eyes. "You come to my booth and get me as soon as you're done, okay? I'll be ready to pack up fast when you get there."

I nod and then he kisses me slowly, for several minutes, until I'm forced to tear myself away. I rush into the convention center, find the correct room, and settle myself into the back row...only a few minutes late. I do my best to focus through the haze that Bo's kiss left me shrouded in.

Mindfulness, presence, stress management. All of these topics that seemed imperative before, are going through one ear and out the other today. Poor Maxine. I need to be learning how to handle my employees with care, and all I can do is fantasize about the guy I have just a few more hours with. But it's worse than that. If only I was free to indulge in thoughts about a future with Bo, instead of constantly having to check myself so they don't get away from me. What weighs heaviest on my mind is how I'm going to explain that he can't call me after I'm home. Bo's a straight-shooter and he's not going to play along with any games. I'll have to be upfront at some point or I'll lose his respect.

By two thirty, I'm up to my eyeballs in information about how to empower my star workers and nurture them for future leadership roles. Good. I've done my duty as an employer. Now I've got to rescue Bo and get a couple moments with him before Maxine meets us.

I head first to our room to put on my swimsuit, then book it to the supplier depot to find Bo already packed up. He must have been anticipating me. I step behind his booth and then give a quick, furtive glance around just before Bo swoops me in for a kiss.

"Ready to go play?" he asks.

"With you? Anytime," I reply, stroking down the length of his arms and back.

Laughing, Bo suddenly grabs me up and throws me over his shoulder, then sets me down on the countertop of the booth and stands before me. An overwhelming heat rushes in, rendering me helpless, almost unable to think. I have to push him back and clamp my legs before anyone notices things getting inappropriate at Big Bo's booth. My mission to establish relevant conversation just became impossible.

Leaving me on the counter, Bo finishes packing up his laptop and places it into a bag along with a couple other odds and ends. He then removes me with one arm, while clutching his bag in the other, and restores me to my feet. Standing at his side with an arm around his waist and the other on his chest, I can feel warmth radiating from the long, muscular thigh I'm leaning into. It's taking everything in me not to get lost in a kissing frenzy in Bo's booth. By the intensity of his stare, I can see Bo's struggling with the same thing...his hot breath so close to my own.

Chapter 20

Bo

Rapt by the gorgeous creature before me, I unwillingly comply when she steps away and takes me by the hand. I don't wanna release her from my arms, yet I'm afraid of what I'll do to her in this booth if she doesn't get me outta here. Anyway, I suspect it's the blind leadin the blind. With purpose, Fiona pulls me through the crowd and out into the cool, open space of the quieter hall. I watch, enraptured by the way she moves in her well-fitted jade green suit...the pull of the fabric against her heart-shaped behind as she walks, the swish of her hair down her back...a shiny stream of caramel against the jade, streaming out from under a large, floppy, leopard-print sunhat. She is the image of beauty and elegance.

Fiona pulls me out into the hot light of day and slows our pace. As we meander down the garden paths, I wonder if Maxine will be at the pool yet. I wouldn't mind havin my lady all to myself for a while, but I know that's an unreasonable wish.

"Got your trunks with you?" Fiona asks, finally breakin the blissful communication that had traveled between us only through smiles.

"I have. Got em on already."

She laughs. "They must not be very baggy to fit under those painted-on jeans."

"They're not exactly oversized," I tell her with a cock of my eyebrows. She looks charmed by the thought.

As we continue walkin, Fiona keeps throwin me glances. She appears to need to say somethin she doesn't know how to get out.

"Bo," she says just as we reach the pool, "about all those phone calls we're planning to have..."

"What about em?" I ask as she strips down to her suit right before my eyes.

Stunning. An elaborately strapped leopard-print suit to match the hat. The sides are cut out, showin the precise curves of Fiona's narrow waist, and her perfectly tanned back peeks out from between the straps. The bottom is narrowly cut to reveal the tantalizing edges of her flawless hindquarters. I've lost my mind and can no longer recollect our conversation.

Entranced, I pull her to me and lean in for a kiss until she stops me. "Not so fast cowboy," she says with a giggle. "Gotta play fair. You get those jeans off."

I'm on it. I shuck my boots and clothes off with haste, laughing as Fiona gasps.

"No kidding these trunks are fitted," she says, reaching out to brush the fabric at my hips.

It's not that I aim to buy miniature shorts; it's just that my quads fill out most pants to the limits of their design.

"Ready to get in that water?" I ask, throwin a squealing Fiona over my shoulder and smackin her butt.

"Wait! Wait! Hang on!" she protests as I hover at the edge of the rippling, aquamarine expanse.

I set her to her feet and run my hand along her elegant jaw, gaze into her eyes and raise her lips to mine. In the next moment we disappear. Nobody else at the pool. No conference. No Florida. No Iowa. Just my lady and me... timeless and forever.

"Bo," she says breathlessly, then kisses me again. "Bo, I'm sorry," she says with that sadness in her eyes, then kisses me while my heart drops like a lead weight.

"What is it darlin? You know you can tell me anything, right?" She hesitates and drops her eyes. "Fiona, darlin, whatever holds you back...you've just gotta share it with me. I wanna hear your fears and doubts. Lay em on me. Go ahead now and just...lay it all out for me."

When she lifts her face back to mine, I see the shine of held-back tears in her eyes. What is it that could have this woman so frightened of a nosy ex and a little distance between states? I'll go to the end of the Earth for Fiona. I just need her to come forward and permit me to do it.

"Bo...shit." I turn to see what's caught Fiona's eye, and find Maxine headin toward us with her jolly disposition.

"It's okay sweetheart. We'll pick this up right where we left off. Just as soon as we can. Okay?" She nods an agreement and turns to greet Maxine.

"Hey Maxine!" Fiona calls out, putting on her best face. "How's your afternoon been?"

"Very relaxing. I'm ready for that awards banquet tonight."

"That's what we want to hear."

"How about I treat you fine ladies to a couple of cocktails this afternoon. What would you like?" I ask them.

"Surprise us," Fiona responds with a wink and a hand gently directing me away.

Damn that mysterious woman. I wouldn't wanna have to pry Maxine for information, but I suspect Fiona reveals very little to anyone anyway. It would do me no good. I order myself a beer and give them a minute while I check out the cocktail menu. The peach sangria sounds appropriate for my peach, and Maxine looks like the frozen margarita type. I purchase the drinks and stroll back to the pool at a leisurely pace, confused when I find Fiona on the opposite side from Maxine.

"Everything okay?" I ask as I hand off the drink.

"Yes, thank you. We were just...talking, and then...we were done talking. So I wandered over here to wait for you," she replies nervously.

"I know now's not the time, but we'll talk after the awards and you can let me know what's on your mind," I tell her, as I guide her back toward Maxine.

Maxine smiles with delight when I hand her the margarita, and Fiona leads us in a toast. We pass the afternoon in a seemingly happy blur of playfulness and light conversation. A celebratory energy runs strong between the three of us, in anticipation of Maxine's potential win tonight, and if I didn't know better I'd believe there wasn't a care in Fiona's world. She's awfully good at hidin her emotions...somethin I need to remember about her.

* * *

The sight of Fiona in a black dress nearly knocks me out. The Convention Center has been decorated lavishly for this event, and we feel like royalty as our champagne is passed out. The girls are still giggly and the place is humming as toasts and speeches are made. I take pride in my patient nature, but tonight my attention is everywhere but the front of the room. I just wanna hear them announce the contest winners so we can get outta here.

My attitude abruptly changes at the arrival of our food, short rib and trout dinners with incredible smelling sides. Fiona and I generously share with each other, havin each ordered a different dish. She becomes adorably flustered and excuses herself after spilling some white sauce onto her dress.

As expected, Maxine wins first place...trophy, money, and all, and Fiona looks so happy and relaxed that it's no surprise when she pulls me out onto the dancefloor later. I've done my share of country line dance and even took a few ballroom lessons way-back-when, in anticipation of one day havin a woman as fine as Fiona for my partner. Well, tonight all that's payin off nicely. And here I thought she couldn't wait to get me alone again, but the DJ's spinnin 80s hits and

Fiona's all over it. She's like a firecracker on the dancefloor till nearly eleven o'clock, and lookin dead sexy all the while.

"I don't know darlin, I'm about ready to get back to the room and settle in. What do you think?" I ask, catchin her from behind and wrappin my arms around her as she tries to escape to the bar for one more glass of champagne.

She spins around and wiggles close to me, kissin me without a care in the middle of the pulsing crowd. "You're right," she replies between kisses. "I need to be cut off."

She goes back to kissin me but I feel leary of her motivation. I wasn't just tryin to rescue the woman from alcohol; I was hoping she'd be as anxious as me to spend some time alone.

I put my hands on her shoulders and pull away, steadying her eyes with mine. "Well Fiona, you're welcome to go grab another glass instead if that's what you'd like. You're a big girl and I'm not here to cut you off. Do I need to be?"

"No...not at all. I don't normally drink like this. I'm sorry...I'm not myself this weekend."

"Well I'm pretty sure that was the real you in bed with me last night."

"Oh yes, Bo...yes...I'm afraid that was all of me. I can't hold back from you no matter how I try," she says, swayin just a little from side to side.

"And why would you ever wanna do a thing like that?"

"Like what?" she asks, lookin confused.

"Hold back from me."

Fiona stares into me with intent, not droppin her gaze. "I appreciate the full honesty and bluntness of your nature more than I can describe," she says, "and I want to live up to these values that you obviously have. But I just don't know how much of my war-torn life I can offer up to a man I just met, on the first weekend I met him."

I appreciate Fiona's directness as well, but that makes her words no less painful. Again, I remind myself that I've known her all my life, in a mystical, visionary way, while I'm a whole new ballgame for her.

"Darlin, that's exactly why I'm gonna call you up every night. Cause I'd like to get to know the woman I spent my weekend makin love to."

I watch as my words momentarily melt Fiona's body-language, but she quickly reinforces with her usual armor. "Tell you what, I saw Maxine leave a long while back. Let's go congratulate her again, because we ought to, and then we'll go to your room and I'll talk."

"Absolutely. Let's do it," I reply, as Fiona takes my hand and begins leading me out. It takes a real alpha woman to drag around a guy like me, and I love it.

When we arrive at their wing of the complex, Fiona slows her pace like she wants to keep me a while longer. I shoot her a questioning look and she turns around and hops into my arms, throwin her legs around my waist right here in the quiet hall.

"Bo...I just wanna tell you, no matter what happens after tonight, this has been the best weekend of my life."

Her words floor me. It's been the best weekend of mine too, but I can't get comfortable with the negative fatalism she projects onto everything. It seems almost like a form of self-punishment. She's stoic and tough in a way I've rarely encountered in a woman. I stand and hold her tight, my sexual energy dampened into a sympathetic angst I can barely sort out.

"Let's just get you back to my room, darlin." I set her on her feet and hold her another minute till she loosens her grip and begins leadin us toward Maxine's room again, swishin and swayin as she walks...teasin me all the way. "What am I gonna do with you, woman?"

"That is the question," she turns and responds coyly.

I smack Fiona's ass and send her into a giggling fit just as she bursts into Maxine's room. So much for findin out whether the poor girl was awake first. We say our congratulations and our goodbyes, and Fiona arranges to meet her at the shuttle at eight thirty tomorrow mornin... finally dropping the charade that she's gonna make it back to their room.

As we walk to my building, Fiona's eerily quiet. Occasionally throwin me a phonily 'reassuring' glance, I can tell she's thinkin real hard about whatever all it is she needs to lay out on the table. Then, just as I unlock my door and close it behind us, her energy shifts another 180 degrees... into a wild tiger. Springing into my arms, she kisses me blind as she reaches for my belt. She's got everything unraveled and ready to hit the floor by the time I can waddle over to the bed and lay her down. Her back dramatically arches and her dress hikes up with the spread of her knees, as she breathes my name repeatedly in that husky voice of hers. It's all I can do not to take her right now, but I have to slow things down. I must get her to be forthright. I can't allow this night to disappear into another session of total ecstasy followed by a hard snooze. How would I deal with Fiona walkin out of my life and into the unknown first thing in the mornin?

I watch her begin to go limp as I re-secure my pants. Her face falls and she closes her eyes, as though giving up on something critical.

"Fiona, sweetheart," I breathe as I lie next to her and take her into my arms.

The first sign of tears appears at the edge of her lovely closed lashes. I pull her face to my chest and hold her as she begins to shudder. Something's terribly wrong, but I need more information to make it right. I decide to begin takin guesses. If I land on the right thing, or the wrong one, that should provoke her to start sharing either way.

"Fiona, you've gotta talk to me. It's time to tell me what's hurtin you," I say, holdin her tenderly. She quietly cries and says nothin at first, so I start to prod. "You weren't serious about that phone tappin business were you? Cause you know, after tomorrow I've gotta have access to my princess."

She raises her gaze and looks at me with desperate, watery eyes. "I don't know Bo. I feel like a crazy person. I tell myself every day that it's ridiculous but I can't banish the notion from my mind. Maybe you were right about it being intuition."

"Shit! Fiona...this is a serious legal situation. You're actually afraid this man's stalkin you? You have to go to the police with this."

"I told you Bo, it's not that simple. Quade has friends all over the local legal system. He was high school buddies with those guys. It's like a boys' club that he's front and center of."

"Woman, you can't go home to Iowa if you're in danger. I would not and cannot let you do that. You can't hide at your girlfriend, what's-her-name's, house forever."

"Holly."

"Right, Holly."

"I know I can't Bo, you're right. But I am planning to take steps. When I get home, I'm going to hire a professional to examine my phone…and my house…to determine whether anything's been tapped. And I'm sure they haven't, but then I can rest about it and call you whenever I want and I won't have to feel paranoid anymore. Okay?"

"And what if they have been?" My question strikes Fiona with renewed concern.

She can no longer hide her level of fear from me. Fiona is genuinely afraid to go home. Somethin doesn't add up with her story about Quade threatenin to take the house. That doesn't incite the kind of primal fear I see in her eyes. But then a lady does become real attached to her safe haven and belongings and all that.

"Then I get a new number and stay at Holly's," she says more like she's askin me a question.

"You see that as a long term solution?" I ask.

She lets out an exhausted puff of air. "Let's just get me home and get everything checked out first, and then I'll figure it out from there."

"And you say this man could take your business too?"

She leans against the headboard and closes her eyes, lookin like she has no plans to answer. Then finally, "Yes."

Her eyes have dried but I can see the rage behind them. Fiona is not a woman who's okay with being manipulated and controlled.

"Fiona," I ask her, "is there any way I can convince you that you don't have to worry about whatever outcome you discover?" She looks at me like I'm a moron, and I feel like one for not being able to explain myself better. "I know you might not be ready to hear this now darlin, but I've got your back. No matter what happens up there, you have my word that Big Bo's gonna help you fix it." I reach down to pull her back into an embrace, but she plants her hands on my chest and resists me.

"I don't want you fixing anything and I don't need it. Can't you see, letting men 'fix' things is exactly what got me into this situation in the first place!"

I see Fiona's point. And I'm also aware she doesn't need me to say anything more, to give her any kind of blessing or permission to do this on her own. I'm not the type of guy to give up, but she leaves me little choice but to drop the subject.

"Well alright then Fiona. I'll just sit down here and wait to hear from you when I hear from you. But believe me, it ain't gonna be easy havin no clue when that might be. So I hope you'll consider borrowin Holly's phone a time or two while you're gettin things figured out," I respond, inciting a nod from Holly.

"Deal," she says. "I'll keep you in the loop."

Still lookin mostly vacant, Fiona allows me to take her hand in mine. Her face is hardened and she seems to be deep in thought, perhaps wonderin what she'll do about Quade... perhaps wonderin what she wants to do right now, with our last few hours in a hotel room.

Chapter 21

Fiona

Feeling like an unimaginable jerk, I sit here with my hand in Bo's...waiting for him to make a move on me. I'm sure I've thrown enough water to smother the heat he was kindling all day, so we're left with the uncomfortable silence of having sort-of fought? It certainly felt like that's where I was going with it, except Bo is so incredibly reasonable that I can't even work myself into a tizzy before he brings me to heel. Which makes me feel like a halfwit.

What I need is a good, loud shouting match, but Bo's too together to even participate in that kind of bs. His greatness neutralizes every laser I think I'm going to throw at him. And here he sits, after trying to help me with his infinite wisdom and being shot down by my jaded bitchery, quietly stroking my fingers and wondering what he can say that I won't bite his head off for. Poor man.

I've already tried and failed to seduce Bo tonight, so there's really nothing I can do but excuse myself back to my room. Yet, that feels like we're having a fight...and we're not really, are we? I know that what he wants is for me to put my whole heart out on the line, and I'm not going to do that. Yes, being in bed with Bo is better than anything I'd imagined life could be, but I'm a survivor.

There's a reason I was okay with remaining in a dull friendship with Quade instead of moving on...I don't need the love of a man. And I'm not going to become addicted to it now. I've come this far in life and all I want to do is save my business and buy my own house, which I'll have the capital for whenever my father kicks the bucket. Quade can have his crumbling Victorian mansion. The shop is almost paid off and I'm finally profiting, rather than breaking even. My future looks bright. No need to complicate things.

Quade had originally agreed that Fiona's Flowers would go in my name after it was paid off anyway. What kind of fool would blow the deal now? That's probably what this whole control thing is about anyway, not because he's got my phone tapped and heard me talk to Bo. What a completely stupid thought. I sound like a paranoid delusional.

My awareness is brought back into the room when Bo leans in toward me and gently squeezes my hand. I look up at him haggardly, not sure what to expect, but his face is relaxed and his eyes compassionate. What I don't see, however, is the flame that was there earlier. I blew it, sure enough.

I've never known a man like Bo. On our final night to share his hotel bed, he won't strip his pants off and get down to business without some promise that I'll let him be my Superman. It's a wonderful sentiment, but not one I can entertain. Bo certainly has more restraint than I do. I'm a whore by comparison. No way could I have stopped the momentum, had he been the one seducing me earlier.

Just as I'm about to excuse myself, which seems like my only dignified option, Bo reaches over, grabs me around the waist, and hoists me onto his lap in a straddle position. He catches me so off-guard that I can't help but laugh, which lightens the mood considerably.

"Bo, what are you doing?" I ask out of mock defensiveness.

"I'm takin what's mine."

The embers are back in his eyes, and my body ignites on the impact of his words. I become heavier in his lap and feel his response from below.

"You are mine aren't you, Fiona?"

My body tells me to say yes, but my mind says I am nobody's. And my heart...I've never heard before and would have no idea what its input even feels like.

"Tell me you're mine Fiona, my woman, the one who was tailor-made for me. At least for this weekend, this night, this moment...which is all we ever have anyway."

I've already given Bo everything, but I was more inebriated the other night. I'm amazed at how he observes my resistances even when I try to shut them down. He knows I want him, but he also senses my body's more invested than my heart. I can appreciate that a man like Bo has higher standards than that.

"Yes," I tell him. "I'll be yours for tonight, your woman for the taking." I give him the sexiest grin I've got, hoping it pulls him back into the mood and holds him there.

He smiles back, but I can sense he's not fully believing me. Just the same, I'm ready to get this show on the road. When I squeeze my thighs around him and lean in for his kiss, Bo's ready to deliver it. I knew he wouldn't let me down; he finds me as irresistible as I find him.

Heat radiates from Bo's hands, as he pulls me tighter against him, and I lose myself in the smell and taste of him. Leather, clove, faint sweat, and an organic pheromone I can't put my finger on...like sweet tobacco. The man almost smells sweet like a horse, enough to intoxicate me.

He moans and grumbles while we kiss, gradually pushing harder against me as I wiggle around him. I can tell he's still reluctant or he'd have me on my back by now, but I'm happy to take the reins. I shimmy down his thighs and tug his hips, till he follows my cue and lies beneath me. Then I remove his shirt button by button and peel it off, unbuckle his thick leather belt, and pull his jeans over his muscles any way I can.

By the time he's down to his briefs, I'm clamoring to get at the rest of him...watering at the mouth. But I hold back and straddle him again, deciding to first get out of my dress. I whip it off over my head and revel in the way Bo moans at the sight of me. Leaning to give him the full view of my boobs spilling out of the dark, lacy bra, I crawl forward to plant my ass right on top of his chest. He pants and heaves forward, but I remain just out of reach.

Bucking and grinding, twisting my hips inches away from Bo's face, I know exactly what I'm doing. Pretty surprising for a woman who's never done any of this before. I feel like a sleek, wild leopardess that's been released from a cage for the first time, and my captive audience is the king of the jungle.

I tug the lacie thong away from my hips and roll it down enough for Bo to just see the top of my tuft, then pull it back up and play with it for a good minute before dismounting and turning myself around. Bo grunts and pants when I straddle him with my ass hovering right in front of his face. I roll my body on and off of his in a rippling motion, the way I saw a girl do on stage once when I visited a strip club with Holly, long ago. Little did I know I'd assimilated something that would come out of my own body one day. The feeling of Bo's hands on my butt is sensational, as he massages and gently slaps it...occasionally brushing his knuckles up the middle, teasing me through the lace.

At last I stand up on the bed and unclasp my bra, dropping it to Bo's face, then slowly slide my thong down over my hips and step out of it. Reaching over Bo's legs, I peel his boxer briefs off and what bounces out is just as shocking as the first time I saw it. I still can't believe I took that inside me, yet I remember everything about the way it felt.

I crawl up the bed, growling and purring, tickling Bo with the lengths of hair hanging down either side of me. Once I reach his middle, I give him the pleasure of a lifetime... employing all the skills I never knew I had. When Bo tries to pull me up, I resist...forcing him to starve for the taste of me. All I want is to serve Bo tonight, to watch him relax and receive, to try to demonstrate what this weekend has meant and how much power he's ignited in me. I'll never be the same.

After I've teased him to the brink of his tolerance, I climb up onto Bo's hard body, mount him, and ride him like a rodeo mustang, frothing and feral, into the night.

The alarm goes off too early, but it's not fatigue that hits me the hardest. I find it almost impossible to get up and walk away from Bo. I thought I could spend the weekend taking advantage of everything he had to offer and head back home relatively unscathed. But this morning I find myself tangled in a harsh combination of newfound inner strength and disgust with what I have to go home to. It's like having my foot on the gas and the break at the same time.

Bo taps the alarm off and reaches out, wrapping his warm arms around me like huge jungle vines. My body disappears against him, so small and feminine. I don't want to leave our love-cocoon, but I have to face reality before I go getting all emotional. He turns me around and we lie in the semi-darkness and stare at each other, not kissing, talking, or even smiling. Just staring like we want to read as much of each other's mind as possible before parting ways. When I finally glance back at the clock and then push away from him, we're still wordless...there's nothing to say.

I put on my things and gather my purse and earrings, all the while aware that Bo hasn't taken his eyes off me. Once I'm ready, he hastily dresses and walks me to my building.

"Are you sure you won't let me drive you to the airport?" he asks, trying one more time as we approach my room.

"I'm sorry Bo," I tell him, holding back tears, "I need to separate now." I don't know how tomorrow's going to go and I have to get my head back into that space. "We'll talk when the time is right. I promise. I'll call to let you know everything's fine as soon as I find out."

"And if you can't get your phone checked right away, call me from Holly's will ya? Cut a nice guy a break?"

I smile, reaching up to cup Bo's face in my hands. "I'll call you Big Bo. You won't be the only one hankering."

What I really mean is, Bo has no idea how desperately I'm going to miss his face, his voice, his body, his hands... every minute I allow myself to think of him. Which is the reason I cannot and will not. Once I walk away from Bo Thompson, all this will have to be over on more levels than he's aware. And it will be the hardest thing I've ever done.

Chapter 22

Bo

Driving home to Fort Myers, I can still feel her on me...all around me, the exact scent of her and the particular way she sighs. In some ways I didn't accomplish what I was hoping to over the weekend, but in other ways I did so much more. I had expected to meet some oblique manifestation of the woman in my dreams, a lovely but imperfect potential soulmate, who would quickly warm up to me and allow me to work my magic. Bond with her conversationally and intellectually. Perhaps share a first kiss before our time was out.

Instead, I got the fairy tale...a tidal wave of beauty rushin toward me with every encounter. An aggressive, self-assured woman with uncontrolled moods, complex motives, and all the realness of an atomic bomb. Legs and eyes and teeth and fingers...magnificent. I had no idea what I was in for, or just how accurate my dreams of her had been.

It's already straining my self-control to be drivin home rather than headin her off in Iowa. Of course if Quade actually is spying on her, the last thing she'd want is a new man hanging around. But I can't take that into consideration as any real possibility because otherwise I *would* drive straight to Iowa. So I'm resigned to waitin an untold number of days for Fiona to call me up and say her phone's not tapped, and that she feels safe. Then I can help her sort out what to do about her life. I know a woman like Fiona won't remain under the thumb of any man, even if it means walkin away from her own business and fortune. If this Quade guy can't be reasoned with, she'll walk soon enough.

* * *

As I pull up to the saloon, I quickly spot Jose's car and smile to myself. He's gonna get an earful. Just inside the bar I stand blindly, allowin my eyes to adjust after the bright, gray light of the parking lot. Eventually I catch Kiana's eye and she automatically grabs a Lagunitas out of the cooler.

"Hey Big Bo! How's it shakin?"

Jose whips around when she shouts my name. "Hey Bo! You're back, aye? How was it man? What happened to you man...you get laid or what?" he laughs as he rises to hug me. "You look like you been laid man! I recognize that look... you devil you. You didn't, did you? Your lady liked you, aye? She good to you man? You look like somebody been real good to you."

I just stand and grin while Jose swamps me with his questions. He knows. I sit next to him silently, still smiling, then take a couple good pulls on my beer while he impatiently awaits my answers.

"Talk man, talk," he says, reachin over to shake my shoulders. "Was it that good, man? Look at you...what happened to you man?"

"It was that good Jose, it was that good," I finally say, allowing myself for the first time to fully take in everything that happened.

I've been fightin it ever my last look at Fiona's face, strugglin with our separation and her vague commitment to future communication. It's almost too much for me to fathom what all went down between us in that hotel room, and all weekend long. Where do I even start? I glance back over at Jose and he's still staring fixedly.

"It was her Jose. Fiona's the one."

"Dude, I don't even know what to say man. Congratulations! You bringin her back here or what?" he asks, slappin me on the back.

"It's gonna take some time bro. This one ain't easy."

"Awwww...she played hard to get, huh?" he asks with a shit-eatin grin.

"Naw, that's not even what I meant bro. I mean...she's mine, and I know I've got her, but I'm gonna have to negotiate to get her in my life in a big and permanent way."

"Oh yeah? Doesn't she know a good thing when she has it?"

"Well, sure, but she's also got her own personal life."

"Oh dang man...boyfriend?"

"Naw, just a few loose ends to tie up. That's all."

"You tell her about your big farmhouse you're plannin to put her in and everything?"

"No Jose. I'm not gonna try to buy anyone. You know that. She'll come to me when she's ready to, and it won't be because of anything else I have to offer her."

"Aw come on man," he says with a doubtful half-smile. "Women ain't like that. You gotta give her somethin to come to."

"Oh yeah? Well, she knows I own Big Bo's and the farm. I'm not askin her to hook up with some broke down guy. I'm only askin her to take a chance on love, if that's what it is. And I'm here to tell you bro, that's what this is. You'll see. You just wait and see."

"Hey, I believe you man. You know I've always believed in you," Jose says, clinking his bottle against my now-empty one. "Another beer?"

"No, thanks man. Just one for me tonight. I got a lot to catch up on out there. I'll be seein you later bro."

A gold and orange sunset brightens the horizon behind me as I drive toward the farm, and my heart folds in on itself...trying to process that Fiona's not here to see this with me, and that I was unsuccessful at layin any plans for a future with her. I pass the next five nights and days in a flourish of farm work...sweatin in the sun, buildin up my calluses, sleepin only a few hours here and there. I've gotta get efficient enough to put aside extra time for workin on the house. I intend to have it fixed up and beautiful by the time Fiona's ready to get serious.

Late Friday night, after the longest week of my life, my phone rings and it's an Iowa number I don't recognize. All day I could feel that this was the night. I've been waitin for her.

As I answer the phone, I can feel the weight of her on the other end...heat, rage, fragility, desire. It's all there, waitin to breathe life into me again. When I put her to my ear, I pause a moment...listening to her atmosphere, knowin I'm about to face the tantalizing voice that's been haunting me nonstop. The voice that puts me to bed at night and then keeps me awake. That runs an opinionated critique over every move I make. The voice that brings me a vision of her eyes, pulsing with longing and pain...a somersault of conflicted emotions.

"Big Bo," I answer as usual, but not in my usual voice.

"Bo, hi!" Her overemphasized words blare through the phone. "How are you? How's business?" she asks with a gratingly phony demeanor.

"All good here," I reply, tryin not to get irritated. "I notice you're not using your own phone yet?" May as well get down to business if she's not gonna be real with me.

"Nope. No...everything's fine, just...being on the safe side."

I can smell her dishonesty from here. "Well did you get it checked out yet?" I ask, knowin I'm treading on thin ice to steer the conversation this way.

"We're working on it," she replies in a voice that tells me there's an unnatural smile plastered to her face.

My soul tears in two as I absorb the implications of Fiona's behavior. She's shut me out, but she realized she couldn't let any more days pass without at least makin the obligatory check-in call. If I don't find some way to fuse together her opposing sides, she might never allow herself to remember 'us'. She'll push our memories deep down into those pockets of her heart she refuses to examine.

"Well that's good. You be sure to let me know how that goes." I decide placating her is my only option for now.

"Oh you bet...I'll let you know," she responds with inappropriate enthusiasm. "Everything's good at the store. Got Maxine's plaque up and the paper did an article on us, so we're all happy," she gleefully announces.

"I'm glad to hear everything's hunky dory then." Somethin tells me I'd better not say anything personal at this time, yet I don't know when or how I'll talk to Fiona again. She's really got me dangling over an abyss.

"Yes. And I'm glad things are good with you," she responds, followed by a couple beats of silence. "Well, I've gotta run actually. I made plans with Holly and I need to get ready."

Panic floods my veins like black ink. I want so terribly to tell Fiona that I love her, but I know she wouldn't be able to hear those words. "Fiona...a wise woman once told me that putting her trust in men is what got her into trouble. Well there *is* a place in this world for putting your trust in another, when your priorities are straight and your motivations are in line. Not for your parents or anyone but yourself. When you decide that I'm what's best for you, you let me know. I'll be waitin." As the words leave me, I feel the blood rush to my head.

Either I just blew it, or something resonated with her. After several seconds of dead air, I can't be certain which.

"Bo," she says in her real voice, almost breathlessly, "I should go. Bye." And she hangs up before I can get in another word.

Chapter 23

Fiona

Holly's knock startles me out of my thoughts. "Come in," I tell her.

"You about ready to go?" she asks, coming over to sit beside me on the bed.

"Sure. As ready as I'll ever be to go out for a dumb comedy." God...I sound like a joykill even to myself.

"I told you it got really good reviews. Come on...up with you," Holly says, standing and pulling me up by my armpits like a bratty toddler. "You look fabulous."

I glance at the mirror on our way out and snicker to myself. What's the point in dressing sexy when I'm doomed to be forever single? Because...that's what girlfriends are for.

"So do you," I toss back, playing along.

And she does, with her long, black hair in its full kinky glory...dangling down the back of a bright orange mini-dress. We always go out on weekend nights when Levi's out of town, or otherwise swamped in; it's tradition. After our movie, we detour for a couple glasses of wine before home.

"At least you laughed a few times," Holly says, prodding me into conversation.

"I told you I liked it. You were right...it was good and I did need to go out. I'm glad you talked me into it tonight." I tell her what she wants to hear, even though I'd rather be at home brooding...which is the worst thing for me. It's so good that Holly doesn't let me get away with that crap.

"So...I hate to ask, but how did the call with Quade go tonight?"

"It's okay...he never called, so I decided to just leave it," I reply.

"But I heard you talking to someone when I walked by your door, right before we left," she explains.

"Oh, it wasn't Quade," I reply, then swirl my wine and stare at it mesmerized...as though it's more interesting than our conversation.

"Fiona..." Now she's on to me. "Did you call Bo?"

The very sound of his name makes me start shaking. Suddenly my wine looks like it's trying to survive an earthquake, so I set it down.

"You did, didn't you?!"

I can't hide anything from this woman. "I did," I reply, nodding.

"And? Come on Fifi, what's wrong with you? Don't you want to talk to Bo? You know, whatever happened in that hotel room...it's not going to go away just because you won't acknowledge it. I think you should keep your lines of communication open. You know you can use my phone every night. I don't even want that thing near me after work hours."

The tragic thing is, Holly's exactly right and I know it. My memories won't go away, although I have hopes of them dramatically fading after the passing of a few more months. Or years. Or decades.

"Oh Holly...the sound of his voice." That seems to be all I can manage without choking up. I stare at my lap for a second to collect myself, then grab my glass and toss the rest of it down.

"I'm getting us a bottle," Holly says, "and we're heading for the hot tub."

A bottle of wine could be trouble for me tonight, but a jet bath sounds divine. Ten minutes later we're home, filling the tub, riesling bottle in an ice bucket, glasses perched on the marble rim. We pour our glasses and lie back on opposite sides, scooting up against the jets and letting them massage our backs.

"Talk," Holly says at last. "I don't know who this quiet lady is who's been tiptoeing around my house the past week, but I wanna hear about this guy."

I put my head back and moan.

"Come on...tell me everything," she prods.

"You know Holly, my world was already completely upside down and now it's catapulted the other way, and I just wish there was something I could do about it but I know I can't."

"So...why are you so convinced this is an impossible situation? I mean, if I didn't know better, I'd swear you really like this guy."

"Well, for starters...because Quade made it deadly clear that he will pull out everything I thought was mine if I displease him. If I even lock my damn door he thinks I'm rebelling against him in some spiteful way. He threatened to take back my house and business Holly. Don't you get that? And I don't give a fig about the house...I mean, I love it but it's too big. I could afford a downpayment for my own house now, with or without any help from my inheritance. But I cannot afford to lose my business. You know that's everything I have. I will literally eat my savings if he takes that from me, and my dad's determined to hang on to all his moneys until he keels over dead. And if I cross Quade... the guy could easily cajole my dad into leaving me nothing." "This is all so crazy—"

"I don't know what he'll stop at Holly. All I know is that he scared me within an inch of my life, and now he wants to talk about 'us'. Can you even believe that? He says he feels like I'm slipping away from him and he doesn't like it."

Holly sits alertly on the other side of the tub, speechless and compassionately angry on my behalf. She's always been there for me, letting me dump everything on her all the time. But I've never been up against a wall like this before, and the poor thing would have no idea what to do with it. I have no idea what to do with it.

"Well sweetie," she eventually responds, "let's just wait to find out if your phone's really tapped and then we'll figure it all out. One thing at a time. How's that going by the way? Heard anything back from the investigator guy yet?"

"No. I've left three messages and now I'm afraid they'll ignore me because I'm a nuisance."

"Well...you're staying at my place, forever as far as I'm concerned, so there's no pressure on you there."

I nod along appreciatively. My wineglass is emptying fast and I'm feeling looser. I have the sense my tongue's about to start operating against my own will.

"So how was the call with Quade on Monday then? I guess he got everything off his chest?"

"Didn't I tell you?"

"No, you've barely said two words all week," she replies, sounding concerned rather than miffed.

"I don't exactly know. Honestly, he didn't say much. He'd built up this huge thing that we were gonna have this stupid, uncomfortable talk about us, and then he just sort of touched base and got off the phone. Said he'd call again tonight and then didn't."

"That's good, right?"

"Um...well...other than the fact that it doesn't change or fix any of the insane things he said and did to me the week before. Thus...me walking around a ticking bomb twenty-four seven."

"You have a point," Holly says, pouring us another round. "Well, I think the best thing might be for Levi to have a talk with Quade, guy to guy...right? Not that he wants to be in the same room with that monster anymore. But... considering we can't really take any legal action, a calm collected conversation might be our best bet. Not to make any excuses for Quade, but I'm sure he's just been all caught up in his emotions and could be reasoned with at a more casual time."

"Oh Holly, I do hope you're right about that. And yes, I think Levi's a good approach." I huff out a slight laugh of relief. "You're a pillar of ideas...I don't know how I'd live without you. I will pray, pray, pray that he catches Quade when he's normal though. Cause I've gotta tell you, the man I witnessed was a psychopath, and he was in no way the one I married, divorced, or have ever been friends with." Silence again. And really, how is a person supposed to respond to that? "I'm sorry, I'm just rambling again."

"No, not at all," she reassures me. "So, tell me about this Bo. What was he like? Where does he live?"

I sink down till the water line is between my mouth and nose.

"I know you hit it off, you couldn't convince me otherwise. You might not wanna talk but it's been written across your face all week."

"Really?" I ask, bursting back to the surface with a laugh. "Don't you think I'd be happy or something, I don't know... in a better mood, if things had actually gone well?"

"No, because you've been brooding. I think something happened, big time, and you don't want to deal with it."

Busted. "Oh God Holly." I mute myself in the water again, while she laughs. "I wouldn't even know where to start. Um...Well, he lives down there actually, in Fort Myers."

"Oh! You know...that's where my cousin Teah lives. I've actually been there a few times, but I was really young and don't remember much."

"Yeah...isn't she the one always bugging you about how beautiful it is?"

"Yes, she's been trying to talk me into leaving the Iowa winter forever, since we used to be so close. And I'm telling you, I've thought about it more than once."

I sink back into the bubbles, relieved by Holly's change of subject...but it doesn't last long.

"So, what does 'Big Bo' even look like?" she asks, putting finger quotes around his nickname.

I guess Holly's not going to let it go, so I may as well give the people what they want. "Well...he's huge, he's a total stud, an absolute southern gentleman, incredible to look at...got this gorgeous, ornate tattoo sleeve of flowers all over one arm. In black ink...it's crazy manly on him. He's bursting with muscles, he barely fits into normal clothes...he's almost a hulk, but completely slim. And I've seen him everywhere," I add with a dreamy eye roll, partially dunking again.

"Fiona!" Holly looks thrilled. "I cannot believe this. How could you withhold this information from me? And by the way, what does huge mean?"

"I'm not exaggerating. I'm serious. I can't exaggerate this guy. He looks exactly like he sounds on the phone. I thought he was an aging ex-wife fantasy but nuh uh. Bo's the real deal Holly, the real deal." Finally I'm smiling. Wine or not, it feels surprisingly good to get all the details off my chest. "Um...he has dark hair, brownish eyes, a perfectly shaped goatee...I shouldn't be talking about this."

"Why? Are you kidding me? He sounds like Superman on a platter! You should be calling him five times a day!"

she shouts gleefully, then hesitates. "Wait a minute, he's not Ulysses all over again, is he?"

"No!" Her question causes me to sit bolt upright. "No way. He's as refined and selfless as any gentleman I've ever met. He's just incredible Holly. Like very, very hard-to-even-believe-he's-real incredible. I'm fucking in love and I have no idea how I'm going to get through this."

"Fiona!"

"Sorry...scuse my French. It's just...I am in deep, deep trouble here. Like my-life-will-never-be-the-same-again trouble."

Holly grins and claps her watery hands together. "Bravo! Fiona's in love! I can't believe it! I had the sense you were secretly into him but...this is Earth-shattering."

"Damn right it is, and I have no idea how to navigate from here. The first day we spent hours at his Expo booth, hanging out together between clients, and everything was going great. And then all of a sudden he started telling me how he doesn't intend to have a fling or take advantage of a 'woman like me'. And I was like, okay...what does he think this is then? So I reminded him point-blank that I was flying home to all my responsibilities in two days. And he just said 'We'll work something out'." When I pause for a breath I'm met with Holly's baffled stare. "Well? What was I supposed to say to the guy? I mean, yes...I wanted to go to bed with him. And I know that's not characteristic of me at all, but I haven't felt this in...actually I've never felt like this about anyone. And I sure as heck wasn't going to walk away from a guy like him, but—"

"Fiona...hang on. Are you hearing yourself at all here?"

"What?"

"You've got a man you're wild about, who insists on not using you, and you sound upset about it. I don't understand what it is you're going for in life. How are you possibly interpreting any of this as a bad thing?"

"Holly, you know my situation. You know as well as anyone that this can't possibly go anywhere."

"But—"

"I can't lose my business Holly. I can't put my livelihood in jeopardy in the wild pursuit of a long distance boyfriend. If Quade ever caught wind of it, and I assure you that one way or another...that would happen, he would pull the plug on everything I am, overnight."

Chapter 24

Bo

Sunday mornin I whip outta bed bright and early. After one full day of hardly movin, I'm ready to get my ass back on the horse. The trick is for me to concentrate on the realness, the life and the love I heard in her voice there at the end. Though she tried hard not to, Fiona gave herself away. And as long as she still feels, I'm gonna draw her back into her light. Damn beautiful woman. What's a man to do?

After hittin the hardware store for some supplies, I do somethin I haven't done in years. I unlock the old house and enter. I detect no mold in here; the place always was tight as a drum, solidly built. Other than about a foot of dust, it's nothin too daunting. Memories hit me in a torrent as I track through the rooms, peeking around doors and opening cabinets.

When I place my boot on the bottom step, somethin freezes me up. Me and Mack's childhood bedrooms are upstairs, and it's strange to think of them still just sittin there suspended in time...all quiet and cobwebbed and unused. I didn't know I was gonna set foot in here when I woke up today. Figured I'd lay in my supplies and then hit the garden. I guess being so close to fixin up the place compelled me to go ahead and have a look.

I've already laid everything out on charts...the new kitchen I'm gonna put in, updates to the bathrooms, modern lighting and ceiling fans, a fresh coat of paint everywhere. The hardwoods are as good as ever. What they need is a nice polishing. I'll replace the nasty old carpeting in the bedrooms and take up the kitchen linoleum. This place will be picture perfect on the day my doll moves in with me.

There's nothin like a hard day's work to take my mind off my troubles. By nightfall I'm dirty and exhausted, and ready to whip up a little dinner. I throw a homemade pizza together and hit the shower, then kick up my heels with a book while it finishes baking. I almost psych myself up imagining Fiona will call again tonight, but my intuition says it ain't gonna happen.

Nonetheless, I can't concentrate on science fiction. My mind is wholly set on gettin the house done and gettin her in it. It's gonna be a long process if I can't find my peace of mind, but it's been slipping me ever since that dern phone call. I'm best off to forget all about Fiona for now, and that ain't an easy prospect. Maybe she'll at least stay out of my dreams for a while.

I finish up my plant chores and settle into bed, quiet enough to hear a pin drop. The cicadas are my only company tonight, and they even sound more distant than usual. I close my eyes and concentrate on lettin go, clearin my head. And then the images come, plain as day. Not dreams but memories...the sounds and scents of Fiona, rushin into my awareness all at once. And the way she looked in the throes of pleasure. Admittedly, my pride's a little battered by how she could just walk away like this. I know what I did for the woman...and I know what she did for me. I honestly thought her barriers would come crashin down.

Which brings me back to wonderin exactly what is up with that Quade fella. If he did tap her phone, will she even bother to tell me? I guess I'll find out when she orders more orchids, but that could be weeks or a couple months out at least. Or maybe she'll just hook herself up with a new supplier.

Naw...now my mind's gone all rotten on me. Fiona is my woman, the woman of my actual dreams. Nothin can come between us. I slam a fist into the mattress and try to fight the urges of my body. The anger at Quade that was filling my veins, now drains and morphs into other aggressive emotions. A low growl develops in my chest and I let it out, thrashing my blankets off and seizing my turgid member. After all my efforts to not act like a total animal around Fiona, the thought of her drives me mad in this endless aftermath of noncommunication. I need her next to me. Under me. On top of me. My right-hand gal for all time.

I give in and indulge myself in the torture of fantasy, wonderin for the life of me whether Fiona's doin the same thing tonight.

Chapter 25

Fiona

"Holly," I say the moment she picks up her phone, "Lieutenant Earnhart called back today."

"And?"

"I brought my phone in and he examined it and told me in about one minute that it was tapped."

"No! No! Are you okay? Your voice sounds a little shaky."

"Oh I'm definitely shaking. And I'm no way okay. I asked Earnhart to examine my house too."

"Is he doing it now?"

"No...I wish. He penciled me in for this fall. I told him I'm not even able to stay at my own home anymore but he said November's the earliest he can deal with it."

"That's insane! So what should Levi say about the phone tapping tonight?"

"Nothing. Quade can't know that I know this. Levi's going to have to play it cool. Maybe you shouldn't even tell him."

"No, I think Levi should know what he's dealing with. You know, so he'll keep his phone close at hand. I don't know how easy it is to tap, but what if he does it to all of us? Or already has?" Holly asks with escalating panic.

"Don't think like that Holly. I've received no indication that he's heard any of our conversations or any calls I've made from your phone." It dawns on me how lucky I am that I essentially blew Bo off a few nights ago. What if Holly's right?

* * *

"Want to hop in the tub?" Holly asks after dinner, when two more hours have passed and Levi still isn't home.

"No...you go ahead without me. I've gotta stay focused."

"You sure? You've been working nonstop ever since Florida."

"Yeah Holly, thanks. Really...I've got a pile of messages to respond to. Busy week of a busy season."

"Okay, well, I think I'll pop some corn and find something to watch...in case you'd like to join me later. Nothing like a good show to take your mind off...oh good, it's him!" Holly abruptly cuts herself off to race downstairs and meet Levi as he comes in the door.

A minute later they're with me in the guest office, Levi looking stricken.

"What did the man say?" I ask with a faltering voice that I pretend isn't faltering.

Levi's eyes are bloodshot, like he hasn't slept in days. I know the feeling, but I have to laugh that just a couple hours with Quade can do this to a person. He doesn't even bother walking over to the couch, but sinks onto the carpet...right next to my desk chair.

"He went to Victor."

"What?!" I scoot my chair back and stand so fast it falls backward. "What the hell did that freak say to my father?"

Levi drops his head like he can't bare to face me with this information.

"What?!"

"Your father...you know, your father's mind is very fragile at this point."

"Yes Levi, I know my father's mind is very fragile..."

"Quade told me you never legally divorced."

My face goes red as a beet. In my periphery I can see Holly slowly sinking to the couch.

"Is that true Fiona? I mean...I'm not trying to grill you or anything, but—"

"Yes it is true. I am so screwed." A long moment of silent dread fills the space between us. "So what does this have to do with my father?"

Levi heaves out another deep sigh and continues. "Quade has convinced your father that you never divorced spiritually either, and that you're now messing around with other men. Which he even had the nerve to try to convince *me* was essentially the case. When I didn't look like I believed it... he told me..."

"What did he tell you Levi?!"

"He told me that you slept with him a couple weeks ago."

"What?!" This gets me frantically pacing the room, wondering who I can trust and who believes what.

The instant I stop and whirl in Levi's direction, he pipes up. "I didn't believe him Fiona. I heard your story loud and clear...I know he's a liar."

"Damn right he's a liar! He's a sick psychopathic maniac and he's out of control!" I heave and pace in silence for another minute...trying to formulate, through my veil of rage, where exactly all this is going. "So I suppose he's talked my father into leaving me out of my inheritance then?"

"I don't think he even had to. I'm sorry Fiona."

"Sorry!? Sorry? Me too Levi! Oh let's see...I'm only about... three million dollars sorry! Oh what was I ever thinking? Daddy was never gonna leave me that money anyway! Tell me something new Levi! Huh? Tell me something new!"

As my breathing escalates into one smooth, rolling, smothering seesaw, the room begins to darken. The red I saw only moments before is a dull gray by the time I look around and notice I'm on the carpet. Holly is beside me, rubbing my arms.

"Fiona," she cries when I look up at her, "I'm so sorry this is happening. It's so terribly wrong and you don't deserve any of it."

"It's okay," I eke out, gathering a little strength to sit up. "I really did know I was destined for the smallest portion of that inheritance. If anything." I sit, gathering my bearings, while Holly rubs my back. "It's that Quade claimed I slept with him...ew! I don't know how to even begin to deal with that one! You know, Levi, that he physically manhandled me that night, that he came onto me in such a fashion as to indicate he was planning to take advantage of me." That last phrase fizzles into a sob and Holly pulls me against her, holding and rocking me quietly.

"I know Fiona. I didn't for a moment believe that Quade was telling me the truth," Levi says, joining in the back-patting.

He goes to fetch tissues, as I continue to cry for a couple more minutes. I accept them, blow it all out, and then pull away enough to look Holly in the eyes.

"I'm okay," I say, offering her a half smile. Then I reach out to Levi and pull him over to us. "I'm sorry buddy. I wasn't yelling at you. I was just...yelling."

"Don't mention it," he responds, handing me a glass of water.

The three of us rise and relocate to the couch. "So, the million dollar question, no pun intended, is...am I going to get to keep my business? If we were never legally divorced, which we weren't, and the law is on his side, and he's unabashed about claiming I'm still with him...and two-timing him, no less, then what have I got? What exactly have I got?" The tears pour forth once more, as I grapple for the tissue box.

"Did you know he's been pumping iron?" Levi carefully asks, after allowing me to calm down for half an eternity.

"Seriously? Yeah...I mean he didn't tell me he was, but it's fully apparent. Don't you think?" I can only hope Levi's question was rhetorical.

"I guess so," he replies. "But did you know he's also been fooling around with some kind of roids?"

"What?" This sounds staggeringly unlike Quade. But then, nothing should still surprise me.

"Yeah, he was cryptic about it, but he mentioned some testosterone boosters. Things I'm unfamiliar with."

"Well that would explain why he suddenly looks like a dorky, balding action-figure."

"Oh no," Holly adds, as if she's just heard the most calamitous news of the night. "Fiona, do you remember my old friend, Isobel, I introduced you to at an open house a few years ago?"

"I think so, vaguely."

"Well her husband of fifteen years got into bodybuilding and started taking some sort of testosterone boosters...it completely changed his personality."

"Really?" I ask with fascination.

"Yes, completely. He started having an affair with a female bodybuilder, left his wife and three kids, became hostile and emotionally abusive. Totally different person than the guy she'd always known. She was devastated...turned her whole life upside down."

I don't know whether I'm more horrified or relieved that we've found a potential explanation for Quade's changes. "Well maybe you should tell him he's destroying himself," I say to Levi.

"Believe me, I mentioned that whatever he's taking... which sounded like an entire cocktail of different things... could be dangerous or change his personality. But he didn't take the hint." Levi stops talking and rubs his forehead.

"Could change his personality?! The guy's a maniac!" Suddenly my irritation is mounting again.

"I know, I know," Levi responds in a placating voice. "But you didn't really expect me to come out and say that to the guy, right? I don't exactly see that as productive."

"So he doesn't have any clue that he's morphed into an asshole?" I ask.

Levi drops his head and groans. "It's so much worse than simply not knowing, Fiona. He said he finally feels like the man he's always wanted to be."

I throw my hands up, caught between coughing and gagging. "Is there anything else we need to know about how it went tonight?" I ask, trying to be composed and polite. It's hard for me not to shoot the messenger, but I have no right to.

"Honestly, that's about it. He spent most of the time bragging about his number of reps of...everything. It was dizzying, actually."

* * *

First thing in the morning, I drive to Silverbell Care Center to pay Dad a visit. I'm in no humor, whatsoever, to see his face. But I have to at least take a stab at reasoning with him. Perhaps he's so far gone that I can get a lawyer over here and cajole him into signing everything over to me after all. For the moment, I just want to get an idea of what I'm dealing with. And it's a fact that I haven't visited in over a month, since the last time he didn't seem to notice I was even there.

"Hi Dad!" I greet him jovially, hoping for the best. If he still remembers Quade so clearly, and that I'm legally married to the guy, shouldn't he be able to communicate with his own daughter?

"Fiona," he responds gruffly. "How I have failed you as a father."

Well this is off to a good start. I pull up a chair and take his hand between mine, eager to hear him finish this thought.

"Your mother and I both, we failed you terribly...and for that I am sorry."

He's quiet for a minute while I try to come up with a diplomatic response to such an obviously correct statement.

"We tried to set a good example in our long marriage, but somehow never taught you how to treat men," he explains, just as I open my mouth to speak.

My mouth hangs open but nothing comes out.

"What you're doing to my son is despicable."

"Your son!?" I finally manage. "Dad, I am your only child! Your daughter."

"No Felicity, that's where you're wrong. I do have a son, a son and a legacy. And he is going to carry on my good name with or without you."

At the word "Felicity" I stand and stagger backward...my blood pressure rising so quickly that my vision blurs.

"Felicity...Felicity?" I mumble inaudibly. "Dad, do you know that I'm your daughter, Fiona?"

Radio silence.

"Dad...dad?"

"Yes I hear you! And no daughter of mine would ever betray a great man like Quinton!"

"Quinton? Dad...you're making a huge mistake here. Quade...Quinton has lied to you. I am not having an affair!"

"You get out of here right now! I won't listen to this scallywag anymore! This is nonsense! Nonsense! Wade would never lie to me...to his own father! The very idea of it! Just where do you get the nerve to come marching in here and try to tell me— "

Before he can finish, I'm out the door and rushing down the hall...teary eyed and panicked. I'd intended to ask whether his will had been signed off on, but clearly his arrangements with Quade make no difference to my world. My father's not going to leave me anything and that's that.

Chapter 26

Bo

A whippoorwill sounds as I finish glazing the last corner of the living room floorboards. In the past month I've recarpeted the upstairs, refurbished the master bath with a deep, jetted soaking tub, redone all the lighting in the kitchen, installed ceiling fans throughout, and gotten my floorboards cleaned up. The place is startin to gleam and I'm gettin excited to move into it, but the idea still falls flat when I think of doin it without Fiona.

I clean up my supplies and head over to the shack to rustle up some dinner. Since our ill-fated phone call, I've learned to direct my thoughts away from Fiona enough to get through the day...but at night they come cascading back, every night. My body doesn't listen when my mind tells it to take a rest, and Fiona's the torturous itch that I keep havin to scratch.

Late summer fades into the milder heat of Florida autumn, and then finally into the relief of our benign winter. But I hear nothing from Fiona. I've decided to drive up and find the woman if I haven't heard from her by next year. By then the house will be all finished, freshly painted and ready to cozy into.

I turn in early and have the first non-erotic dream about Fiona since we met, and this one's alarming. She's yelling, crying and alone, distressed by the collapse of a series of mountainous towers surrounding her. They crumble to the ground one after the other, as if detonated, while Fiona screams in protest. Once they've all fallen, she stands straighter, unballs her fists and looks out at a new horizon...a dry, flat field with nothing visible at first. Then, as the dust clears, emerald green grass appears at the perimeter. Fiona stares at it, transfixed, and then she's gone.

I awaken sweating. The thought of my lady in emotional torment perhaps bothers me more than the thought of her axing me from her life. And the combination is hardly tolerable. As I stare into the darkness, unable to get back to sleep, I remind myself to keep my faith. Fiona is my love, and I am hers. She'll find her way out of her darkness and back to me. I've waited so long for her, I'll never give up now.

Chapter 27

Fiona

"Hey Cookie," Quade breathes into the phone. "How's my favorite girl? A little bird told me you haven't been showing up for yoga lately. Those classes are expensive. I paid for an entire year of classes and someone's been skipping out. I don't think that's fair Cookie. Do you think that's fair?"

"Oh! I...plan to continue going. I...very much appreciate the classes. I just lately have been...oh what the hell Quade!? Now you're keeping dibs on my yoga therapy? How's that supposed to be therapeutic for me? So every time I can't go, due to the maddening task of running my own business, I have to feel guilty that you're gonna take it personally if I didn't show up? Oh that's really going to create deep inner peace in my life, Quade. Thank you very much...I'm so deeply indebted to you for saving me in every single way! I just don't know what I would do without you and all your precious therapy money!"

Upon hanging up, I feel justifiably elated. But in a mere matter of seconds shock sets in as it dawns on me that I just chewed-out the antiChrist, followed by fear over how he's going to respond...followed again by a knowing confidence that there isn't much he can do that he hasn't already.

The store's been booming since Maxine returned from London, and all the work has been a very welcome distraction for me. I smile to myself as I drive home for the night, pull into the driveway, and find Holly and Levi hovering around the grill.

"Look who's finally home...you look happy," Holly says, hugging me before I can escape past her. "You should be cause we're making your favorite," she says, as she lifts the grill lid to reveal a load of fat, red lobster tails.

"Holly, those look amazing!" I hug her again and then remove my heels, sitting to stretch my toes in the cool air.

"It sure is nice to see you smiling. Anything interesting happen today?" Holly asks, as though something exciting could possibly happen in my life.

"Oh not really." She looks at me with a question mark. "Just that I chewed Quade out and hung up on him about ten minutes ago. I'm basking in the afterglow I guess."

"Whoa! I kind of can't believe you did that, but I'm so glad you did. What have you got to lose anyway?"

"Exactly."

"Wait," says Levi, snapping his tongs at me and looking confused. "I thought you were on pins and needles that Quade might pull your business any day."

"Nah, I've done some research. Even if he confiscates it tomorrow and sells it out from under me, I believe he'd have to give me fifty percent because we're married and I've been working there. Not that I'd be okay with that, but at least it wouldn't leave me destitute."

"I sure hope you're right about that," Levi retorts.

"What would you do?" Holly asks.

"Take my half and open another place that's really truly mine. At this point, half the value of the store would be more than what he took out for the original loan. But seriously, I don't think he'd do it no matter what. I think it was an empty threat."

"Really?" Holly asks, looking not so sure. "He's followed through with everything else, hasn't he?"

"Oh yes, more than you even know. I had another call with my investigator this morning...guess."

Holly's eyes go wide. "No..."

"It's unbelievable Holly. They found cameras at each possible entrance to the house and guest house...what did I tell you?"

"He is so busted! What did he have to say about this?"

"I didn't mention it...how would I? I figure he'll only get creepier if I call him out on his creepiness. I'm sure he's already furious that I've outsmarted him by staying away from the place."

"Don't you have a case with all this evidence?" Levi asks, removing the lobster to a platter waiting with lemon-butter.

"That's the real kicker. Earnhart says it isn't illegal to rig your own house, whether you live in it or not. Plus he says that since we're legally married, I don't have much of an argument, especially since he didn't actually find cameras *inside* the house. It turns out that not divorcing Quade was the stupidest thing I've ever done. I cannot believe all the ways this is coming back to haunt me."

"I don't know...cameras at the entryways...don't you think maybe Quade was just trying to keep you and the house protected?" Holly interjects.

"Come on, he had no business not telling me about this. What it actually means is...if I'd ever brought any man into that house, Quade would have known who it was, what time of day or night, and exactly how long they stayed." When Holly glances back up at me, she has a look of apologetic understanding...but I'm always surprised by how she still wants to give Quade some benefit of the doubt.

We change the subject and eat our incredible dinner in the dining room, as the patio temperature had rapidly fallen. Afterward Holly nestles next to me in the guest bed, and we space out in front of a mediocre romcom...the absolute last thing I want to be watching.

"Oh cheer up Fifi," she says to me when it's over. "If that didn't make you laugh, nothing will."

"It was dumb," I say with a smirk, trying not to come across too harshly. But it *was* a damn waste of time.

"I thought it was pretty good...come on," she chides.

"So two people who have been vaguely corresponding finally meet and they immediately hit it off and wanna jump each other's bones. Bravo. How often do you think it actually goes like that in real life? Give me a break already." Holly stares at me blankly, like I'm the densest person she's ever known. "What?" I ask, laughing, trying to lighten the mood I just killed. "I generally go for more realistic plots, that's all."

She continues staring and blinking, like I'm missing some obvious point. "Let me ask you something," she finally says. "Do you remember how me and Levi met?"

"Sure," I relent, "and it was love at first sight. Obviously it really happens...look at you now. It's just...I don't know... such a lame stereotype for something that's radically unlikely to occur."

"So...am I the only woman you know who's ever had that experience then?"

"Definitely," I reply, wondering where Holly's going with this.

"Okay," she says with feigned resignation.

"What's your deal?"

"My deal is that a few months ago you told me you were in love for the first time in your life. Does that ring any bells at all?"

I feel my face flush with some nasty combination of embarrassment, anger, and a resistance I can't identify. "Yeah," I tell her. "Yes, it rings a bell. And guess what else...I was in the tub with you that night...drinking."

"Ah, I see. So it was just the alcohol talking."

"Of course."

"Uh huh, okay. So, I guess then that even though Quade's already tapped you out of your own home and phone, plus stolen your inheritance, and even if he forces you to give up your store, you'll still remain single because you've just never met the right guy."

"Can we not talk about this? I'm tired Holly and I wanna go to sleep. My imaginary love life is not a hot topic."

"Sure, I'll get out of here and let you sleep now," she says with undisguised frustration. "Since a devilishly handsome flower farmer who's a superhero in bed couldn't be of any real interest to someone like you, I guess there's nothing to talk about. Goodnight." She gives me an obligatory peck on the cheek and then waltzes out, leaving me tongue-tied.

Bo Thompson, a devilishly handsome flower farmer who's a superhero in bed. It's been so long since I allowed any of those thoughts, that I feel like my world's disintegrating around me. I brush my teeth and undress in a daze, knowing I should go apologize to Holly but unable to find it in me to do so.

My room is warm but the bed-sheets are cold when I shiver into them and pull the blankets up. Sleep evades me as I lie in the glow of the deck light that was never turned off, attempting to steer my restless mind in its usual directions... mostly upcoming client work and Maxine's latest design ideas. Then there's the question of which side of town I want to buy a house on, and when I'll feel completely comfortable living alone again, not to mention how I'll afford one if Quade takes my business.

As my thoughts become increasingly worrisome, I struggle hard to redirect them to the holiday party Maxine and I are arranging for next week...but they take another turn. This time not focusing on my situation, but settling into a dark place in my psyche where all I can feel is an indiscernible sense of lack and grief. I hover over the thought of my father assigning the inheritance to Quade, an obvious knife in my chest, but that doesn't banish the idea that I'm not facing the true source of my devastation. What more could a girl need to make her feel lower than ground level? And then, that imprint I've pushed to the back of my awareness blinks its way to life and shoves all other thought aside.

Holly's flippant statement about Bo Thompson resurfaces in the foreground of a series of images of a hotel room... spinning through my memory like a movie reel. I arch my back and squeeze a pillow between my thighs, overcome by a painfully familiar warmth I'd committed to walking permanently away from. Tears stream out of me, and I pound a clenched fist into the bed. I can't identify who I'm angry at; I am just so angry. But then, why would I be crying if I was angry? That question only makes me more furious until I'm thrashing back and forth, kicking blankets everywhere and hurtling pillows at the far wall...a snotty, hyperventilating mess, cursing under my breath and hating myself for being such a weakling. Who cries when they're angry? What the hell is wrong with me?

After my head is filled with so much oxygen I can't function, I go limp and struggle to wiggle my fingers until sensation seeps back into my arms. Too weak for any more tantrums and too pathetic to control my thoughts, I drift back to that hotel room as my body sinks into the mattress. I never do this, but just this once...I indulge in a bodily memory so palpable it's as though my cells deliberately locked it in. Does my body want me to exist in a state of tortured conflict forever? I relax my face and stretch back, tossing my arms above my head and finally breathing fully and deeply, returning to the homeostasis I experienced once. Bo's hot breath on me, hands stroking down my length with all their texture and smoothness. His rock hardness teasing me through fabric that is soon to come off. Longingly I writhe under the weight of his phantom body...visiting and entering me right here, in the quiet, half empty room of someone else's home.

Chapter 28

Bo

Fiona's house is almost finished, and it's perfect. Large enough for guests but still cozy, and with a kitchen that inspires. I'll be seriously bustin out my a-game when I introduce the woman of my dreams to some gourmet home cooked meals. Veggies fresh out of the garden and greenhouse, peaches and plums from the orchard, mangoes straight off the tree.

It also happens to be an idyllic, sunny, early January day; meanwhile it's abysmally frigid up in Iowa. After half a year, I'm ready to charge into action like a medieval warlord. By next week I'll have my plants in order and loose ends tied up, ready to turn the farm over to my workers for however many days necessary.

I really can't imagine what awaits me. My memories are almost a constant that I have to battle my way through in order to function each day. I tell myself I'm working them off, but they're always lurking in the background of whatever else I'm focused on.

They make me feel like I'm losing it, as though I've got anything left to lose. Separated by over thirteen-hundred miles, Fiona couldn't care less for all I know. I've always been a man who wears my heart on my sleeve, but even Jose's tryin to talk me down from this one. What a fool he is to think I have any other choice.

Chapter 29

Fiona

I still feel mixed emotions every time I drive by and see my magnificent house for sale. I guess my hanging up the phone was just too much for little Quade to handle. The holiday season used to be fun and festive at the store, but this time it's passing me by in a blur of gray days and monotonous planning. I'm no longer able to find motivation for the things that once made me tick, so I'm putting in the bare minimum and letting Maxine run with the rest. Thank God I have her. She's talented enough to compete, but if Quade takes the store I'm sure she'll decide to come with me.

As I pull up to park outside the showroom, a familiar number rings my phone. My heart leaps into my throat when I register that it's a Florida number...the only one I've ever memorized on sight. Being that I still use my tapped phone so Quade won't steal my business, I cannot answer this call. So I pray he doesn't leave a message of any kind. Even the quality of Bo's voice, in a purely professional context, would cause Quade's little remaining hair to stand on end.

Simultaneously I receive a text from Holly.

Are you at work yet? I just got out of a meeting and missed a call from a Florida number. They didn't leave a message.

Thanks Holly. They called my phone too but I was busy. It's just a flower vendor.

Well come home at lunch and call them back?

I can't, have to work through lunch today doing party prep. I'm just going out to pick us up Subway.

I toss my phone into my purse, relieved when I never get a message tone...yet conflictingly disappointed that I don't get to hear Bo's voice. I take a couple deep breaths and march into the store to pretend I'm having a perfectly normal day.

"Morning Fiona!" Maxine is her usual sunny self.

She's been dating a pilot ever since her trip to London, and seems to be high on life. Why do some of us have all the luck in love?

"Hey Maxine. How's it coming along?" She holds up a bouquet of red roses filled in with evergreen sprigs and gold-dusted berries. "Looks like a holiday miracle. I love it."

I wish I was in the mood to let on over her beautiful work, but I just want to be quick and efficient right now. Knowing I'll call Bo back, against my better judgment, is going to make this day insufferable.

I become foolishly exuberant when my phone rings again, but the excitement morphs into disgust once I see that it's Quade. I excuse myself and go back to my car to sit and take the call.

"Hello."

"Hey Cookie, you at the store?"

"Yes. I was. Helping Maxine prep for a huge New Year's Eve party we're decorating tonight." I'm trying not to sound too exasperated, but Quade knows I hate being interrupted at work without good reason.

"Well that sounds nice. Getting into the New Year's spirit?"

"Come on Quade, Maxine's waiting on me. What's up?"

"Oh is she really? I thought Max was fully self-sufficient by now?"

I break out in goosebumps as it occurs to me that Quade probably has my store cameras rigged to send him footage as well. Does he actually know Maxine's working away without me right now? I look down nervously at my plunging neckline and wonder if he knows what I'm wearing.

"No you're right. She is. I just have a lot to help with if we're going to make our deadline tonight," I gently grovel.

Quade takes his time letting out a huge sigh into the phone. "Okay Cookie, well...I'm in town tonight if you want to grab a bite with me. I could pick you up at work. I'd really love to come in and see what you're doing in the store windows these days."

I freeze up, sputtering for a response while my head fills with blood.

Quade hasn't requested my company once since our incident, as though he hoped I'd forget the details over time. He always calls to let me know when he's in town, acting like we're still friends, but then comes up with an excuse for not getting together. "I'm sorry Quade...I told you we're doing a party tonight," I respond, thankful to have my own excuse this time.

"Let Maxine do it. Call Laura and whoever else to help her out. You shouldn't have to be hustling at these parties anymore Cookie. It's undignified."

"Undigni...Quade...what?! This is a major annual client and they want me there, okay? The place is called Fiona's Flowers for a reason you know, and clients need me to show a little interaction and interest from time to time, right?!"

"I'll pick you up at five sharp."

"What?! Quade...I can't just...I can't!"

"Is it not your store, Cookie? You can do anything you please. You'll make arrangements with your girls, and then be ready for me by five."

I sit holding the phone like a speechless idiot for an entire minute after Quade abruptly disconnects. It takes every fiber of my control not to hurl my phone through my own windshield. Fat lot of good that would do me. I instead slam it into the passenger seat, grip the steering wheel with both hands, and scream like a banshee...then thrash around flailing my fists into the windows and ceiling until I'm bruised everywhere. Good thing we closed early today. I'm not sure exactly how your typical holiday bouquet shopper would interpret my parking lot behavior, not that it would even stop me if we were open and teaming with customers.

I get out and slam the car door, then pace the sidewalk for several minutes trying to sort out what's got me more infuriated...the fact that Quade thinks he's the boss of me, or that I now won't be able to call Bo at five o'clock. How ridiculous I am to even be thinking about something so frivolous at a time like this. I head into the store once I feel almost collected enough to deal with Maxine.

"Max...something's come up. You've got this, right?"

"You mean...can I finish all the prep by myself today?"

"Not exactly. How about I get Laura in here to help you with whatever you need, and she'll do the party with you tonight?"

I feel slightly pleased to see Maxine's disappointment, when she sharply inhales with surprise. "But you were all excited. I thought you wanted to do this party," she says, looking dismayed.

"You're right kiddo. I really did...but I can't. Family emergency," I respond, just realizing how harshly neutral I sound.

"Oh my gosh...are you okay?" she sweetly inquires.

"Yes, I'm fine. Everyone's fine. I just...forgot about something I can't get out of or my head will be on a platter."

"Oh geez. Okay, well...I'll miss you tonight," she lies, looking utterly puzzled by the thought that I could get in trouble with anyone. Maxine's used to me calling all the shots.

"You'll be fine kiddo, and I will too." I rest my hands on the counter and drop my head, taking a couple more calming breaths. When I raise my head, Maxine looks lovingly concerned and unconvinced. "I'm gonna call Laura and then I'll do odds and ends till lunch. No guarantee I'll make it back in this afternoon, but I'll have my cell on me. So call me if you need anything, okay?"

Maxine nods as I dial Laura and head to the front of the store to check the freshness of our latest window arrangements. She agrees to come in after lunch, and I go sit in my car again to call Holly.

"Hey Fifi. Taking lunch after all?"

"You bet. There's been a change of plans and I'm not working that party tonight. Quade's in town and wants to take me to dinner at five sharp, so Laura's going to help Maxine."

"Oh God, uh...that sounds nice."

"Yep, so...are you eating at home today or what?"

"Sure, no plans. Why don't you just come on home and I'll whip up a frittata."

"That sounds heavenly. Be there in ten."

When I arrive, Holly isn't there yet. So I sit in the living room to meditate for a few minutes...soaking up the bright sun streaming in through the skylights, trying to ground myself for the all-consuming task of hearing Bo's voice without losing my stability. Even my visions of punching Quade have been put on the back burner for now.

As I hear Holly enter through the kitchen, I try to take a minute to come out of meditation but it's impossible. My eyes pop open of their own accord, and I rush over to meet her extended hand...snatching the phone like a child and dialing Bo's number without a thought.

"Thank you," I mouth, as I head back to the privacy of the den, leaving Holly to bang her pots and pans in the background.

"Woman," Bo growls in his caveman voice.

I go weak in the knees, and my breath catches when I try to respond. "Bo," I finally whisper.

His laugh begins like always, as a hollow rumble deep in his chest. I can see his crooked smile as I hear it.

"Still waitin for you darlin," he says at length. "Thought I'd give a call and see how your holidays are going."

I continue breathing into the phone, unable to speak as memories of Bo envelop me like an ocean wave. If I wasn't clear on it before, I know now that Bo Thompson is the love of my life. And my life is in ruins. I refuse to beg any man for help, and I don't know what a farmer could really provide me anyway, but I can't sweep this one under the carpet forever. So I make a monumental decision...to tell the truth.

"Bo...I'm not so great. I mean...I've had better years. Not at the store...in life in general, I mean."

"Well sure. I notice you're still not talkin on your own phone like a big girl. That can't be a good sign," he responds with all the confidence of Conan the Barbarian.

"Well I still have my store," I reply, immediately getting defensive, "and that means everything to me. So things could be much worse." My stupidity rings loudly through the silence as I wait for him to respond.

"Alright then darlin. I'm glad you've got everything that means somethin to you," he says so nonchalantly I want to slap him.

"That's not what I meant!" I holler, then remain quiet for a good half minute during which Bo patiently waits for me to explain myself. "I'm just glad I still have my store," I mutter, embarrassed, feeling on the brink of tears.

"Well alright then. You just keep side-steppin it and we'll keep talkin on Holly's phone if that's what suits you."

I know all Bo's doing is giving honest responses to my cryptic information, but it's making me feel more helpless and dimwitted by the moment. "I never said it suits me to talk to you on Holly's phone," I say, lashing out in anger... my auto-response to being cornered into my own bullshit.

"Okay darlin, I'll call you on your own phone from now on if that's alright."

"From now on? Bo...it's been what...six months since you called me?" I feel tears welling up, as I transition from angry to sad...then back to angry.

"Well to be fair, I did leave the ball in your court."

"So you think that's how you're supposed to treat your woman? You just sit back and wait, take your sweet time, play around with your...your plants and all that...good little farmboy stuff...and leave me on the edge of a cliff forever... waiting for a man to call me?!" I yell, pacing frantically back and forth.

"Aw darlin, you know I wanna talk to you. You just seemed a little...underwhelmed...last time I called is all."

"Well you know what Bo, maybe my life has got me *overwhelmed*, and I've got things to take into consideration...

strategies for how I can survive and get through all this because I'm a survivor and I don't want anyone's pity and I don't need some big man to come along and try to rescue me. So yeah...maybe I was a little underwhelmed by you!"

Tears finally break over the damn of my lower lids as I fully absorb what I've just done. My body slides to the floor while my lungs struggle to assimilate the size and speed of my breaths. As the silence lengthens between us, my head fills with the sound of words I cannot bring myself to say... Bo, I love you more than anything. I need you desperately. My life has fallen through my fingers like a sham and I just want you to come pick me up and carry me away...

"Well Fiona, if that's how you feel," he finally ventures in a beaten-down voice.

Another wave of sobs pours out of me, as I cover the speaker so I can't be heard.

"I sure wish you'd let me be a part of your life strategies, but it sounds like you've got things covered on your own," he says.

"I'm sorry Bo," I manage in a whisper, followed by another expanse of silence before I disconnect my phone.

Chapter 30

Bo

"Hey man...what's up man? You look beat," Jose observes as I stagger into the saloon with a headache.

I raise a finger toward Kiana and she automatically comes over with my usual. "How's it goin Big Bo? Haven't seen you around lately. You're not goin dry on me are you?" she asks, leanin over the bar to the full advantage of her low plunging tank top.

"Naw...just busy doin winter things, putting final touches on the house and...keepin to myself too much I guess."

"What's on your mind bro?" Jose asks, readin me like a book as usual.

"You might wanna order another one for this." Kiana takes the cue and sets a beer in front of Jose, who's now turned sideways on his stool...giving me an expectant glare. "I'm gonna drive on up to Iowa and surprise her."

"What...for New Year's?"

"I guess so, except I won't be able to make it till New Year's Day."

"You're crazy man. What are you trying to do, torture yourself? Woman doesn't talk to you for half a year and you put your heart out on a limb...man that's crazy. I wouldn't do it! That's all I'm saying."

"It gets worse," I tell him with a faint smile, knowin he's gonna laugh when he hears what a fool I am. "I called her this morning...and she told me she's underwhelmed by me."

This sets both Jose and Kiana into whoops and hollers of side-splittin laughter, dramatized by fists poundin the counter and knees being slapped.

"You? Underwhelming? Underwhelming?! That's creative...I gotta hand it to the woman. I don't know how she came up with that one to describe Big Bo," Kiana says with many shakes of her head, as she begins fixin cocktails for a group at the other end of the bar.

"Why Bo? Why? What are you doing man? You've got beautiful girls eating out of your hand man. Wish they were after me like that...it ain't even fair man." He shoots Kiana a mournful look under his black lashes, but she doesn't take any notice.

"She said somethin else too." Jose braces himself for the worst. "She said she's my woman."

"What? It sounds like she's loose all up in here," Jose says, rotating a finger around each side of his head.

"Okay, okay." I say, finally laughing. "*She* was pissed at *me* for not calling in half a year, and she said that's no way to treat your woman. Now, I don't know what to make of all that...but I'm sayin she still likes me."

"I heard that!" Kiana shouts from the end of the bar. "Of course she still likes you, you big dumb oaf!"

The group before her laughs as I turn back to Jose in a more private tone. "I've just gotta see her again bro. The call was short and unmeaningful and...somehow I blew it again. I need to see Fiona. If she gives me the boot, it is what it is. But I'll tell you somethin...that woman wants me, and she's wound up tighter than the inside of a golf ball." Jose finally nods in earnest as I gulp the last drop of my beer and begin to rise. "Big Bo's gonna ride into town and bring that woman to her knees," I declare in a voice slightly louder than intended, inciting an eruption of hollers and 'hell yeahs' across the bar.

"You headin out already man?" Jose asks as he grips my hand in a dap shake.

"Yeah buddy. I've got some work in the greenhouse and a lot to think about."

"Damn straight Bo. You be thinking about it. If you come back home a broken man, I've got your back bro."

"Ain't gonna happen Jose," I assure him with a fond smile.

"I'm just sayin bruh," he shouts over the din, as I open the door to exit.

Chapter 31

Fiona

Holly finally heads back to work, after sacrificing two hours in an ungratifying attempt to console me while I blubbered and refused to talk. I splash water on my face, redo my eye makeup, and drive to the shop to make myself useful till Quade shows up. Glancing in the rearview mirror at a light, I can see how unsuccessful I was at de-puffing my face. But I'm pretty sure Maxine and Laura will take me as I am. They've got their work cut out for them today.

By five o'clock I've successfully dropped a two gallon bucket of water, pissed off the cake designer, and assembled half a dozen table centerpieces before noticing I left out the all essential roses. The girls are loading the van to head over to the clubhouse when Quade pulls up to get me, and I'm certain they're glad to see me go.

A wave of nausea overtakes me, as I see Quade's face for the first time since he decided to turn my life upside down. My favorite thing about the past few months has been not seeing him. Although I miss the friend Quade used to be, I'd have been happy to never lay eyes on him again after the night he tried to...seduce me? I still don't know what exactly that was, and some mental block always prevents me from thinking about it too hard.

He gets out and grins goofily at my storefront, pretending to take an active interest in what goes on around here, then comes to open the passenger's door for me...his typical display of pointless chivalry. I can't find it in myself to manage a thank you, but I afford him a convoluted half-smile as I step away from his Rolls-Royce.

"I'd like to take my car," I tell him.

"No no no...allow me, please," he says with pleading eyes and a vulnerable tone.

"Quade, you've brainwashed my father and stolen my inheritance. We are not friends!" I blurt out, already breaking my inner vow to keep my cool tonight.

"Not friends? Come on Cookie...please don't do this here. You're embarrassing yourself."

"Embarrassing myself?! How am I embarrassing myself Quade?! You think I'm concerned that people driving by are gonna turn their heads and judge me for yelling at my ex in the parking lot of my own store? Do you really think I give two craps what the neighborhood thinks right now?"

"Okay, okay Cookie...calm down—"

"No, don't change the subject on me Quade! You come to town calling me up, marching into my life like you own it, requesting that I change *my* plans on a dime...after you've already taken almost everything from me. And you know what...you can have the store. Go ahead and take it Quade! Is that what you're here to do tonight? You wanna determine whether I'm nice enough to allow me to keep my precious store? Well guess what...I'm not! Go ahead and take it Quade! See if I care!"

A minute after I slam my purse into my car and put it in reverse, Quade calls...sounding sadder than I've ever heard him. He was cheerier than this when we were in the throes of our separation.

"Cookie, you know I have a plan for you. I only want what's best for you. I know you better than even you do, and you've always been on a path of self destruction. You need someone to look out for you. I'm only trying to save you from yourself Cookie."

He sounds so morose and honestly concerned...I have to wonder if he actually believes everything he just said. Am I really self destructive? I'm disgusted with myself when Quade's patronage causes my emotions to break for the tenth time today. My eyes flood with tears as I quietly continue driving in the opposite direction, back to the safety of Holly's condo.

"Come on Cookie...how does sushi sound tonight?"

I struggle not to let Quade hear my cynical laugh. Yes, sushi is my biggest weakness, but food is the absolute last thing on my mind. Suddenly he's almost reduced to someone sweet and innocent...imagining he can make it all better with a little sushi dinner. What a childish buffoon.

"Come on Cookie...I'm sorry. You know I'll always be here for you. Let's just talk things out, okay? We just need to talk," he coaxes as I pull into Holly's driveway.

My face crumples into a sobbing grimace as I drop my forehead onto my steering wheel and feel myself give in. Defeated, I put it in reverse and drive away from all that is safe and sane.

"Okay Quade, okay. Meet you at the sushi joint?"

"I want you to meet me back at the store. I want you to get into my car and let me take you out tonight. You think you can do that? Let your oldest friend take you out for a nice dinner tonight?"

I have to admit that Quade sounds like the same old placid guy I've always known. Has he always been controlling and manipulating me like this? To think that all my life I believed he was *my* puppet...how could I have been so unaware? I try to calm my mind by imagining the cozy, dim lighting of the sushi place, Quade making pleasant chit chat and reassuring me of all the ways he plans to invest the inheritance for the best interest of my future. Looking after me as always, my future, my inheritance. My inheritance. Quade patronizingly doling out all the ideas he has for *my* inheritance, that *my* father is leaving to *him* because Quade is the model child Victor really wanted.

Having failed to sufficiently calm myself, I absentmindedly pull into the parking lot of Shokai before remembering I was supposed to meet Quade first. "Quade," I say, after dialing him up to profess my error, "I'm sorry, I forgot what I was doing and drove straight to the place. Why not just meet me here, okay? It's a one minute drive from the shop."

"How do you know where I was going to take you?"

"You said sushi. There's only one place we eat sushi in this town."

"How do you know I was going to take you somewhere in town?"

"What? Quade—"

"I was in fact planning to take you to Iowa City for something really special tonight."

"But Quade...I'm tired. I...don't want to spend that much time in a car tonight. Please..."

"So...my Rolls Royce is too tiring for you to spend time in?"

"That's not what I said!"

"Fiona, I wouldn't thwart my plans if I were you."

"Is this some kind of a threat?! Gee I'm sorry if you feel thwarted, Quade. I mean...I'd never intentionally thwart a guy!"

"Okay, okay Cookie. Are you gonna let me take you to a nice place and talk things out, or what?"

I feel my resolve slipping as the words leave Quade's mouth. Is he honestly trying to give me a platform to discuss everything that's gone down between us? Does he somehow not know that I'd like control over my own money and life? What will he ask of me for the privilege of letting me keep my store, the product of my own blood, sweat, and tears? And most importantly, if I turn down his offer tonight...will he punish me for it?

I'm an inch away from saying yes, but can't quite bring myself to get into a car with the guy who stalked into my house, into my bedroom, held my wrists while I panicked, then followed me across town threatening me as I scurried barefoot and naked through the streets. The memory hits me of Quade's voice coaxing me to get into his car that night, and how I was almost afraid for my life at the time.

After so many months of being left alone, it seems fantastical now...like a nightmare I had, or maybe a misunderstood encounter my mind blew way out of proportion. Then I think of the cameras and phone. No, I'm not the crazy one, and the nightmare is real.

"Quade, let's be reasonable," I say in the most soothing tone I can muster. "I'm tired and I've got to be in the showroom in the morning. How about you meet me at Shokai and we'll get that little table in the back where we sat last time. I'm looking in now and the place is practically empty...I'm sure we can get our table."

"I don't want our table, Cookie. I want to take you somewhere special. Please don't make me resort to anything regrettable. All I want is an audience with you in the atmosphere of my choosing."

He sounds as calm as a summer breeze, yet his phrasing is downright disturbing. How can he expect me to respond nicely to this?

"Quade, I'm tired and I'm going to have to say no. If that forces you to do something you regret, it's on you," I say in a voice that feigns confidence.

He lets out a huffy sigh. "Okay, I'll meet you at Shokai. Be there in a sec," he replies before disconnecting. I knew the bastard was bluffing.

When Quade walks in I'm seated in the back, as promised, pouring a cup from the tea service that's already arrived. I struggle to hide the instant state of repulsion his presence puts me in. His body looks bulkier than ever...thick, rounded muscles bunched stuffily onto a frame that can hardly support them, his face revolting. I never thought Quade was good looking, not even in our early days, but I've never seen him through these eyes of knowing before. I pray for the strength to hold a civil conversation in his overbearingly distasteful presence.

"Hi," Quade says breathlessly, as he stares in wonder like he's never seen me before. "You look stunning."

As he comes around to kiss my cheek, while removing his coat, I try to make it unapparent that every cell of me is cringing away from him. I thank my lucky stars I changed into a conservatively high-necked sweater this afternoon. He sits across from me and continues gazing, taking no interest in the menu. I crack a smile in an effort to act decent. If I'm going to agree to meet Quade, I may as well pretend I still think he's human.

I pick up my menu and instinctively hold it in front of my face, hoping it will magically deflect Quade's gamma rays. After some minutes he succumbs to picking his up, and together we select five rolls of sushi...in our traditional collaborative manner. After placing the order and making a short trip to the ladies room, I'm out of activities to hide behind. So I force myself to participate in Quade's gaze. He has the nerve to stare at me as though waiting for me to begin a conversation; I meet his eyes with an expectant glare until he gives in first.

"Well Cookie, I guess you're wondering why I've decided to take charge of our finances."

"*Our* finances?"

"Well, technically mine, but I have every intention of sharing."

"How very generous of you," I respond, seething.

"Let me spell something out for you Fiona...I didn't ask Victor for your money. I didn't have to. He thrusted it into my lap because he wanted me to have it from the bottom of his heart."

"From the bottom of his insane, senile heart."

"Now that's not fair. Victor may be slipping in his final years, but he's always made it clear how he felt about me. And frankly, I wasn't surprised when he announced that he wanted me to inherit his financial legacy. I feel honored."

"Oh good for you Quade! Bravo for winning over a dying chauvinist on his last brain cell."

"Thank you," he says, smugly folding his arms across his chest and sitting back in his seat. "Now, about what I plan to do with our money. First of all, I'm investing in your new home. The Victorian was turning into a money pit...I had to get rid of it," he says, catching me way off guard. My violent anger simmers ever so slightly. "Second, I'd like to open another store in Iowa City. How about turning Fiona's into a small chain?"

"Oh my God, Quade! That...yeah...that would be a dream come true. With Maxine, I could get out from under all shop duties here and just manage the two stores."

"That's exactly what I was thinking. I was going to show you the site of your future new location tonight. There's a prime lot open on South Clinton Street that I've already put a deposit on."

As much as we should be discussing *my* money and *my* decisions, I can't argue that I'm not thrilled about Quade's plans for it. After all, he is right. My father never had any intention to give me that money.

"After dinner, I'll take you to see the new house. I hope you don't mind that I took the liberty to move some of your basic furniture over already...I can hire movers for the rest," he says as the waitress lays our rolls before us.

I pick up my chopsticks and begin eating with a somewhat softened facial expression, still fuming that he would arbitrarily sell the house and buy another one without consulting me in any way. Granted, Quade knows my tastes well and I'll probably love it, which is entirely beside the point, and hey, at least he's aware he was taking liberties when he...moved a few pieces of my furniture! What the hell is Quade's actual sense of priority, anyway, that he feels compelled to use apologetic language around moving my furniture...into a house he bought without even asking me?! How very decent of him! Idiot.

We eat for a few minutes while I mull over the best way to launch into the topic of his camera habit. And also the fact that I'd never spend a night in a house Quade's had access to, without changing all the locks first thing.

"So," I start in with a roll stuffed into my cheek, "where's the house?"

"You'll see soon enough," he replies with his patronizing smile.

"Quade...what side of town is it on? Come on...just tell me what part of town it's in," I insist, beginning to raise my voice again.

"Nah ah ahh." Quade rests his chopsticks to lift his hand and wave a naughty finger at me.

I swear with everything I am that I want to murder my ex husband. Right. Now.

"Quade...I hate you," I say without sarcasm.

"Sweetie, come on. Settle down," he responds with a laugh.

"No! Don't tell me to settle down. Are you laughing at me? You have the nerve to sit here and...and actually laugh at me?! Are you out of your mind?!" Our teacups rattle as I abruptly rise and slam my polyester napkin onto my plate, grab my purse, and book it for the door.

"Cookie! Cookie...sweetie!" he calls after me before saying something to the waitress.

I continue marching toward my car, but Quade dashes out of the restaurant and heads me off within seconds.

"You left without paying?" I ask to change the subject.

"No...I just told her to hold my card. That's not important right now. Cookie, listen to me," he says pleadingly, as he physically blocks me from entering my car. "Why do things have to be like this? We used to be best friends. We *are* friends. What's...what's going on with you these days?"

"I'll tell you what's going on Quade. Here's what's going on...first of all, I know about the phone tapping." He stammers out a half-laugh and shrugs like he has no idea what I'm talking about. "Oh yeah, I know all about it. And...I know about the cameras." His face goes white as a sheet. "You, my dear friend, are a very sick man...and—"

"Oh my God, Fiona...how could you have not told me about this?" Quade asks as though stricken.

"Not told you what? That I know what a psycho you are?!"

"Cookie, my God...how could you have not told me someone tapped your phone? And what is this about cameras?"

"Bullshit Quade! This is bullshit! I'm calling bullshit on you right now," I shout, not about to lose my conviction.

"Ulysses."

"What?"

"Who else? I knew there was something wrong with that guy. You should have never gotten mixed up with a guy like that."

"Oh my God," I mumble through my fingers. "Wait... no...wait...you mean it wasn't you?"

"Fiona, how could you? How could you even think such a thing about me?" Quade timidly asks, looking devastated.

"Well I...I...well. Well there was that one night when you broke into my house and came into my bedroom and held my arms so I couldn't go and acted like you were going to have me against my will. What about that night, Quade? Remember that one? Why wouldn't I think that the same creep who did that would also tap my phone and rig my home with cameras?! Huh?!"

"Cookie I'm...I'm so sorry about that. I was confused about...your signals. I guess I got the wrong idea. Can you ever forgive me?"

"Um, maybe. Except that then you followed me across town naked to assure me that going to the law about it would be useless. How about that little detail, Quade?"

"I'm sorry...look...I was hurt, okay? I thought you wanted something more and I was wrong. I was just trying to get you into my car so I could get you home safe Fiona. Clearly with that maniac, Ulysses, on the loose...you need someone watching over you."

Quade's tone is so pitiful, and his eyes so crestfallen, I know he must be telling me the truth. And I couldn't be more surprised by his ability to apologize and confess that I wounded his ego that night. I still have nightmares about the whole thing, but suddenly the perpetrator seems so small and insignificant. It's just Quade, my goofy ex, the one I've watched a thousand movies with while consuming ten tons of popcorn.

I rub my forehead as another wave of tears threatens to flood me. Did I somehow blow the events of that night out of proportion? I was dead asleep when Quade entered my room, and I do have a history of scary experiences during sleep paralysis. The more I struggle to remember, the hazier it becomes. And to think that all this time I was being stalked by Ulysses, which makes total sense.

But before I can go getting too sentimental, my body is wracked with a sickening, wormy shudder of remembrance that I allegedly slept with Quade a couple weeks back. I won't even hazard to confront him on that one or I might actually lose my dinner, and I'm feeling a peculiar faintness as it is. I have the sudden urge to claw my way out of my stifling, hot sweater as I collapse onto the passenger seat of...Quade's...Royce. What the hell am I doing in here? Why would I ever put myself in a position where he has complete control over the rest of my evening? My fading last thought is of spoiled sushi, as he closes my door and the world goes black.

Chapter 32

Bo

At the risk of lookin like a jerk, I never planned to warn Fiona I was gonna come see her. I thought I'd just show up and find out if she's really prepared to turn me away forever. Not to mention, I always have the feelin she's hidin a bunch of stuff I'd wanna know about. All the more reason to surprise her. If the woman ain't gonna talk, Bo's gotta take the proper measures...ain't no harm meant by it.

Eight hours on the road, I screech to a halt pullin into a gas station when a beautiful cat dashes right out in front of my truck, freezes in a dead staring contest for about ten seconds, then disappears into some bushes. Now if that ain't an omen, I don't know what is. I literally shivered as her eyes penetrated straight into my heart, and a guy like me don't shiver.

"Hello?"

"Yes ma'am, is this Holly?"

"Yes?"

"My name is Bo Thompson and I'm an old friend of Fiona's. I just had a queer feelin I needed to call her up right now is all. Would she happen to be available?"

Several seconds pass with no sound from Holly. I wonder if the gal's hung up on me. By now she's probably heard I'm no good anyway.

"Bo? Oh my gosh...yeah. I mean, she's out right now but she'll definitely call you back when she gets in. Should be any time now."

"Well thank you very much Holly," I say before pausing awkwardly. I guess I imagine that if I can keep her on the phone, Fiona will show up quicker. "I'll just wait to hear back from her then." Somethin in me does not wanna hang up, but I know that makes no sense at all.

"You bet Bo, soon as she gets home. Nice talking to you."

"Nice talkin to you too, ma'am."

After returning the gas cap and wheeling back onto the interstate, I tighten my grip on the steering wheel and put the pedal down. Somethin don't feel right, and I wanna either finish the next twelve hours of drivin right now...or be on the phone with Fiona. I need to hear her voice, damnit. Why didn't I ask where the hell she is tonight?? Because it would be invasive and it's none of my damn business. That's why.

"Bo?"

"Yeah, I'm sorry ma'am...it's me again."

"Oh that's okay," Holly responds cheerily. "Did you just want to leave a message or something?"

"No, no I...I guess I was just wonderin if there's anywhere I could try reachin her right now. I know she doesn't like for me to use her number, but maybe if you could just tell me where she's at." I have to pause when I hear how fanatical I must sound. "I'm sorry Holly. You don't have to tell me nothin that's none of my business," I say with an inauthentic chuckle. "I guess I just have no patience tonight is all. Men can be like that, you know? I hope you'll forgive me for it."

"No Bo, no need to apologize at all. Distance will sure do that to people. I'd be more than glad to tell you, except she's just out and about. She had to meet up with her ex husband, Quade, tonight, and there's nothing in the world she hates more. I'm not trying to get you worked up over anything, but she deals with him as little as possible anymore. So I'll be waiting near the door till she gets home. I'm sure she'll be in a mood, but she'll be happy you called. Just cut her a little slack if she's extra grouchy," Holly says with a laugh.

"I'm much obliged Holly. I'll treat her with kid gloves tonight. Thank you again."

"You bet Bo. Don't you ever hesitate to call her on my phone, any time."

I'm surprised that I feel somewhat appeased after hanging up. I hope it don't make me less of a man that I feel relieved Fiona's with her terrible ex, but it explains away the feeling I have in the pit of my gut...and I guess that's what I needed.

I throw on a classic rock station and lean back to ease my mind till I hear from my princess. Gotta get my head in the right space to make her feel the way she ought to feel. I smile to myself when You Wreck Me comes on, Tom Petty... tellin it like it is, the only way the man ever knew how. But

I won't be wrecked. Fiona will be in my arms again...of that I'm certain.

Every Breath You Take floats through my speakers next, exactly what I don't need right now. I struggle against tears as the song develops, wonderin what the hell's wrong with me. Why would I let a silly song get to my head? Every smile you fake, every claim you stake...it's Fiona to the last note. I click off the radio to get an emotional grip, but the atmosphere refuses to lighten. As darkness sets in and my foot weighs heavier on the pedal, I know beyond doubt that I won't be hearing from her tonight.

An image of the parking lot cat is burned into my retinas, in all of her beauty and distress. Although she communicated volumes in the few seconds that passed between us, it was no easy reading, and I'm not sure how I should translate it. Every time I try to make heads or tails of the experience, I sink into a mire of despair over the undeniable sense of alarm it initially gave me. According to that cat, Fiona's in a lot more anguish than she usually is when navigating her ex. I'd even hazard to say I get a sense of danger, except I cannot let my mind wander that way. There are still almost ten hours between me and her, and I've somehow gotta keep my cool.

The next two hours disappear in a blur of intense focus, as I press into increasing speed...twenty miles, then twenty-five over the limit. Benefits of night driving on the open interstate. I refocus in time to notice it's eleven o'clock in Iowa. Just as I thought...no calls from Fiona tonight. My shoulders slump as I mentally run a horrible scenario of showing up only to be turned away by a neutral, if not hostile Fiona. I tell myself that's too bad to be true, but the doubts keep returning. I sensed she wasn't gonna call, but can't get a good feel of why she didn't. Everything I'm pickin up on is conflicting, like she would have wanted to call me but somehow couldn't. It just don't make no sense.

Maybe I should've listened to Jose all along. Maybe I need to reassess the decades of dream visits I've had from Fiona. I suppose there's no guarantee they ever meant she was my soulmate. Perhaps they were tryin to tell me somethin else, and I just wanted to believe what I wanted to believe. Although these heavy thoughts don't deter my momentum, they do make me wonder what I'm drivin into. It just feels like a bad situation, and I hope one or both of us won't come out of it hurt. But it's her choice if she wants to turn me away. I can't force her to choose a life of marital bliss in a Florida dream home with the man who worships her. Damn it woman. You have no idea how long the last six months have been for —

I physically jolt when my phone startles me out of my increasingly negative thought stream.

"Fiona?"

"Hi Bo, it's Holly."

"Holly — "

"I'm sorry to bother you, I know it's late in Florida. I just wanted to let you know not to wait up. Fiona's not even home yet."

Suddenly my veins are erect, my blood is boiling, my foot's even heavier, and I'm exhibiting all the signs of full blown dread. And it ain't good old fashioned jealousy either.

It's that even Holly doesn't sound okay. All my senses tell me somethin ain't right.

"Well Holly, I reckon you're off to bed soon, but maybe you could leave a note somewhere she would see it? You can trust me when I say I'll be waitin up for her. All night," I finally say, tryin to let her know I'm serious without betraying my level of concern.

"You bet I'll do that Bo. In the event I go to bed. To be honest, I'm a little worried about her."

"Now why would you be worried about a big girl like Fiona?" I ask, pretending that I'm not.

"I'm not sure," she says hesitantly.

I give her a long moment of silence before gently prodding again. "Well now what's got you bothered there, Holly?"

"Well, first of all...I'm pretty sure she'd murder me in my sleep if she knew I was talking to you about her. So please, can I say something to you in confidence?"

"Absolutely. I'd never rat you out," I reply, still soundin calm but feelin like a dozen firecrackers goin off in a bag.

"Thanks Bo. I feel I can trust you even though I don't know you. It's just...Fiona's painted a good picture of you in my mind."

"Really?" Finally Holly's got my attention on a thought that's not disturbing.

"Oh of course. Not that she goes around talking about you much, but when she first got home from the conference... she said some things," Holly says with a blush in her voice.

I clear my throat waitin for her to continue.

"I just want you to know that she has, or had, very strong feelings for you. I've really never heard her talk that way about anyone. But she just...has this mechanism where she shuts people out. She had a very lacking relationship with her parents and I think that has a lot to do with it. She doesn't want to let anybody in where she could get hurt. And I've really never seen her get hurt, ever. But it's not because she's indestructible. It's because she puts a wall up, you see?"

"I do see, Holly. I can see that clear as day about Fiona."

"I knew you were a good one," she says with a smile I can hear.

"Question though, if she's wanting to avoid me, what would that have to do with her stayin out late tonight? Assuming she still doesn't even know I'm tryin to reach her."

"Oh goodness Bo, that's where it gets weird. Please promise again that this information won't make it back to her? I probably already overstepped when I revealed who she was out with. Fiona's exceedingly private about her personal business, especially if she knew I was telling it to... someone she cares for."

I feel silly when that last comment lights me up inside. Our brief history provided ample evidence that Fiona cares for me, but there's somethin about the woman that challenges my confidence in a way it's never been challenged before.

"I don't suppose," Holly continues, "that Fiona's told you much about her relationship with her ex-husband, Quade?"

"Just enough to let me know I wouldn't wanna fight alongside him in a trench."

"Yes, well...to say the least. But what I find truly irksome is...they were always such good friends. He's always been the nicest guy, and then all of a sudden it's like he just turned."

And what I find truly irksome is the way Holly's beatin around the damn bush. "So, by "turned" you mean they're not friends anymore?"

"I'm afraid it's worse than that Bo. Fiona's father's dying of dementia, and..." Holly stops and lets out a heavy breath. "I hate to be the one telling you all this. Fiona's afraid to let you into her life because she doesn't want to rock the boat with Quade."

"I'd gathered that," I reply, tryin not to sound as impatient as I feel.

Holly lets out another huge sigh and goes quiet for a while, during which time I hold my breath like I'm waitin for a bomb to go off.

"I'm a little worried about her, Bo," she ekes out after an interminably long period.

"Well alright then Holly, I think we've pretty well established that. What I'm wonderin is...what is there to be worried about? What exactly do you mean when you say Quade turned against her? And if you don't mind my askin, I've gotta wonder what her business is tonight with a man who's no longer her husband or her friend."

"And you have every right to ask Bo, and I think you have every right to know."

My jaw clenches against my gritting teeth as Holly pauses once more.

"Bo?"

"Yes ma'am?"

"Several months back, before you met Fiona at the conference, she had an altercation with Quade."

"Altercation?!"

"Yes, now...try not to get upset. There hasn't been anything like that since and I think they're on peaceable terms...as much as they can be. But Quade's become moody in a way that he never was in past years. We don't really understand it."

"Now Holly, you have got to give me the straight talk here. Did he lay a hand on her?" Silence. "Did Quade lay a hand on Fiona?"

"Yes, but it didn't seem violent."

"Didn't seem violent?!"

"As far as I know, he frightened her mostly."

"Did he threaten her?"

"No, not verbally."

"He threatened her physically?!"

"Not exactly. Bo, you have to calm down, okay? He intimidated her and threatened to take her store...and her house. That's all I really know. She won't talk about it anymore."

"Why would he do this to her? How long have they been divorced?"

"Years, forever. He's just...I don't know. He's become possessive of her. We suspect he caught wind of her interest in you, and now he's trying to win her back."

"Win her back?! By threatening her?! What kind of a maniac is this guy? He tapped her phone and threatened to take her life away so he could win her back?!"

"I don't know what else to tell you Bo. Quade was always sort of a wimpy guy, nerdy...you know...a wuss. I think he's figured he can finally impress Fiona by suddenly being the man. Except she's not going for it in any way. Everything he's done has completely and totally turned her off, believe me. She's furious with him, wants as little to do with him as possible now. He completely destroyed their nice friendship with all this."

"Nice friendship," I mutter under my breath, disturbed that Holly could even mention that as one of the losses in all this.

The great loss is Fiona's freedom, her trust, her peace of mind. Meanwhile it's pushing midnight...and where the hell is she?

"Well Holly, in order to figure this out, let's just put our heads together," I say, hoping this will be an effective strategy for extracting more information. "Now what is it she needed to meet with Quade about that could have run her so late?"

"I actually don't know. She doesn't tell me anything. She came home at lunch to use my phone to call you, saying she had to meet Quade at five sharp tonight, then —"

"Now hang on a second here...are you tellin me that Fiona's been with an asshole she doesn't even trust for seven hours? Have you called her? Have you searched for her? Have you called the police?!"

"I did call, yes," she replies soundin put on the spot, "right before I called you, but she didn't answer...of course. That's when I decided to notify you. My boyfriend's up late doing paperwork at his office tonight and he could go out searching for Quade's vehicle. Levi should be home any minute."

"Well how about you put him on the task right now because it's midnight!"

"Okay Bo. I just need to...get off the phone...with you."

"Not a problem. I'll expect a call back with news that Levi's on the trail. Please don't make me drag the police into it."

"Okay, I understand. I'll call him right now," she says apologetically before hangin up.

I cannot even believe what I'm dealin with here. I'm sure Fiona's best friend is a great gal and all that, but I wouldn't want her in my trench either. Fiona, on the other hand, is a fighter...and I trust she's in no danger tonight. In all probability she's chewin Quade out for once and for all, layin down the law.

If I make my gas stops quick and keep the pedal down through the night, without sleep, I should roll into Fairfield, IA at about eight in the mornin. I'm sure Holly will call back any moment and put my mind at ease, but I have no need for sleep. Pure, raw adrenaline is pumping through my veins, drivin me toward the goal like a bear to a hive.

An hour later I'm pressing, pressing, pressing toward the Midwest, when finally my phone rings. I can feel that it ain't Fiona...somethin's still wrong.

"Hey Bo, this is Levi. I have scoured this town for Quade's car and I have not seen it. It's a Royce too, real easy to spot. Quade recently confided he'd bought Fiona a new house, and admonished me to keep it a surprise at the time. He wouldn't tell me the address, but Holly keeps track of every house on the market and somebody just purchased a great big brick Victorian...I highly suspect it was Quade. I've cased the place and all the lights are off, no car in the driveway. If it's in the garage I've got no way to tell, but the place looks dark and empty to me. I'm afraid I just don't have any other leads."

Once Levi finally stops for a breath, panic overtakes me. Fiona's literally a missing person. At least Levi's on the ball, not to mention he has some efficiency at doling out information.

"Well damnit Levi, call the police?"

"You bet. Doin it right now. Over and out."

I like this guy. I trust him. There has to be a simple explanation for this, and Levi sounds like he's ready to get to the bottom of it. In ten minutes, when I haven't heard anything, I ring Levi back.

"You're not going to like this Bo," he tells me in a downtrodden tone, "but the cops don't take a report about a missing adult out with her ex husband very seriously. I tried to explain that Quade's exhibited abusive behavior toward her and the guy actually laughed into the phone. When I raised my voice to cut back in, he told me I was out of line. Said they'd do a drive around and search for his car, which I told him I've already done."

"Did you tell them he's got her in that house?!"

"I did tell him about the house and he said they can't break and enter without real cause. He told me to call in if she doesn't show up tomorrow."

I'm so angry, I fear I'm in serious danger of running off the road. I look at my speedometer and it reads 105. It's all I can do not to stop and find something to pound my fists into, a sign, a tree, the side of my own truck...but it's imperative I get to Fiona without interruption.

"Levi," I say with measured steadiness, "you promise me you'll go find a way to get into that house. Jimmy a lock, open a window...if it's an old Victorian I'm confident you'll figure it out."

"Okay Bo," Levi heaves out with a sigh. "Fiona's her own woman and I'm sure she's having some kind of heart to heart with Quade that she doesn't want to interrupt, and she just hasn't thought to call home. She gets caught up in the moment like that, you know? She's used to living independently, not feeling obligated to report her whereabouts to—"

"Levi! Focus! You know better than me that somethin ain't right between her and that weirdo she used to be married to. I don't care how independent she is...somebody better get in that house and find her, pronto. I've got a sixth sense about this stuff and there's a real bad feelin in my gut tonight. Understood?"

"Well I sure hope you're wrong about that Bo, but I do understand. Let me go tinker around with the windows over there and I'll call you back," Levi says before abruptly hangin up.

Out of nowhere, my vision takes focus in a conscious way and I notice signs for Murfreesboro, Tennessee. The last time I had any comprehension of my surroundings, I must have still been in Florida. At the rate I'm drivin, I'll be in Iowa in seven or eight hours...incredible timing. I'm very lucky the state troopers are asleep tonight; some guardian angels surely are on my side.

"I checked everything and that house is tight as a drum," Levi reports an excruciating twenty minutes later.

"Well break a window, damnit!" I say with immediate regret. I don't wanna piss off the one guy that can possibly help Fiona.

"I don't know, Bo. If I break into that house tonight, the cops will obviously know who—"

"Are you tryin to tell me you're gonna leave your own friend at the mercy of a deranged man because you're afraid of gettin a slap on the wrist from local law enforcement?!" Silence. "That ain't cool Levi. I know you believe everything's probably okay and there's an easy explanation and Fiona don't wanna be bothered and all that, but what if you're wrong? And if you're not willing to bust into the only location we have reason to suspect she might be, then what exactly would you suggest doing instead?"

"No, you're right. You're right. Shit...I don't even have tools in my car."

I start to grumble, wonderin what kind of man I'm dealin with here.

"There's a stack of old firewood in the back. Maybe I could break a window with one of these logs."

By this point I'm fuming, wishin to God I was there so I could just ram my fist through a pane of glass and be done with it. I swear nothin would feel better to me at this point. I hear the garbled scratching of bark against bark, followed shortly by a sharp bang. Then another one.

"Dang, these old glass panes are sturdy," Levi mutters between heavy breaths before a final clang rings deafening through my phone speaker.

"You okay there buddy?" I ask out of politeness.

"Yeah, I'm alright. Wow...when it finally broke, the glass shattered all over the place. I've gotta pick a few giant shards out of the frame before I can squeeze in. Should I call you back after I'm in?"

"Okay," I reply reluctantly. "Actually...Levi?"

"Yeah?"

"Why don't you keep me on the line. I'm just thinkin... in the event Quade *is* in there and he ain't happy to see you comin, I'd like to bear witness to whatever goes down, right?"

"You bet Bo. Sounds like a smart idea, now that you mention it. Okay, well...I guess I'll just...scoot on in the window then and...check the place out."

"I'm right here waitin buddy. You got this. Just take it easy."

"Should I call out to her, or try to be sneaky about it?" Levi asks, and I hate to admit I have no good answer to that.

"Levi, I'm sorry to ask you this but...do you own a gun?"

"No! No I'm afraid I sure don't. Look Bo, I really don't think Quade's exactly a dangerous man or anything. I don't know the details of the night he freaked Fiona out, but from what little he's said to me about it...he didn't mean to frighten her or anything. I don't know...I think he just showed up late and accidentally woke her out of a deep sleep, gave her a start. You know how that sort of thing goes."

"Mmm..." I grumble indiscernibly, "it sounds like that's open to debate Levi, and I don't know anything about it either because the woman don't tell me nothin. But what I'm concerned about is you walkin in on somebody who isn't expecting company and has no forewarning that it's you.

Assuming Quade isn't armed either, he could still strike you with a beam or somethin if you come up on him in the dark, you hear what I'm sayin?"

"Oh yeah Bo, I hear you loud and clear. So...what the heck am I doing in here then? To tell you the truth, this whole thing's giving me the creeps."

"Okay, okay, stay calm now. No need to get wound up over anything. Here's what you can do...call Fiona's name and say 'Hey it's Levi, we're worried about you. Are you here?' That way he'll know you're not a burglar, okay? And turn on as many lights as you can, as fast as you can navigate through the house."

I immediately regret this, knowing Quade could potentially hide or escape if he has that kind of forewarning. But unfortunately I'm not there, and I cannot, in good conscience, coax a guy into sneaking up on another man in the dark.

I listen with beagle ears for about ten minutes, as Levi cases the place before concluding he's the only one in the house.

Chapter 33

Fiona

It vaguely dawned on me that I was entering Quade's car, but I was too sick, weak, and faint to stop myself. Certain I'd collapse if I didn't sit immediately, it seemed I had no other choice. But when I open my eyes a moment later, my existence blasts into stark disorientation. Suddenly the world has become black as ink, and I have no idea where I am.

As I realize I'm no longer sitting upright, I begin violently thrashing...instinctively terrified that I've been stuffed into Quade's trunk. But my hysteria quietens once I notice the padded nature of the surface beneath me, and come to realize I can move all my limbs freely. I sit up to ponder what exactly happened tonight.

Clearly I was asleep or unconscious during the transport part of the evening. Which raises the question, where in God's name am I? And where is Quade? I feel around for my purse, to check the time, but it's nowhere to be found. I scoot off the edge of the bed and pat my way along the wall, searching for a light switch. After running my hands over what feels like a bookshelf, and then some other bulky furnishing I can't distinguish, I conclude I'm getting colder and start running my hands back the other way. Once I reach the bed again, I sweep my palms up and down the expanse of flat, plain wall...desperately searching for something I never find.

But what's much odder than failing to find a light switch in the pitch dark, is that I never come across anything resembling a door. I never feel a doorknob, a door frame... even a window frame. As I clamber back in what I believe is the direction of the bed, I almost faint from fright when I trip over the leg of something and a sizable object rattles off with a crash as it hits the floor.

"Quade!" I yell at the top of my lungs. "Quade, where are you?" As the sound of my own voice pierces the quiet, nausea sets back in...compounded by a headache like nothing I've ever felt. My foot hits the mysterious object just as I arrive at the edge of the bed. I sit back down with great relief, then reach to the floor and grope a little...quickly identifying the object as a globe. I set it around the corner of the bed, where I can't fall over it later.

A globe? I scoot back to the end of the bed and sweep my hands around until I scoop the globe up again. Turning it with one hand and running the other along its surface, I notice a couple of things. This globe is contoured, its mount has a precisely familiar size and shape, it has a chord sticking out of the bottom...because it's a lighted globe. My lighted globe. In the event the lightbulb didn't blow out when it hit the ground, and that I can grapple my way to an electrical outlet in this hellhole, I'll be in business.

I begin my miserable search through the darkness again, continually surprised my eyes aren't adjusting to something by now. I must be in a basement room, but I don't detect any odor of mold or familiar coolness of a basement. It's actually rather stuffy in here. Slowly making my way back to the area of the alleged desk, I begin frantically pawing the wall around it...in the space under its legs, to either side of it, between the wall and the desk frame itself. Nothing. Eventually I help myself onto the desk and methodically feel my way to the ceiling like a nincompoop.

My temples pierce like a cracking coconut when I let out a holler of frustration and drop to my knees on the desk, brushing over it one more time in search of anything with a plug I might have missed. But there's almost nothing on it at all, no computer or lamp, just a tape dispenser and what feels like a small metal file-organizing rack. With my head in this condition, I simply have to get back over to the bed. Too groggy to resort to screaming my lungs out or beating on walls, rest feels like a priority over rescue...strangely enough. After struggling across the room and back to my soft surface, I'm down for the count.

***

"Cookie, honey, wake up."

My head feels no better as I try to reassemble my awareness, piece by piece. Opening my eyes, I'm amazed to see...the lamplit room around me. And Quade hovering above, holding me like an infant, with tears in his eyes.

"Quade, you fucker!" I attempt to yell, as I instead break into a bawl, my fists clenched and gently pounding at his arms with the only trickle of strength I have. "What did you do to me? You left me here. Where were you? How did I get here?" I stammer out between sobs.

"Cookie, it's okay," Quade whispers, brushing my hair away from my face. "You got very sick last night and I brought you here to sleep."

"But, but...where's my purse? You left me in the dark. What is this place...there aren't any lights in here!" I yell, pushing myself away from him.

"I'm sorry honey. I don't have the house set up yet. I thought this would be the best room for you to sleep in. I...didn't want you to wake up and spoil the surprise by seeing the rest of the house without me."

"What?!"

"I had to run some errands. Cookie, it's almost eight in the morning."

"You had to run errands at eight in the...why didn't you take me to Holly's? Did you call her?" I immediately read the guilty 'no' on his face. "My God Quade, she must be frantic," I attempt to yell, though my head still won't let me.

"You're a grown woman Fiona. Since when do you have to call home to somebody?"

"Quade, I've been living at Holly's for over six months now. I *live* there...don't you get that? She could think we drove off a freaking cliff or something."

"Well...we do live in a town surrounded by cornfields, so...no real likelihood of that," he says with what looks like the beginnings of a smirk.

Just when I want to slap him for being such a smug ass, the screwdriver in my head twists itself again and I flop over in helpless agony.

"I'm sorry," Quade says under his breath.

"Sorry for...what?" I ask, barely recognizing my own voice as the words drip out of me like tiny, molten droplets of wax.

"Nothing," he says, tears welling up again. "Just everything."

As I slowly turn my head to face him, I hear the thunder of heavy footsteps coming up stairs. They sound massive, yet somehow distant. Like this house must be amply spacious.

"Who is that?" I manage as my eyes close again.

"I have no idea," Quade says irritably, apparently not ready to have our space intruded upon.

"Well geez Quade...it's probably Levi or someone... coming to find out why I never made it home."

"Sounds about a hundred pounds heavier than Levi," Quade whispers nervously, as though we have reason to fear.

And he's probably right. The footsteps sound nothing like Levi's, yet...everything in me wants this random intruder to fling open a door and discover us. As I open my eyes and gaze around woozily, I find that I was right last night in the darkness. There is no door. I have a million questions about this mysterious, impossible space we're in, but not enough energy or even clarity to form them into words. Does it make any sense that I'm hoping some random, unwieldy burglar will come bursting into this bizarre claustrophobic room? Not in the slightest, yet somehow I'm not at all rooting for our continued privacy.

The enormous steps slowly make their way closer, sounding as though they've stopped in each room and opened every door. Clearly there is either an attempted burglary taking place, or Holly's got the police searching for me. I glance at Quade, and his eyes meet mine with breathless intensity. He looks like a scared rabbit. For the longest minute, we remain locked in a stare-down...Quade's eyes telling me not to make one single sound, mine somehow giving away the fact that I'm thinking about it.

On a wild impulse I attempt to holler out, but Quade's hand seizes my mouth in an instant.

His face distorts into a grimace as his fingers dig painfully into my cheeks. A moment later, our strange island is surrounded by a confusion of noise...the muffled sound of hands frantically tapping and searching the outer walls.

"Fiona!"

Quade tightens his grip when I try to respond to the oddly familiar voice. It must be the cops, and for some reason Quade does not want them to find us.

"Fiona!" I hear again.

This time I let out a squelched scream through Quade's palm. It rumbles from the back of my throat, rendering it raw. Combined with my still persisting headache and general wooziness, my mind begins to play tricks on me. I have the most ridiculous notion that the stranger on the other side of the wall is Bo Thompson. I guess the cop's voice did sound a little like Bo, but why I would choose now to indulge in absurd fantasies is beyond me.

Quade whips his head around with a panicked expression, perhaps searching for a quick place to stash me, then releases me all at once when a leg the size of a tree trunk kicks through the drywall. My relief combines with utter shock as a huge man ducks to step into the perfectly rectangular cutout he kicked in the wall...apparently a pre-cut panel that had been invisible to me before. Once his face appears in the opening, I'm certain I'm going to pass out again.

My consciousness swirls into a spiral of confusion as I struggle to fully awaken. If all of this is a dream, then where am I actually sleeping? I should wake up any moment in my bed at Holly's, but something feels so real about the present. I decide I should try to stay in the dream forever when Bo Thompson stomps over and picks me up off the bed like a ragdoll.

And it's the darndest thing. Bo doesn't introduce himself to Quade, doesn't question him or his intentions, asks nothing about why I've been trapped inside a non-existent room. In fact, I'm positive Bo doesn't even so much as glance down at quivering Quade...because he maintains eye contact with me the entire time he's carrying me out of the hole and into what appears to be a large attic space.

My heavy head supported in the crook of Bo's arm, I continue to stare at him, entranced, as he navigates our way out of a sizable house. After several turns and two flights of stairs, I feel a blast of frigid air as he opens the door and continues carrying me to his truck. He lays me gently in the back and turns on the ignition, aiming the vents in my direction, but I'm still feverishly hot from my time in that room and...whatever illness I've come down with.

Unable to form words, I lie still...staring and blinking in and out of my delirium. Bo returns to the back seat, propping me against a lush, full sized pillow he's leaned against his thigh. When my head and neck relax into the softness, it feels like heaven. If there even was a pillow on last night's bed, I never found it in my state of exhaustion.

"Princess," he says, stroking my cheek and gazing down on me with clear, stern eyes. "What's happened to you, my love?"

"Bo," I whisper, reaching up to touch the face I couldn't believe was real only moments ago. "I don't know...I...my purse...we have to find it."

"Hang on darlin, I'll head right back in and fetch it. Do you know where you left it? Is it in that room?"

"No...I don't know. I haven't seen it. I woke up in there...I don't know what happened," I say in a voice that's so faint and weak I can hardly hear myself.

"You seem very, very sick princess. I'm gonna leave you out here with the heat blasting for just a minute, and then I'll be back with your purse, okay?"

I nod a miniscule affirmation and then Bo's gone, leaving me to wonder how he'll extract my purse from Quade. I can't hide my surprise when he arrives back with it in a couple of minutes.

"What happened? He just gave it to you?" I ask.

"Well did you think he was gonna say no to me?" he asks in reply, making me feel silly as it dawns on me that no man would refuse to cooperate with Bo Thompson. "Now," he says as he restores my beloved purse, kisses me on the forehead, and moves up front to the driver's seat, "let's get you to Holly's where you can get warm and rested. Why don't you try to tell me a story about last night. You came down with a little flu, I take it?"

My first attempt to respond fails as my lips go rubbery and my mind goes blank. I only wish I knew how to answer. "I guess that's what happened," I eventually manage. "We ate sushi and I became very suddenly ill, right as we were leaving. Quade wanted to show me the new house and I must have passed out. I remember sitting in his car, and then I woke up...hours later, in that room. It was dark with no windows...I was alone...couldn't find the way out. I passed out with a headache. When I woke up a while ago, Quade was there. My head's throbbing."

"Wow Fiona, you must have eaten somethin really off. How much did you have to drink?"

"Nothing at all. A little black tea, no sake, no alcohol," I reply, as I limply riffle through my purse to find everything still intact.

"Has this happened to you before? Blacking out from food poisoning like that?"

"Never. It's the strangest experience I've ever had... almost."

Bo takes a heavy breath and then goes quiet for a while, during which time I begin to formulate all the questions I have for him. But somehow nothing seems pressing except the fact that I woke up in a hidden room with an ex-husband who desperately didn't want us to be discovered.

"So, Quade got himself a new house, aye?" Bo asks with trepidation.

"Not exactly," I respond. "He sold his old house and bought this one instead."

"Sounds like a new house to me," he says with a slight tone of amusement.

"Yes but, the house he sold was my house...the house I lived in. He bought the new house for me."

"That house I just dragged you out of is yours?" Bo asks with something between surprise and alarm.

"No. Nothing is mine. This is what Quade does. He took the other house away...now he's bought me a new house... also in his name. This is how he plans to run my life forever, Bo." I cringe at the pathetitude of my own words as I say them.

After the appropriate social introductions, Holly hands me a glass of Alka Seltzer Plus and Bo's warm, pulsating arms scoop me up and carry me off to my bedroom. Although I currently couldn't detect a sexual bone in my body, I don't want Bo to leave. I want him to tuck in behind me and wrap me up in those pythons, breathe against my neck the way he did one night so long ago. What I'd believed was a fading memory is now flooding back to me in full color.

Respectfully, Bo tucks the blankets up around me, kisses my forehead again, and pulls the curtains closed before quietly shutting the door and heading back downstairs. Too weak to protest, I close my eyes and sink into another deep sleep. Only this time when I awaken, my headache is gone and my brain seems to have been switched back on.

My eyes pop open wide, and I snap to an upright position...trying to add some chronological order to the jumble of events in my recent memory. I was with Quade, I passed out...and then I had a series of nonsensical dreams. Images of an impossibly small, black room mingle with the dark vibes of malicious intent. And then there was a most lucid series of images...Bo Thompson, the unquestionable love of my life, literally bursting through the wall of the room and carrying me away. Some words exchanged that I can't remember, and then the dream fades out.

I rise to open the curtains and let in what looks like dim, early evening light. How many hours or days have I been sleeping? When did Quade drive me back to Holly's? Why did I pass out? That last question ricochets off the walls of my mind like an echo. I sit back on the bed and drop my head into my hands to think. Images of Quade come back to me...me and Quade, inside the dark, hidden room. And then the feeling of malicious intent again, followed by Quade's sickening, flimsy apologies. 'I'm sorry,' he'd said. 'Sorry for what?' I remember asking in the dream. 'Sorry for everything.'

But the oddest thing, despite the confusion of having a carousel of bizarre 'memories' injected into my head, is that I don't remember ever relieving myself of whatever made me so sick. I'm quite clear that I never vomited or even visited a restroom. I simply...blacked out and ended up back at home.

Next, it occurs to me that I'm starving. I'll go down and see what Holly and Levi are doing for dinner. I'm sure they can help to fill in some missing details of my night out with Quade. Quade. Night out with Quade. Sushi with Quade. Sushi and hot tea. Quade bought me a new house. I had sushi and tea with Quade and he bought me a new house. I was sitting in Quade's car. Why was I sitting in Quade's car? Why would I ever get into Quade's car? I was going to drive my own car to the house...I'd insisted. I clearly remember insisting on driving myself that night. How did Quade get me into...I went unconscious in the front seat of Quade's Royce. I remember his face as he opened the passenger door and guided me onto the seat...calm, unconcerned. I suddenly fell so terribly ill that I couldn't make it to my own car and Quade didn't even look phased? Quade didn't ask me why I changed my mind about riding in his car? He just...opened the door...and I sat my ass down in the passenger seat and fell into a deep, black sleep?? Oh yeah...because that makes total sense that that happened. Of course that happened!

The dimness of my room lights up red, as a familiar wall of rage clouds my vision. I squeeze my eyes closed and drop my forehead into my hands again, randomly conjuring up a series of insignificant details. I see myself returning from the Shokai restroom to the sight of Quade topping off my hot tea. 'Thank you,' I say, 'but I don't need another cup of caffeine tonight. Plus, I had the sugar level just where I wanted it.' Then I proceed to nervously demolish the tea during our meal, just for something extra to do with my hands. And I never had been able to get the sugar quite right in that second cup. It just had a bitterness that wouldn't quit. My heartbeat pounds in my ears, as anger transmutes into total alarm, then pounds even harder when adrenaline hits me like a fist. A familiar voice rumbles deeply from the hallway, followed by heavy footsteps.

"...go check on her," I hear just before my door cracks ever so slightly open. "Princess, you up? May I come in?"

My body turns to jelly and I melt back onto the bed, as Bo's face appears around the edge of my bedroom door. Bo Thompson is in Iowa, in Holly's house, in my bedroom... right now. And he's wearing the exact shirt he wore in last night's...dream.

I have no words. I simply extend my arms from my reclined position, and Bo Thompson is suddenly lying parallel to me...hugging me flush against him as he strokes my back and whispers my name repeatedly, like a mantra.

"Fiona...Fiona...Fiona...are you all better? I knew somethin was wrong. I knew I had to find you. Please try to tell me what's goin on...why you were in that room. I have a real bad feelin that I just can't shake this mornin," he says, the bass of his voice reverberating through his chest and into mine.

A horrific idea of what really happened is gradually dawning on me, as I thaw out of my daze. But ultimately I feel safe, unmolested, and eager to put the experience to rest. If Quade was on a mission to tamper with me, I could see in his eyes this morning that he failed...shame and regret radiating from his apology. And what's more important, my clothing's intact and my deepest intuition tells me nothing happened.

Bo pulls back just enough to look at me.

"Bo," I say, as I reach up to touch his face. "Bo," I say again, barely able to think any other sound. "How are you here? When did you come here? What's going on?" I ask to divert him from the immediate situation. If I were to express my suspicions about last night's 'illness', Bo would undoubtedly take the kind of action that would land him behind bars...considering local law enforcement wouldn't lay a hand on Quade.

"Well darlin, I just had to come and see you. That's all. Just couldn't wait any longer. I tried to call you last night on the drive up, and when Holly told me—"

Bo pauses for breath when I lift my face to his and begin nibbling along the edge of his jawline. The intoxicating aroma of his skin and hair mingle with faint sweat, a novel yet familiar smell that ignites my nostalgia. I can only hope this isn't a dream.

The myriad reasons for battening down my stable life are evaporating with each inhale of Bo's breath, as his face hovers inches from mine...gazing into me with the pleading look I remember. As though I'm the most rare and precious thing he's ever beheld.

"I can't believe you're here," I whisper. "I thought I'd never see you again...thought surely I'd driven you a—"

Bo's lips find mine before I can finish, and he takes me back to paradise. A place so sublime, I can't fathom why I thought having a home and business could possibly compete. I must have been insane. Nothing is as good as this.

Chapter 34

Bo

I don't want to take advantage of a woman who's been ill, hasn't even seen me in half a year, and obviously isn't sure how she feels about me, but Fiona's sendin every possible signal that she wants this...right now. The way her feet delicately coil around mine, strokin my insteps with her toes, her fingertips at the nape of my neck, the escalation of her breathing. Her breathing...

I match her intensity with my own, our noses and mouths playing with the space between us, teasing out the connection and then locking it together. A beautiful dance between senses. She's everything I remember, and her absolute abandon tells me she's all mine. But then...I recall thinking that before, only to run headlong into her wall of unwillingness.

Casting that thought aside, I go instead with Fiona's cues. She arches her breasts toward the ceiling as I pull her sweater up over her head, then gives me the look of longing when I reach down to unfasten her jeans. As I stand at the foot of the bed and begin peeling them off, she bucks wildly, wiggling out of them and thrusting in anticipation.

"Bo, I can't believe you're here," she says again. "I can't believe it."

She reaches up to pull me into another kiss, before I can get my own clothes off, wrapping her legs around me and grinding closer.

"Woman, you didn't think I was gonna let you slip away now did you?"

"I'm so glad you didn't," Fiona responds, reaching down and grabbing me.

She clambers for me when I roll away to tug off my clothes, then moans resoundingly at the site. I hop back onto the bed, straddling her to unclasp her lacy, white bra, while her hands roam everywhere...palming the muscles of my chest and stroking down my torso, her ravishing mouth contorted into an expression of awe.

I've left her panties for last, hesitant to take her again without stating my full intentions. Cupping her incredible tits and rubbing them in gentle circles, I attempt to form coherent thoughts. But talkin really ain't what I wanna do right now, and it seems impossibly awkward with Fiona buckin around underneath me.

"Fiona, darlin," I start in the best I can.

Her eyes focus on me, but her writing does not let up. "Yes Bo," she responds with expectancy.

Good, she's in the right space. "I'm takin you away from here. We'll start up a new store that's all under your name. Down in Fort Myers, okay? The Florida sun will work with your complexion." The words spill out, quicker than I'd intended, yet Fiona doesn't flinch.

"Okay Bo," she says with lust in her eyes, "that sounds perfect."

I know Fiona cannot be taken on her word at this moment, but at least my intentions are out on the table. Fair enough. Finally I touch her, my fingers barely grazing her hot, drenched flesh through the silky fabric of her panties. Her eyes roll back and she loses herself in desire, begging me now to enter.I carefully rim the edges of the lace with my fingers, slowly teasing them down and off of her while she pleads for me to hurry. When I stop to visit her exquisite parted region, she quickly pulls me up to meet her. The goddess wants me inside her, and I'm honored to oblige.

My hugeness slips into her, tightly but completely, as she grabs my back and cries out. I gaze down at the miracle in my arms, the woman I have longed for, too precious to be believed. Yet I can hear, smell, and feel her realness all around me. She is woman, and she is mine.

I kiss the tears off her face as I make love to her for the next hour, healing her wounded heart, cleansing away all the hurt that's been done to her. I can feel her pain as she trembles in my arms, vulnerable at last...in a state of real surrender.

I long to know Fiona through words, but I do know her at the deepest cellular level. Somehow I always have. She is the prize I've worked my whole life for, and I'll never stop working for Fiona. I get up in the mornin to create a world that's good enough for a woman so fine.

And here she lies limply in my arms, still moaning... ever so softly, in the aftermath of our crescendo. With some difficulty, I remain silent despite the thoughts that are re-entering my mind. Is she really gonna walk away from a new house? Admittedly, it was a nice one. And what exactly is her relationship with this sniveling rodent, Quade? I'm sickened as images of his jealous face take over my thoughts, cowering and guilt-ridden. Not what I wanna be thinkin right now.

I try to refocus on the goddess before me, but my discontent only escalates at the site of her. The way she's been caged for so long...it ain't right. Does she even know who she is anymore?

Fiona's eyes blink open and she speaks, as though having heard my very thoughts. "Bo," she says with a welcoming smile, "how long are you here? Where are you staying?"

"That's all perfectly up to you, darlin," I answer as I reach down to massage her irresistible legs. "I've left the farm with my help for however many days I'm away. I can count on those guys for anything."

Fiona stares at me as though wantin to say somethin she can't quite formulate. "Bo," she says after a long pause, "I'm not moving into that house. I'll never set foot in there again."

"Well alright then. That's an awful nice house, but I agree you shouldn't," I respond, resisting the temptation to express how proud I am of her resoluteness.

I wanna wrap up the details I mentioned earlier, about her comin to live with me, but I'm afraid of soundin too abrupt. I've learned to take baby steps with Fiona.

"Just tell me one thing," she says, "You carried me out of that house and went back in for something, right?"

"Well yes, darlin. I went back in for your purse," I reply, dismayed that she was sick enough to forget that detail.

"Oh yes, I remember. So...what did Quade say to you? How did he react to everything?"

"Well now that's the weird thing, Fiona. When I went back up, he was still standin in that little room. He hadn't moved an inch and he looked like he was in a total state of shock." Fiona's lips spread into a grin at my answer. "And well, I guess he thought I was The Terminator or somethin. When I stepped back in through that wall panel, he started shakin and put his hands up like he was about to beg me to spare his life." Fiona barks out a laugh and claps her hands. "It took me about two seconds to spot your purse, sittin just behind Quade on a desk back there. I walked straight toward him to fetch it and he looked like he was pissin himself, hands spread up in the air, head shakin back and forth. I believe the guy thought I was comin back up there to kill him...and that sure made me wonder what it is he was feelin so guilty about. I walked right up on him, reached past him to grab the purse, and then turned around and walked out while I was ahead. Cause I'll tell you right now, my fist was all balled up ready to punch him one for good measure. I do not like the guy."

Fiona seems beside herself with mirth, hands over her mouth tryin not to laugh...but she can't control it.

"Now I've got a question for you, darlin," I say, eager to run with the opportunity Fiona's created. "Why in God's name did Quade have you stashed away in an attic closet, too sick to even call home, instead of bringin you back here to your own bedroom? And why didn't he call Holly? Levi called law enforcement with a missing person report last night...fat lot of good that did."

Fiona's face ripples through the full spectrum of petrified, to worried, to somethin surprisingly bordering on guilt. "Because Quade's a total ass," she finally blurts out, much to my satisfaction. "When I first started waking up, he told me he'd stashed me in that room because he didn't want me to see the rest of the house without him."

"So, let me get this straight...Quade left you, sick, in an empty house all by yourself?" I don't know whether I'm more disgusted by his irresponsibility, or relieved that he didn't spend the night in there with her.

"Well, he said he left in the morning to run some errands...I really don't know Bo. I have no excuses for Quade at this point. I thought he was the best friend I'd ever had, but now I'd be happy to never hear his name again," Fiona says, her voice cracking on that last syllable.

Her usual bitterness has lost its edge to a sorrow I can hardly fathom, the betrayal of a friend she was once married to. I hope she now realizes what a better place she'll be in without Quade, a man whose total demeanor reeks of a lack of integrity.

"Fiona, princess," I say, scooping her back into my arms, "I know you're your own person, and a very strong woman, but there ain't anything you need to say about last night, is there?" She looks slightly affronted, as though being accused, so I decide to rephrase. "I mean, there wasn't any harm that came to you...other than being sick, that Quade would have inflicted?"

"Bo, what are you implying?" she asks forwardly, but without hostility.

I decide to speak frankly. "I'm only implyin that it don't look good to walk in on a man with a deliriously ill woman, in a room that's damn near impossible to find, on a night when she never showed up home and nobody ever called to share the reason why. It looks incriminating, if you really wanna know."

Fiona nods in agreement, offering no defense of Quade. "He absolutely should have called, but I wouldn't worry about it. Quade's ability to make decisions just gets switched into reverse around me anymore. He'll choose the wrong thing to do, every time. I don't know how to get him out of my life, but I'd walk away tomorrow if I could."

"Well about what I said earlier—"

"Where is Holly? Is she home? I don't even know what time it is. I really should talk to her," Fiona cuts in before I can finish, in her usual goal-oriented manner.

I immediately sense that she's put up her old familiar barrier, as though the past couple hours didn't even happen. She's selectively forgettin what I told her about comin to

Florida, but she's got all the time in the world. I've decided I'll set up camp in Fairfield until she's ready to leave with me. No way I would drive outta here after whatever went down last night. Fiona's gotta make a decision, and I'm here to help her make the right one. Even if she rejects me in the end, I've gotta get her to examine the truth of her situation... from all sides.

Chapter 35

Fiona

In my immense struggle to keep from spilling the beans about my suspicions, I feel that I have to get out of Bo's space for a while. Right now I want to collapse on his chest, pound my fists and scream. No, I do not believe I was compromised by my ex-husband last night, but yes...certainly his intentions were sordid. If I were to tell Bo I was roofied...he'd either dismember Quade beyond recognition, or be made to feel impotent when our local police laughs him out of their office. Neither is an outcome I'm willing to risk.

But the more clarity I get around last night, the more I recognize that Quade has a sick obsession with me. I'm certain he drugged me, then essentially caged me while trying to figure out how to undo our regrettable situation.

And that room...in my new house? As a windowless and doorless room, it must have been something that was built into another storage type space...a preplanned area to hide or trap me inside. This had to have taken some serious forethought on Quade's part.

I could go mad thinking about the level of sickness that would drive him to pursue something like that. Visions of being chopped to pieces flood my mind, as I quickly kiss Bo on the cheek and race downstairs to distract myself with Holly.

When I find her in the dining room, she rushes up from her mug of tea and embraces me like I've been gone a year. "Fifi, sweetie, how are you?" she asks. "You were so sick when Bo brought you home this morning...that must have been one awful headache. Did you sleep it all off up there?"

"Yes, somehow I did. It was something else."

"Next time I see Quade I'm going to slap him across the face. I can't believe he wouldn't think to call and tell us what was going on."

"Well you know, he insists that I'm an adult and shouldn't need to check in with people. I tried to explain that after six months of sleeping here...you'd be a little concerned. But we didn't even have that talk till this morning. I was out like a light last night."

"Poor thing," Holly says, pulling me in for another hug. "Can I make you tea?" she asks.

"Sure, I'd love that," I lie, suddenly wanting to return to Bo now that Holly's seen me alive.

"So," she starts in, as she places a tea bag in my mug and refires the kettle, "were you as surprised as us when you-know-who showed up?"

"Oh yeah...completely. I knew nothing about this...still know nothing. Do you have any idea what compelled him to drive all the way up here?" I ask, happy that she settled onto my next topic of interest.

"I don't know! You mean he hasn't explained that yet? What exactly did you two do up there all afternoon?" Holly asks with a grin.

"Okay okay, to be fair...I mostly slept." She's not buying it. "Mostly," I reiterate with a knowing smile.

"Fiona, seriously, that's the man you've been avoiding and putting off all year? Do you have any idea? I mean...I don't even know where to start..."

"What?" I prod.

"Fiona, that's one of the most attractive men I've ever met. Not just his looks...his voice, his conduct, his integrity. Levi called the police last night...as futile as you might imagine, and then went to that house to see if you and Quade were there. We'd suspected Quade's purchase on it. Anyway, he couldn't see into the garage so he gave up," she tells me, and I'm riveted to be getting all the little details I'd started wondering about. "So guess who prompted him to break a window and go in looking for you."

"Really? But—"

"But Levi didn't find you. Right. So what we didn't know was that Bo was already in his truck driving up here... must have been driving like a madman. A few hours later he comes pounding on our door, ringing the doorbell. Levi flies downstairs and opens the door to this gigantic man, and he's like...are you with the police? Honestly, it scared Levi senseless. He thought they were here to notify us of something we wouldn't want to hear. And then Bo goes 'what's the address of that house? I'm going over there to find Fiona', and just like that...he disappeared and came back with you draped across his arms not a half hour later."

My mouth gapes as I listen to Holly's account of my actual rescue. No wonder she's taken with Bo. The guy really is a superhero...and I just...slept with him. Again. What have I been thinking all these months? If only I weren't so goal-oriented, so business forward. I just can't wrap my brain around deprioritizing the store, and I really have no time for a relationship.

I change the subject for the duration of our teatime because I don't know how to continue dodging Holly's attempts to hook me up with Bo. But now that I've experienced him again, not to mention he's probably saved my life as I know it, I'm not sure how to dodge my own mental bullets. I don't want to deal with or even see Quade, ever again. There can no longer be any pretense of civility between me and a man who would commit unspeakable atrocities against me.

Perhaps his sense of shame will cause him to back down and allow me to keep my store, without any interference. But some part of me has dislodged from all of that. I can't imagine even setting foot in the place again. I don't want to see anything that reminds me of Quade, that feels like part of a joint effort between us. I need a long vacation.

"What's Bo doing anyway? Is he still upstairs?" Holly finally asks, interrupting my endless dark tunnel of thoughts.

"I'm sure he is. He wanted to give us our space since I hadn't seen you this morning. I remember drinking Alka-Seltzer, but I have no idea who gave it to me."

"That would be me," Holly says, raising her hand. "You were really far gone Fiona. It scared me. Bo told me you said you didn't drink anything...must have been some seriously bad sushi. You should probably report that to the restaurant."

"Quade ate all the same rolls I did," I respond with a sober tone. "I'd better go check on Bo, let him know it's okay to come out," I say to break the tension, then walk away leaving Holly perplexed.

I find Bo lounging upstairs in a sitting area of the hallway, slouched back with phone in hand.

"Hey Big Bo," I purr to him, already longing to drag him back to bed. "What are your plans?"

"Plans?" he asks. "No plans except bein here for you. As I said, I got my guys takin care of business on the farm. I was just now checkin in with them. I've already got a room booked so I can stay out of everyone's hair."

This news shatters me, though I refuse to show it.

"I hope you'll consider joining me...maybe offer us a little more privacy than we have here," Bo adds, to my relief.

"Yes! Yes," I respond, checking my enthusiasm. "Let me pack an overnight bag and tell Holly quick."

Half an hour later we're in an outdated hotel, ignoring the gaudy smell of deodorizers sprayed over musty old carpeting. "I'm sorry I couldn't come up with somethin better. Slim pickins on hotels around here."

"That's quite alright Bo. It's about the best you can do in a town this size," I respond, reaching out my arms to lure him into them.

Bo's got that familiar apprehensive look, like he wants to talk before getting carried away, and I know we have a million things to cover. But I still don't really know what to expect. I've tried to forget that he mentioned me going with him to Florida, but I have to admit I've been turning it over in my mind. Nonetheless, I won't be the one to bring it back up.

"How you feelin?" he asks as he slips my shoes off my feet. "Do you think you could get any more sleep after a full day of it?"

"Yes, believe it or not. I feel like I could sleep for days on end. But I'm perfectly fine other than that," I reply, stretching my toes and then relaxing them into Bo's warm hands.

"Lay back and close your eyes," he says.

I do so, and soon my awareness drains into a drip-line of pleasure from my feet to my head. Within minutes, I'm hazing in and out of sleep until the blackness wins over. The next time I awaken, the bedside clock reads ten a.m. I'm tucked under the blankets with my clothing still on, Big Bo breathing peacefully by my side.

I gaze at him in the bright light stream filtering through the room's thin, low-coverage curtains. My normal energy levels seem to finally be restored, and the sight of him fills me with intense desire. If only he weren't such a gentleman. I wish he'd woken me up last night, as I've got to rush over to the store this morning.

I linger for as many minutes as possible before forcing myself out of bed. Soundlessly, I slide just close enough to feel the warmth of Bo's breath. It dawns on me that he must have gone a good thirty-six hours without sleep. Not to mention the concentration it would have taken to make a trip that long in a single night. The greatness of this man seems increasingly impossible the more I think about him. Maybe Holly was right all along. Maybe I should have thrown everything to the wind and allowed a long-distance relationship with the guy.

As much as I want to 'accidentally' wake Bo up, I slip out of the sheets and get changed like a ninja. Knowing he'll still be here this afternoon sets me up for a most pleasant day. But a sickening sensation wracks all the way to my gut when I turn my phone on to find it blown up with calls from Quade. What could he possibly think he could say to me now, that would make anything remotely okay between us?

As I start my car, my mind charges furiously through all the things Quade has done *in spite* of my good behavior. He rigged my house, devastated any semblance of privacy in my life, accepted my inheritance...which he could have talked my father out of if he'd tried to, sold the house without asking...roofied me and trapped me in a creepy room!? I still can't wrap my brain around that one, don't even want to.

By the time I pull into Fiona's, something else comes to mind with instant clarity. Quade tapped my phone and blamed it on Ulysses, and I bought it hook, line, and sinker. The continued occasional presence of Ulysses, in this town, has been more annoying than creepy. Why would I believe for a moment that Quade is innocent about anything? Quade is a liar who would stop at nothing. Of course he wasn't going to come clean when I called him out on my tapped phone. He had a perfect alibi.

My disgust only increases when I remember the false sense of safety I felt, as Quade announced with concern that Ulysses must be my phone tapper. Maybe I still wasn't ready to come to grips. My ex husband, and best friend of seventeen years, is a complete creep. Too much testosterone drugs gone to his brain or whatever...he is not the man I married, nor the one I cared for all this time.

What I struggle the most with is when, exactly, this transition began taking place. Thinking back, Quade's general demeanor had been icking me out for quite some time...but not too long. Come to think about it, his attitude changes probably were synonymous with the physical changes his body underwent. At first I felt so proud of him for deciding to whip himself into shape, and then it started to feel like he was flirting with me. Something he didn't even know how to do when we first met.

I'm still reeling from this train of thought when I find Maxine in the back cooler room.

"Maxine, how's it going with the Endrigo account?" I ask, feigning normality.

"It's going great. I pretty much have everything sketched out already, just have to make a few more decisions about what types of blooms to use," she replies.

"Great. Wanna show me what you've got?"

"Yes! And I also need to talk to you about something. Personal. Something personal that affects my work life. Something that pertains to me and you."

For some inexplicable reason, a sense of dread overcomes me at those words. I wait, in stunned silence, for Maxine to continue...fearing the worst.

"Um," she says, guiltily clearing her throat, "should I show you my sketches first?"

"What is it Maxine?" I ask, with approximately zero patience remaining in me this morning.

"Well, on New Year's Eve, Ivan asked if I would move in with him."

I'm confounded.

"We've been pondering our future a lot, and trying to figure out how my career fits into it. Ivan's offered to put forth the funds to help me kickstart my own business, so I can ultimately leave the shop and become more mobile. Maybe open a store in London or Chicago."

"Okay," I respond, "so you're saying you wanna quit here and go somewhere else?"

"Well, yeah. You could put it like that. It doesn't need to be right away, just whenever you find someone you're comfortable replacing me with. I can train them before I move to Chicago. All my stuff's in storage since I've been in Zenovia's house, so that won't soak up my time."

During her diatribe my phone vibrates with a text. Great. My lunch meeting has been canceled. And hey, you know what? Who cares? Why not have as little responsibility in my life as possible now. I've got no home or future finances, just lost my star employee, and I'm sure Quade was going to pull the carpet any minute anyway. Whatever was I thinking?

"That won't be necessary," I inform her. "You're free to go whenever you want. Just let me know if you need me to get someone to take over the Endrigo wedding."

"Oh no! I'll definitely finish everything I've got open first. We didn't even discuss a timetable on this, so I'm very flexible."

"Up to you," I say with a deadpan expression, as I make tracks for the door. I'm not about to give Maxine the satisfaction of believing I care, yet I really don't know what I'd do if she'd bailed out on that wedding. "I'm out of time now, got an early lunch meeting," I lie, "so you'll have to show me the sketches on Friday. Remember to do closing and lock up today because Laura won't be back in till morning."

Suddenly glad about the canceled meeting, I burst out the door and strut to my car. I've got the whole afternoon ahead of me now. In fact, I've got my whole life ahead of me, Fiona's Flowers and Quade and my house and my phone and my privacy and my inheritance be damned. I've got Bo Thompson snoozing in a hotel right now, waiting for me to show up and turn him on like a power plant. I'm on my way, Big Bo, I'm on my way.

Chapter 36

Bo

I'm still sleepin like a bear when Fiona steps through the door, as I wasn't expectin her back until after her lunch meetin.

"Sweetheart, I'm sorry I'm such a slob," I say, pushin myself upright in a sudden state of alertness. Fiona gets my blood flowin faster than anything ever has.

"Bo, do you have any idea how glorious it is to walk into a dim room, containing nothing but a bed, and find you sprawled across it in a state of partial undress?" she asks, beginning to laugh as she falls into my arms.

"Oh woman," I grumble as I pull her tight to me.

I wanted to brush my teeth, but already she's kissin me, giggling and smiling...lookin happy and relaxed at long last.

And somethin tells me it ain't cause she had such an amazin mornin at work either.

"I thought you had a noon meeting."

"Oh...I blew it off. I couldn't wait that long to see you like this."

"You blew off your meeting?" I ask with pleasant surprise.

"No, not really," she answers as she nuzzles me like a puppy. "It got canceled. But I wasn't disappointed," she says just before losin herself in our kisses.

Fiona's long fingers and hands move sensually over my chest hair as I lift the pretty, pink dress up over her head, exposing another beautiful lace bra and panty set. I pause to take in the sight of her before removing the rest. She's such a vision, I could buy Fiona lingerie sets for a lifetime. But I've brought no such bribes with me to Iowa. I need her to take a leap of faith on non-material terms.

We remove the rest of each other's clothes with vigor and make love like we're the only two residents in the hotel. Fiona's every bit as wild as I've imagined her to be...takin charge and climbing on top, ridin me hard while she belts out her guttural cries of satisfaction, slappin my back and pullin my hair with exactly the right amount of pressure. The woman's a rare talent.

She glides into a frenzy of pent up energy and finishes me in under an hour, sooner than I would have liked but I couldn't hold her eagerness at bay.

I soak up Fiona's radiant afterglow, spoonin and caressing her until her breathin slows. She appears to sleep for maybe ten minutes, then opens her eyes and turns around to face me. I'm a little jarred by her expression...so different from before. Her typical look of concern is back, and I wonder what's on her mind.

"Bo?" she asks before I can figure out where to start.

"Yes buttercup?"

"There's something we haven't discussed that seems really odd we haven't."

"Yes?" I ask her with a smile, knowin where this is goin.

"What in the heck are you doing in Fairfield? Why did you drive all the way up here in the first place?" she asks with curiosity rather than confrontation.

"Just like I said, I came up here to see the woman I haven't had much luck tryin to talk on the phone to."

"Well...but...that's a long drive. What if I'd been too busy? What if I hadn't been available?"

I attempt to formulate a serious answer but find myself laughing instead. "Then I reckon I'd have done somethin to make myself irresistible. Like, you know, show up at the store wearin my best jeans or somethin," I answer with a smirk.

"Oh you," she says, pawing at my cheek. "You think I'm that easy, huh?"

"Now I didn't say nothin about you bein easy, darlin. All I'm sayin is...I'm that hard to resist."

At this Fiona breaks character, and all the tension disappears from her face as she giggles into my neck... tickling the back of it with her fingernails.

"You scoundrel," she teases. "So how long do I have you here, really?"

"About however long it takes me to talk you into runnin off with me." Fiona giggles again, but I remain sober...lookin her in the eyes so she can feel my sincerity. "I really mean it Fiona. I came up here to tell you somethin serious," I say, watchin her every reaction. "I know this is gonna sound premature with all the time that's kept us apart, but I need you to hear somethin I wasn't even gonna try to say on the phone."

I can clearly see apprehensiveness on her face now, but this is my only chance. I have to speak the truth, yet it suddenly feels awkward in a way I hadn't expected. Fiona's moods turn on a dime, somethin I've long been aware of, and it's difficult to express myself through the onslaught of her challenging nature.

"Fiona?" I manage to say.

She responds with a raised eyebrow and slight cock of her head, as if waitin impatiently for me to make a fool of myself.

"I love you Fiona."

In my mental rehearsal of this moment, those words bubbled out like refreshing spring water. But the reality of her blank expression has filled me with a kind of fear I've never felt before. An eternity passes while I wait for some kind of response...anything.

"Bo," Fiona says at last. But not in her bedroom voice. There's an undeniably hard edge to my name comin off her lips this time. Her wall is back up in all its titanium glory. "Bo, you're a good man. No...you're a wonderful man...a wonderful...man. But my life is full of the kind of complexity and drama...emotions...you should never get involved with."

"Is that so?" I ask, not meanin to sound uppity.

"Yes Bo, it is so!" she retorts with just enough moisture in her eyes to keep me from losin my cool. "I'm losing everything...have already lost it. Everything! And all I can do now is fight to keep something going for myself that I can be proud of. I'm not a farmgirl Bo. You can't just stick me out on a piece of flowery dirt somewhere and expect me to thrive. I have goals. Things to accomplish. I have to push forward no matter what, and if it means starting everything over from scratch...that's exactly what I'm going to do."

Fiona's words strike me like darts, but I respond with all the sweetness I can muster. "Well then darlin, if you're willin to start from scratch...why not come open up a nice new store right there in Fort Myers?" I ask.

"Oh Bo, you're a wonderful, simple man...aren't you. Wouldn't it just be so simple for me to uproot and begin a whole new life in—"

"Uproot what Fiona? Uproot the life you don't even have anymore?"

"Excuse me?" she says with a blaze in her eyes.

"Well darlin, you do the math," I say, digging my own hole deeper by the word. "If you're not gonna move into another one of Quade's houses...I guess you'll just be roommates with Holly and Levi forever then?" She crosses her arms with an indignant stare, but doesn't offer any answer. So I take the opportunity to continue at my own risk. "And you think I'm too simple to handle an emotional woman?"

"Bo, that's not what I—"

"Lemme tell you somethin about me and emotions. About when I was fourteen in a fierce lightnin storm, Pappa strugglin to get a hysterical new mustang into a stall between claps of thunder. Me watchin from the dining room windows when I see a great big bolt hit the roof of the barn and spread out over it in every direction, engulfing it in flames a second later. I run out and take off runnin towards the barn, but I can see through the open door that they're in the back corner pinned by that stallion. Everywhere the hay ignites like gasoline, all of them surrounded by a blinding blaze of yellow within the first minute. And all I can do is stand out in the rain and watch my parents disappear. The only saving grace...I couldn't hear them over the screamin of the horses."

The horror on Fiona's face tells me I've said too much, her eyes glazed over and hands coverin her mouth. And I don't know where the hell all that came from anyway, things I haven't thought of in decades...details I've never uttered to anyone before. Ever.

"I'm sorry darlin," I say in a softened tone, finally snappin out of my trance. "I should never have brought all that up...I'm sorry—"

"Bo," she cries, breakin down like a dam and reachin out for me. "I'm the one who's sorry," she says between tears. "You're the most amazing man I've ever met and I can't possibly deserve someone like you." Fiona's havin a full blown sob now, a monumental event I thought I'd never see...and I'm so honored to witness it.

"That ain't true Fiona. You deserve everything a woman could ever have—"

"No...no!" she cries in a state of near hysterics, pushing me away and shaking her head violently.

And then her heart explodes open with the painful revelation I always knew was buried deep inside her. "My daddy doesn't love me! My daddy doesn't love me! My daddy doesn't love me!" And there it is. Fiona pounds her fists against my chest as she screams.

I let her go to exhaustion until she crumples over beside me, calm like the aftermath of a hailstorm. I bring Fiona the tissue box and begin strokin her hair and back. She thanks me shyly, blows her nose a couple times, and then collapses back down...curling around me to receive my rubs.

"I'm your daddy now," I tell her, and the faintest smile forms at the corner of her mouth.

Chapter 37

Fiona

Never had I thought Fort Myers would be so quaint, with its historic brick buildings and cobblestone streets. And then when you want ritzy...voila. A handful of skyscrapers, and row after row of beautiful waterside restaurants and bars. Incidentally, it's a perfect location for starting up my new store, whenever I get the itch to do it.

But even all that pales in comparison to my first experience of seeing Bo's farm. A rainbow planted across the countryside...and the farmhouse of my dreams. Not that I normally dream of farmhouses, but had I enough sense to do so sooner...this is the one I would have envisioned. And what turns me on most is the thought of Bo doing all this with the strength of his own hands. The lighting, the fireplace, the kitchen island and backsplash, all the detailing in the bathrooms and bedrooms, the gorgeously restored hardwoods throughout.

I spy out the living room windows as Bo finishes his evening field work, checking on each precious row before calling it a night, then washes up under the outside water pump. Although I have little experience with cooking, I've always had a slight knack that I wanted to explore further, and Bo's turned out to be the perfect mentor. I get butterflies as I watch him stride toward the house to dine on my pasta dinner, featuring sausage, fresh garden kale, and a white wine parmesan sauce. I've had little appetite lately, but I'll pick at my pasta between stolen glances at Bo.

"Wow," he says, as he steps through the door and lays eyes on me for the first time in...almost two hours. He walks up and wraps an arm around my waist, pulling me into a kiss. "This is how I love to see you," he says, referring to my t-shirt and jeans.

It took me a while to get used to leaving my suits in the closet, and some days I still throw one on for a thrill, but the casual lifestyle is so much more doable than I would have ever thought.

Throughout dinner Bo fills me in on the progress of numerous plants, while groaning over my pasta, until my phone rings and I'm filled with the certainty it's Holly. "Go ahead," Bo says with a nod when he sees my face light up.

"Holly!" I answer, picking up my almost clean plate and walking to the sink.

"Hey, how's everything going down there?"

"Oh...wonderfully," I reply, throwing a smile at Bo as I head to the couch to relax.

"Really? Still not hankering for work?"

"Mmm...I have other things to keep me entertained."

"Oh I bet you do. Living the dream or what?"

"Definitely, definitely living the dream," I reply a little quietly, feeling slightly self-conscious about Bo overhearing us.

Holly goes silent for a minute, probably detecting I'm still too shy to launch into a lot of detail. "Well, something tells me you won't be too upset to hear Fiona's is now a salon," she says at last.

"Really? Whose is it?"

"I'm not sure," she replies, "not anyone we know."

"Oh well. Good to hear the planet is still rotating," I respond, feeling not the least bit sentimental about it.

"And...you won't be surprised to hear Quade's already put that house back up for sale. I wondered if he was going to rent it or what, but I guess he just wants out from under it now."

My arm hairs stand on end at the mention of 'that house', and I wish Holly hadn't said his name out loud to me. But of course, she doesn't understand the breadth of the repulsion I feel for my experience there, so I respond casually. "Well good for him. Managing a rental would be a lot for him not being around town more often than he is."

"Definitely," Holly responds before pausing again. "So, guess what else," she says, sounding like she's bursting to tell me something.

"What?"

"Well, Levi and I have decided to take a week off to come down and look at some of those houses in Teah's neighborhood."

"You're kidding! Already?!" I'm so excited, my heart's fluttering.

"Yep. I'm already bored without you."

"I knew you would be! When are you coming?"

"In just a couple weeks. I'll give you the dates once we have our tickets."

"Oh Holly, I can't wait for you to see our gorgeous farm."

"I can't wait to see it! So...any exciting news for me?" Holly asks eventually, obviously fishing for details again.

"Volumes worth, Holly. Absolute volumes worth," I tell her as Bo walks in and stands in front of the couch, looking like a caveman with the evening sunlight streaming in to backlight him from the windows. "I've gotta go, but one quick thing," I say with a smile so big I'm certain Holly can hear it. "He signed the papers. In ninety days I'll be a free woman."

"Fiona, that's huge! Congratulations!"

"Yep, thank you. I'll catch up to you later."

"You'd better!" she yells, just as Bo bends down and scoops me off the couch.

"Woman," he growls, then hauls me upstairs to the master bathroom. "I haven't showered yet and I'm a dirty man."

"Oh!" I exclaim as laughter rolls out of me. "What are we gonna do about that?"

"Here's what we're gonna do," Bo says, setting me down on the bath mat.

He opens the glass door and turns on the shower, then pulls my shirt over my head...exposing black lace. "Whoa, whoa...what is this?" Somehow Bo never gets used to seeing me in my lingerie, and I love it every time. "We cain't just strip you down and toss you in the shower. A bra like that deserves a little respect," he says, turning off the water and carrying me to bed.

I sigh as Bo pulls off my jeans and runs his massive, warm hands down the length of my torso and legs, then comes back to grip my panties in his teeth. And when Bo growls, it's not phony, not a sexy act just for show. It's who he actually is, primal and unbridled whenever he's in my presence.

He drops my panties to the ground and sniffs his way back up my legs, tickling me everywhere with his goatee, opening his mouth to breathe against me as he journeys up my torso to my chest...where he buries his face in my cleavage, deeply kissing it as he reaches underneath to unclasp my bra.

He slides his fingers under the straps to slip them off my shoulders, then peels the bra off slowly, very slowly, reveling in each new centimeter of my golden round mounds as they're revealed. When the black lace is snagged just on the edges of my nipples, he clamps his lips over it and breathes onto them...one at a time, nibbling lightly through the lace.

"Bo...Bo," I whisper, barely able to contain my yearning for him...still mounting by the moment.

He slides the bra off and then gets up onto his knees to fling off his own shirt, uncovering his tremendous chest, sinuous arms, and six-pack abs. I reach up to pet his curly chest hair as Bo unbuttons his jeans; he hops off the bed to remove them before I can swipe my hands any lower.

I prop my head up on an arm to take in the view that gets me drooling every time, as Bo stands gazing at me... posed with muscles naturally flexed and nostrils flared, like a rodeo bull. I can see him loving the way I stare, until he lunges onto the bed and wraps himself around me in one swift, aggressive motion.

When he rolls over and pulls me on top, I grind against him and kiss his breath away...unable to contain the full height of my need to have Bo inside me. But he allows me to mount him for only a short while before lifting me up and hauling me back to the bathroom, my legs still clinging around his waist.

Bo turns the water back on and I watch as he lathers up a big, soft sea sponge with moisturizing gel, filling the steamy shower with the sharp, edible scent of yuzu citrus. I'm forced to pry my eyes away as he gently turns me around and begins sponging my back in long, delicious strokes.

I arch my back into the sponge, soaking up the massaging sensation while also longing for more. Bo moves forward just far enough for me to feel his response to my body language. My urgency for him triples, but he makes me wait while he proceeds to wash and condition my hair...rubbing my scalp into a state of deep relaxation.

Once Bo's finally finished, I take the sponge and rub it across every muscle of his body, tracing over the lines of his tattoo...roses, lilies, orchids, and vines emblazoned in the finest detail. I squat down to soap between his tree trunk thighs, taking in a spectacular view, until Bo's patience reaches its threshold and he beckons me upward toward his gilded ride to ecstasy.

Chapter 38

Bo

"I love you too much," Fiona tells me later, just before I turn out our bedside lamp.

"Nuh-uh, you can't love me too much," I return.

"I love you too much," she insists.

"Wait...what? What was that again?" I ask.

"I love you."

"What now?" I prod. "I keep forgettin."

"I love you," she tells me once more, laughing now and hittin me with a pillow.

The last thing I see before sleep is the silken back of the head of a goddess. I still can't fully process that she's here, no matter how many times I tell Jose all about her...tryin to solidify that my own reality is real. That I'm not gonna wake in the mornin to find it was all a big beautiful dream.

Yet I do still dream about Fiona. She manages to haunt my days and nights with equal magnitude. But, for the first time, I enjoy the waking side even more than the dream side of life. Watching Fiona by the pool, in the kitchen, strolling through rows of flowers to pick indoor arrangements to her heart's content. My eyes just can't get enough of her.

Lyin in bed at night, dreamin away, the images of her are different than they used to be. She comes to me out of the shadows still, long hair hangin around her like a shaman woman, but her eyes are alive and forward...searchin through me like I'm made of glass. All the tension is gone. She used to appear as a woman on a mission, intently focused if not distressed, but now those eyes blaze ahead like sun pillars... sweepin over the landscape of possibilities as it expands out before her. She stands tall but not rigid, her expression sober without being hard.

Sometimes the wind whips around her wildly, blowin her hair and skirts into a flourish. There's a far off look in her eyes when her vision of the future becomes muddied in the stormy swirl, and she finds me watchin and turns to me in the dream. I hold out my hands to her and say, "Follow me Fiona. Follow your beautiful, sacred heart."

A Note to My Readers (contains spoilers)

As *Fiona's Fury* incorporates themes of domestic abuse and criminal activity, I'd like to address any ambiguity about the characters and their actions.

Quade's long-term obsession with Fiona resulted in turning to the use of steroids in an attempt to remake himself and earn her attention. The end of the novel suggests Quade's epiphany and repentance but doesn't go into his rehabilitation. Because Fiona would not harbor secrets that could cause threat to other women, the reader may assume that Bo will uncover the truth and take matters into his own hands, or that Fiona will seek lawful retribution, or that Quade will discontinue drug use, seek help, and reform.

I hope readers will revel in imagining their own conclusions, based upon how they'd most like to see the future unfold.

What you could do in a similar situation:

Roofies remain in the body and can be tested for 12-72 hours after ingestion.

Roofies can be detected via hair analysis for up to three months after ingestion.

Roofying is a federal offense and can be reported to local police as well as FBI.

If you suspect that you or someone you know has been roofied, do not hesitate to report it and take legal action.

National Sexual Assault Hotline 1-800-656-HOPE (4673)

National Domestic Violence Hotline 1-800-799-SAFE (7233)

Domestic Violence Resource: www.thehotline.org

Finding Love Again is a series of three
interconnected standalone novels.
Be sure to read the others:

Some Kind of Angel
Fiona's Fury
A Letter to Elise

Acknowledgements

First I'd like to thank my small but precious team of brilliant beta readers, who have been stoked and encouraging from the beginning, Michelle Burton, Basilio Light, Jerry, Sophia Landis, Robert Klostermann, and Jeremy Bergan. And my promotional efforts would have gotten nowhere fast without Jeremy's incredible tech support talent.

To Rick Lite and his team at Stress Free Book Marketing, thanks so much for all your hard work.

Shoutout to my dear trail buddy, Ted G. Fleener, for gifting me my very first romance novel, *Bridges of Madison County*, and in some small way starting this whole thing.

Special thanks to Sophia for your priceless edits and endless friendship, support, and fandom, Robere for inspiring certain scenes and themes and being a tireless friend and supporter, Bud for supporting my existence and encouraging the emergence of all my different shades, and Jerry for being that one friend who repeatedly said... You're a writer. Get out there and write, write, write!

Diane Frank was fundamental to my confidence upfront, telling me that my books must be published and read by as many people as possible. Thank you Diane!

Rudy, you are one of my all time great author and creativity inspirations.

A huge thanks to the women in my family who are sharp-as-a-tack editors, and to my Fairfield family that has always believed in me and elevated me as a person. You all know who you are.

And most of all, thanks to all my wonderful readers and reviewers.

XOXO,
Roxy Blue

P.S. If you love my books, taking a minute to leave an Amazon review will help them to reach even more readers!

Join my newsletter: www.authorroxyblue.com

Follow me on Instagram: @authorroxyblue

Enjoy the following chapter of *Some Kind of Angel*, the prequel to *Fiona's Fury*.

Here is a sneak-peak of my book
Some Kind of Angel

The Breakup

I have been here before...at this long, gaping moment of emptiness where life transitions away from ecstatic-fulfilling-relationship, and slowly meanders down the crooked path toward preparing-to-possibly-love-again. It's not the worst state you can be in, nothing traumatic, challenging, or terribly heartbreaking about it. It's simply...a doldrum. A continuous fuzzy gray haze with occasional color running across it, like an old TV channel that won't quite come in. It's your downtime, and you have to sit quietly here until your dues have been paid to the gods of all punishment and reward, until it's time for the pendulum to swing to the other side of the balance. Until it's time for joy again.

* * *

The long drive back from Texas had flown by in my state of excitement to get home to Wesley. I tiptoed up the

345

steps assuming he'd be in a deep sleep at that ungodly hour, padded into the bedroom, and slipped out of my clothes without a sound. But as I pulled back the blankets to get in, Wesley appeared to awaken with a start. Gasping, he turned to face me, reached out his long, powerful arms, and pulled me down into a hard kiss. In the next moment he was on top of me, breathlessly kissing me with a fervor he hadn't had in months…making love to me in an almost frenzied state.

I was more elated than I'd been since the early days of our relationship, reveling in the thrill of our renewed connection, believing Wesley had finally beaten the fears he'd been harboring around my latest revelation. For weeks before taking the temp job in Texas, I'd been rehashing my thought stream to him…hoping he was resonating with it. And I'd ignorantly believed he was.

I'd tragically mistaken his falling tears for some powerful moment of emotional letting go, of an internal shift that was harmonizing and aligning him ever more deeply with me. Not for the tears of agony they truly were, tears of acid pain that were disintegrating his vision of our perfect union…at last melting through the solidity of his unwavering heart, the permanency that was his love for me. But here he was… caressing me like a flower and loving me with the force of a hurricane.

Afterward he held me and finally spoke. "You were with someone, weren't you?"

As a guy who claims to not believe in things like intuition, I couldn't have been more surprised he knew.

"Yes," I answered. "I made out with somebody, that's all."

Wesley dropped the subject and closed his eyes. I hadn't been planning to keep it a secret anyway. So I'd had a little fling with someone on the job, a tan-skinned guy with alluring brown eyes, a thick boyish bowl cut, and the butt of an eighteen year old quarterback. The fact that Wesley had apparently 'known' all this time, was proof my behavior was a turn on, and a huge one at that. At last, I thought, he's unafraid, reinvigorated, ready to forge into our long future together. Everything felt perfect by the time I fell asleep, exhausted and happy.

That night I slept long and deeply, awakening late to the bustling sound of movement downstairs. I threw on a t-shirt and headed down to find the source of last night's revelry, and get some more where that came from. But what I saw, as I rounded the landing of the steps, caused my heart to skip several beats. Wesley, industrious man that he is, had our living room filled with taped-up boxes...several of them loaded onto a hand truck. He did not greet me with a smile but remained focused on the activity of taping and stacking boxes, his expression morose.

Bursting into tears, I sank to my knees...screaming. "What are you doing? Why are you doing this? Why would you do this? You can't do this! Are you crazy?!"

My vocal pleas did me no good. Wesley refused to respond as he continued with his mission like a heartless machine.

"I didn't sleep with that guy! How can you do this after last night? Why would you do this now?!" I cried out in a state of hysterics. "You're crazy!" I continued. "Do you know how rare it is I'm even attracted to anyone? Do you know how rare that is for me?! Do you think we can just go out and find someone else to have this with? Please don't ruin this…last night was more connected than we've been in months! Why would you destroy everything we have? You can't do this! This is insane!"

The wailing continued as Wesley trucked his boxes out to his company van, load after load, then tapered off as the shock set in. He was serious. It was over. I was devastated.

Feeling suicidal for the first time in years, I resorted to desperate tactics to get his attention…force him to talk. "I'll break it!" I yelled between clenched teeth, as I picked up his acoustic guitar and held it over my head like a battle club.

In an instant, Wesley yanked it from my grip and smashed it to bits over the corner of the wooden futon frame. Our mutual pain was real, and it was ugly.

The storm ended peacefully with Wes hugging me as I sobbed, while he continued to say nothing…as was his usual, stoic style. The apartment he was moving his things into was actually one he'd quietly rented months before, waiting to find out whether I'd really go through with my notion to have an open relationship.

After officially moving into it that day, he continued to spend many nights and weekends at my place…though he never again gave himself to me with the same abandon. Wesley and I floundered through a loving but relatively flaccid friendship for years in this way, stuck in the dreary purgatory we'd built for ourselves. Wishing desperately to go back in time, but knowing somehow we never would.